HESTER ON THE RUN

HESTER HUNTS FOR HOME • BOOK ONE

LINDA BYLER

Good Books
New York, New York

The characters and events in this book are the creation of the author, and any resemblance to actual persons or events is coincidental.

HESTER ON THE RUN

Good Books books may be purchased in bulk at special discounts for sales promotion, corporate gifts, fund-raising, or educational purposes. Special editions can also be created to specifications. For details, contact the Special Sales Department, Good Books, 307 West 36th Street, 11th Floor, New York, NY 10018 or info@skyhorsepublishing.com.

Good Books is an imprint of Skyhorse Publishing, Inc.®, a Delaware corporation.

Visit our website at www.goodbooks.com.

10 9 8 7 6 5 4 3 2 1

Library of Congress Cataloging-in-Publication Data

Byler, Linda.
Hester on the run / Linda Byler.
pages ; cm.—(Hester hunts for home; Book 1)
ISBN 978-1-68099-058-4 (trade pbk.: alk. paper)
—ISBN 978-1-68099-112-3 (ebook)
1. Amish--Fiction. I. Title.
PS3602.Y53H47 2015
813'.6—dc23
2015024221

ISBN: 978-1-68099-058-4
eBook ISBN: 978-1-68099-112-3

Cover design by Koechel Peterson & Associates, Inc., Minneapolis, Minnesota

Printed in the United States of America

Table of Contents

CHAPTER 1

OUTSIDE, THE RAIN FELL STEADILY, SPLASHING ON the glossy green leaves of spring, sliding off in tiny rivulets, dancing from one leaf to another. The sky was pewter gray, the day's light dimmed by the heavy clouds of a rainstorm in spring. Beneath the great white oaks, the lofty maples, ash, and cedar trees, the undergrowth received the raindrops, spurring the lush grasses and bushes to renewed growth.

Nestled by the side of a sizable ridge, built to avoid the harsh winds of winter, a small house made of logs stood in the rain, the weathered shake roof glistening with moisture as the rain slid steadily from the edge, plunking like a curtain of water in front of it.

There were four small windows made of glass, with six small panes divided by a dark wooden framework. Only one of the windows glowed with a yellowish glow, beaming warmly through the muffled light, the dripping darkness of the thick forest surrounding the house.

The front door was made of oak planks with a chunky forged iron latch that was closed securely against the wild creatures of the night, or marauding Indians, the residents of the wild mountains of Berks County, Pennsylvania.

The year was 1745, and Pennsylvania was a land of forests, mountain ranges, rivers, and creeks, unspoiled and, for the most part, lightly settled by Europeans. Now a small community of immigrants was hacking away at the great trees, building homes, clearing land, making a life for themselves in the New World, America.

They came from Switzerland to escape religious persecution, their forebears having been called "Anabaptists," or "re-baptizers." This particular group was descended from Jacob Ammann and was known as "Amish."

Beside the glow of the oil lamp by the window, a young Amish couple sat side by side, their heads bent low, his brown hair almost identical to the color of his wife's. A heavy beard lay along his facial contours. His hair was cut straight across his forehead, falling to below his ears on the side and straight across the back of his head at his hairline. He had a wide forehead, high cheekbones, and full lips. A strong, swarthy man of twenty-nine, he was dressed in a dull, homespun shirt of unbleached muslin. Nine buttons held his broadfall knee breeches securely.

His wife wore the traditional white head cap, sewn in the old style adopted by their people in Switzerland. It was made of Swiss muslin, a wide band in the front with pleated fabric attached to it, and tied beneath the chin by wide strings of the same material.

Almost all of her head was covered. Only a thatch of severely combed hair, parted in the middle, remained visible. Her forehead was narrow, her nose a goodly size, but it was her eyes that dominated her features, the one beautiful aspect of her otherwise plain face.

They were large and the blue of a robin's egg, the color turning with the changing of her emotions, which happened as frequently as her words came. That dancing color of blue that went from indigo to the shades of blue sky on a sunny day, was what had captivated Hans.

And so Catherine had placed her hand in Hans Zug's, repeated her soft answer after his, at her place by his side in front of the Amish bishop in the Rhine Valley, and became his wife.

She was known as Kate.

She wore a linen shortgown, over a linen petticoat, as well as a linen kerchief and apron.

Barely visible on her lap was an infant, swaddled in serviceable blankets. Her thick, jet black hair shone almost blue in the lamplight.

When the baby turned her head, her small, oval face was the color of a red squirrel's ear. She was perfect, this tiny foundling.

Her eyelids were already beginning a curtain of brilliantly black lashes over the contours of her wide, flat eyes. The small brows arced like the symmetry of an eagle's wings. Her nose was a tiny bump, with nostrils so small, Kate feared for her ability to breathe normally.

Oh, she was so beautiful! Not of her flesh and blood, this foundling, but hers, all hers. And Hans's. At long last. Kate held in her arms her heart's desire after nine long years of waiting and hoping while her womb remained barren.

The desolation of sleepless nights, when the yearning for a baby of her own caused hot tears to squeeze between her eyelids, the ache in her chest a physical pain, were now things of the past.

She had gone to the spring swinging her wooden bucket, her step heavy but sure as she made her way down the path from the house.

That April, a sharp wind bore winter's reluctance to lighten its grip on the daily temperature. Kate held her shawl tightly around her neck.

A few dandelions waved their brilliant yellow heads, accompanied by the purple violets growing along the side of the spring. She had bent to gather a handful to grace the windowsill by her spinning wheel when she heard it. At first, she thought it might be the plaintive call of a catbird. A mewling sound.

She stopped picking violets and sat on her haunches, holding very still. There it was again. A kitten? But they hadn't brought any cats to America. Rocking back on her heels, she flattened a few dark green ferns, oblivious to anything but the beating of her heart.

When she heard the thin, wailing cry once more, she scrambled to her feet and stood motionless, holding her head to one side. A shiver chased itself up her spine, across her shoulders, and down her forearms, causing the hairs to lift across them.

Suddenly, she felt as if she was being observed. Making a turn to the right, she lifted her blue eyes to the surrounding wooded slopes, quickly scanning with her experienced eyes. More shivers sent an involuntary shudder through her, as her eyes raked the deep forest surrounding the spring. Was this small cry a trap?

Always, the Amish settlers needed to be wary of the Indians, the ones who had rightful ownership of this land. Always, there was the danger of meeting a group of hostile native men, in spite of William Penn's endeavors to keep the peace, as he offered more treaties to that effect.

When the cry came again, she knew it was not a bird or a kitten. It had to be an infant. Neither the danger of hostile red men, or anything else, could stop her now. Her mother's heart responded, and she became a woman possessed, weaving through the undergrowth, bent over, her arms thrashing, combing the ferns, grasses, and bushes with an intensity that sprang from her very nature.

She came up empty-handed and stood uncertain, the loud beats of her heart filling her ears.

When the cry came again, she lurched toward it, stumbled, slipped on wet rocks, then resumed her wild searching, raking aside the heavy ferns and mountain laurel that spilled across her face.

She gasped audibly when she came upon the small brown bundle. A fawn? Was it only a bleating fawn whose mother had been killed? The deerskin was so soft, it had to be from a young fawn. Tentatively, she reached out, touching the deerskin with trembling fingers. She bit down hard on her lower lip, and then a cry escaped her when she found the black hair, the brown face that scrunched up and emitted another mewling sound.

"Mein Gott," she breathed. She sank to the ground, unaware of her full skirt trailing in the icy spring water

as she put both hands beneath the bundle and lifted it gently onto her lap, crying now, laughing, chortling to herself.

In the dappled sunlight that played between the moving leaves of the forest, she saw the baby for the first time, and her heart swelled with an indescribable longing. The baby was beautiful.

Quickly, furtively, she stole a glance. Yes, it was a girl. A girl baby.

"*Ach, mein Himmlischer Vater*" (Oh, my heavenly father)*!* It was all she had ever wanted. Mumbling now, talking to herself, half in prayer, she examined the infant from her head to her tiny red feet. So perfect.

Again, her eyes swept the hillside, searching for answers. Would someone come to reclaim her if she took her to the house?

A strong smell came from the baby's furs, an unwashed, unclean scent that made her recoil. Her first instinct was to bathe her, rub her skin with oil of lavender, dress her in clean clothes, swaddle her with soft blankets.

The trees rustled around her; the spring bubbled and tinkled merrily over the rocks; the wooden bucket lay on its side, forgotten, with the clutch of purple violets beside it.

Quickly, she held the baby to her chest, and with a swift movement she was on her feet, glancing hurriedly behind her now. Gaining momentum, she walked fast until she was running, out of breath by the time she got back to the house, barring the heavy door behind her.

Only then, the thought came, what would Hans say?

In fact, Hans said very little. He stated, matter-of-factly, that very likely a scared young Indian maiden had left the infant by the spring purposefully, hoping the white people would care for it.

By the baby's features, he believed her to be of the Lenape tribe, often mistakenly called the "Delaware." The rich golden brown color of her skin. Her straight, thick, glossy hair. Her well sculpted eyes and brows. Yes, they would keep her, he said. He never doubted that God had heard their pleas for a newborn baby.

Kate's love for her husband sprang up, flowering into a new and beautiful thing, deeply appreciating his manly ways, this sure choice he made now.

She heated water in the heavy, black, cast-iron pot and swung it across the flames in the fireplace. She shaved small bits of lye soap and worried the warm water with her hands until bubbles rose to the surface.

When Kate placed the small brown infant into the water, she opened her eyes wide and became very still, and Kate giggled and laughed with the sheer joy of being able to bathe this wonderful little being.

That first night, they boiled a cloth to purify it, then dipped it repeatedly in warmed cow's milk, laughing together as the powerful little mouth suckled until their fingers hurt.

Kate would not lay her down, even after a soft burp came from her throat. She held her, possessing the baby, her face lit with a radiant fulfillment that came from her mother's heart.

They couldn't get enough of her. They wept together at her first smile. They marveled when she grew, her cheeks filling out from the good cow's milk.

Word got around, the way these things do, and only a few weeks elapsed before Kate's mother-in-law was at the door, tall, formidable, and completely disapproving. Kate clutched her precious foundling to her breast, a sick feeling mushrooming in her stomach.

Taking her outer wraps off in one jerked movement, the irritation on her face playing with her lowered eyebrows, Rebecca was a scary figure in Kate's life. Especially now. Bending to peer at the sleeping infant, Rebecca breathed out in a disdainful whoosh of annoyance, "She's red as a beet."

"*Ya*, Mam." It was all Kate could think of, a sort of agreement, a subservient answer, a bowing to higher authority that was deeply ingrained, the teachings of childhood branded into her conscience.

"What makes you think you can raise her Amish, with Indian blood?" Rebecca inquired, tersely, tight-lipped with disapproval.

"I don't know," Kate mumbled.

"She's a heathen child."

Quite suddenly, Kate broke out with a swift denial, pleading the infant's innocence, as her mother-in-law stood over her with fiery objection.

When the door latch lifted and her father-in-law, Isaac, appeared with Hans behind him, Kate's voice drifted off quietly, and Rebecca's features rounded into a caricature of pleasantness.

Isaac shook hands solemnly with Kate then bent to peer into the small wooden cradle Hans had just completed.

"*Ach, du lieva*" (Oh, my goodness), he murmured softly, quick tears springing to his nearsighted blue eyes, with the dozens of wrinkles and crow's feet spreading around them. *"An shay kind"* (A nice child).

Hans beamed, clasping his hands on his shirtfront. Kate blinked back the awkwardness of the moment, her mother-in-law's censure a cawing black crow stuffed into submission for now.

"So tell me how this all came about," Isaac said, kindly.

Willingly, Hans launched into Kate's experience at the spring, ending his story by surmising that a young Indian woman left the newborn there, intending that they would find it.

Isaac nodded, his blue eyes alight. "It's risky business, but perhaps Kate is right. Time will tell. Just be prepared to give her back if the mother would turn up at your door."

Kate sat up, opened her mouth to defend herself against the unlikeliness of that very thing, but glanced at her mother-in-law and decided against it, withering against the back of the chair she sat on.

"Do you have a name?" Isaac asked.

"Hester."

Hans spoke her name quietly, reluctantly. Kate looked down at her hands, clenched so tightly in her lap.

"Why such a name?" Rebecca said sharply. "No one is named Hester in the *freundshaft*" (extended family).

"It is the name Kate wanted," Hans said curtly, echoing Rebecca's own tone of voice and leaving her without a reply, since she had been taught to let male figures take the dominant role, even if they were younger.

"Why not Esther? It's a Biblical name. Queen Esther was sent by God to save her people." Isaac's voice was kind, so Kate could speak more freely.

"*Dat,* I had a friend in school, a French girl, named Hester Elizabeth. She was nice to me, in spite of my being Amish. I loved her a lot. And, well, I wanted my daughter to be called by her name."

"She's not your daughter," Rebecca spat out, saliva spraying across Kate's face, little wet pellets that made her draw back.

So Kate learned to live with the deepening gloom of Hans's parents' disapproval, although Isaac's kindness lessened the sting.

Each day was filled with a kind of heady gladness as she went about the tasks of running the house smoothly, interrupted only by the sweetness of little Hester's cries. Kate would go swiftly to her cradle, lifting her out, so glad she was finally awake so she could watch her perfect mouth lift into a smile, her black eyes sparkle with recognition.

She was at last a mother, like all her friends. She had a small gift from God, a benediction, a sign of his favor. Hans loved the baby so much, his love for his wife multiplied.

Spring turned into summer, and Hester grew into a healthy child with round cheeks and glowing skin the color of maple syrup.

Kate washed the baby's clothes in the great wooden tubs and wrung them out with strong, capable hands. She rinsed them in hot water with a dash of apple cider vinegar in it and hung them on the rail fence surrounding the house.

She scrubbed floors, the wide golden oak boards planed to a shining smooth texture by Hans's brawny arms.

She planted a garden, with Hester cooing from the blanket where she was placed. Curious butterflies flitted above her, the birds sang and twittered, diving around her, and Kate told Hans that she knew Hester's eyes followed the birds and other flying things. Hans never doubted her.

Hans had built their house against the ridge, which rose in back of it to the north. A gentle slope fell away from it, toward the south, down to the barn built of stone and log. The barn's sturdy roof was made of split shakes, overlapped from the peak to let the rain tumble down over them, keeping the cow and calf, the heifer, and two horses snug and dry in winter.

A split rail fence surrounded the barn, ensuring the animals fresh air in the wintertime. The large pasture was dotted with stumps from the trees Hans had felled and rose away beyond the small barnyard, up the side of another ridge to the east.

Little by little, Hans's acreage spread out, allowing him to plant wheat, rye, and spelt. In any spare time, he felled trees and split them for more fence rails or logs for neighbors who had use for them.

Hans was a good manager and a hard worker, squirreling away every coin he possibly could. His fields were planted, hoed, and harvested in time. He fed his horses well so they could work long days in the sun, tilling the soil, and harvesting what grew in it.

He was the blacksmith for all the Amish families of the settlement, spread out in a radius of fourteen or fifteen miles, give or take a few.

On the days Hans went *gile chplauwa* (blacksmithing), Kate enjoyed a sort of freedom that gave her a great and secret pleasure. She spent idle time arranging wildflowers in redware cups, sometimes washing her hair and arranging it in different ways in front of the small wood-framed mirror above her sink.

Without her cap, her hair was soft and wavy, but she always pulled it back into a tight bun, jabbing combs sharply into the tight coils on the back of her head.

It was shameful to wash one's hair too often, a sign of pride. So she didn't tell Hans, figured he needn't know, for he was strict in some ways where she was concerned.

If her friend Naomi wore a new green shortgown, and she expressed her wish for fabric of such a beautiful hue, he would become quite angry, grasping her arm and giving it a small shake, saying she was going against God's will, being consumed by the lust of the eyes. So she learned to satisfy any desire for beauty when he was blacksmithing.

Once, she dyed a length of plain linen fabric with the juice of pokeberries, turning it into a delightful hue between purple and pink. She was so pleased with the results that she set about immediately sewing a curtain for the east window beside the fireplace. Wouldn't it turn into the color of wild roses when the sun arrived over the treetops, the rays piercing through the brilliant fabric, infusing the house with color?

Her disappointment was crushing when Hans said he would have none of her worldliness, ripped it off its rod, and took it away. She never found out what he had done with her handiwork, until she helped him shovel manure the following spring and discovered slivers of fabric that had once been brilliant, like the rubies Hester Elizabeth had told her about.

The stone in her chest had caused her great pain, but it had dissolved as she forgave her husband and berated herself for being so prone to cave in to her worldly desires. It was the way of it, being Amish.

But now, with little Hester, Hans changed completely when it came to dressing her as an Amish baby. He came home from Reuben Hershberger's with a swatch of blue linen the color of a bluebird's plumage, so blue it was a sort of purple. Smiling, his eyes alight, he asked Kate to sew a little dress for Hester. They would be taking her to church on Sunday.

Pleased, and convinced he would allow her prettier fabric, Kate set about sewing the small garment, her needle weaving in and out with tiny stitches that would hold for years.

She sewed a row of tucks in the sleeves that could be taken out to lengthen the sleeve as she grew. Around the hem along the bottom of the shirt, she did the same, thinking how this beautiful little dress could be worn for quite some time. She made a small muslin cap for her, too, much like her own. They tried the cap on Hester and laughed together when her thick, glossy black hair refused to remain beneath it.

Kate darned Hans's socks, but when a pair was no longer worth patching, she turned them into small black socks for Hester. Hans was so happy about her thriftiness, he told her that together they would turn this little homestead into a productive farm, a real place in the Amish community.

The gentle summer rains made her garden a lovely picture of growth, the pole beans climbing up over the crooked poles they tied together at the top, a tripod of support for the fast-growing vines.

Onions grew in straight rows, their tops reaching for the sky like scrawny fingers. Beets grew large and heavy, their red-veined leaves spread luxuriantly between the rows, adjacent to the field of corn and tobacco.

Kate kept the weeds at bay with endless hoeing. Every morning, before Hester awoke, Kate was in the garden, hoeing, collecting bugs, and drowning them in hot tallow, following well the ways of her mother.

She fed kitchen scraps to the chickens. She gathered the eggs and washed them, storing them in woven baskets in the cold cellar Hans had built behind the house. He'd take any extra eggs along when he made his horseshoeing calls and then put any coins he received beneath the floorboards under their bedstead.

Somehow today she couldn't shake a disgruntled feeling about the brilliant blue dress for Hester. She had been delighted, reveling in the sewing of it, bending over her needle and thread with a gladness that was hard to explain. Why now, here washing the large, brown eggs, did this feeling creep over her?

Was it jealousy? Longing to have one of her own? Quickly, she scolded herself, muttering aloud. How childish. So shameful. Of course she must stop any such thoughts that crept in. They were of the devil.

Hans was the best father she had ever seen. How many times had she helped her friends with their screaming babies, or injured toddlers wailing out their indignities, and watched their husbands in animated conversation, oblivious to their wives' frustration as they struggled to take care of all the babies and young children?

No, Hans was exceptional, and it was only her own childish selfishness that brought on this gloomy foreboding. Or was it her woman's intuition?

Chapter 2

The Pennsylvania forest stretched before them like an endless green sea, the trees as restless as the ocean currents, tossed about by a strong wind, setting the treetops into a sort of constant, ever-changing dance.

Hans urged the dependable driving horse, Dot, into an easy walk. The heavy leather strap, called the britchment, dug into her haunches as she leaned into it, working hard to hold the cart back, to keep it from careening down the steep, rocky incline. The road was barely visible because of the washouts from the thunderstorms of late spring.

Dot lowered her head, picking her way easily between the ruts as the cart bumped and swayed, sending Kate's shoulder bouncing against Hans's. She relinquished her hold on Hester, ignoring the ache in her elbow as she held the sleeping infant inside her brown shawl.

The morning was crisp and cool, the sun lighting up the deep greens into many various shades, from near black to joyful lime green. It was a bit chilly, with the wind whipping the small branches over their heads, turning the leaves inside out, worrying them frantically with each fresh gust.

Hans laid a thick hand on the top of his black felt hat and pushed down, ensuring the headgear's tight hold on his head, then turned to look at his wife. He could see nothing but the wide front of her cap, her face hidden behind its broad front piece. He knew her mouth would be set in a straight line of endurance, unwilling to admit how weary she was. They had come about three-fourths of the way, probably twelve miles, and her shoulders would be aching, he knew. They were on their way to church services, being held that morning in the home of Amos and Mary Hershberger, a distance of sixteen miles from home.

Soon the forest would give way to an open area, the fields and pastures having been cleared by Amos and his sturdy sons. The cart lurched, rocking from side to side as Dot picked her way carefully down the incline. When they came to a level area, the sun's rays changed the light to a yellow-tinged hue, a constantly moving play of light and dark colors. The road became a carpet of pine needles now, pierced only by a few wild blackberry bushes springing up from the acidic soil beneath the ancient pines.

Kate breathed in deeply, savoring the sharp odor of pine gum. Her eyes followed the movement of a red squirrel, chirring at the invaders from his perch on a low branch. Her full-fronted cap effectively obscured her side vision, which was perhaps the reason for its wide rim. The eyes of women should not wander or seem bold or brazen, but should be kept lowered in humility.

Today, Kate would need to pray for humility. Already her heart was thumping, her breath quickening at the thought of carrying her perfect child into the house, the women rushing to see, the gasps of admiration.

Hester was hers, all hers. Kate's moment of glory had come. They rode on in silence, swaying together in the cart. Hans had suggested the cart, because of the distance. It was lighter and easier on Dot.

Kate had given her consent, but after twelve miles, her back ached horribly, her elbow felt frozen into place, and she resented Hans's lack of forethought. They should have taken the box wagon, but Hans didn't want to exhaust Dot.

Soon, from the money he'd been saving from his horseshoeing, they could afford four new wheels. He would make a lighter cart himself, and it would be a fine one, she knew.

Kate turned her head, straining her neck to see the Stephen Fisher homestead. She was curious about Barbara's garden, the animals. Had their Belgian mare given birth? Barbara had spoken of the upcoming event in hushed tones two weeks ago.

The leaves on the trees obscured much, leaving Kate with unsatisfied curiosity, but since Hans did not speak as they drove past the Fishers, Kate thought it best to hold her words.

It was, after all, the Sabbath, the day of holiness. Let your *ya* be *ya*, your *nay* be *nay*, always, but especially on the Lord's Day. Her thoughts were to be on spiritual matters, not wondering about her neighbors' material worthiness.

Kate tugged at her flat hat, pulling it farther front, as if the width of it might ensure heavenly thoughts. She could not resist one furtive, backward glance, however, and much to her great triumph, she caught sight of a thin, blond, long-legged colt cavorting among the tree stumps in the pasture. So the mare had her colt. Kate smiled, well hidden from her husband's steady gaze.

"Oo-oo-ah." Hans began a slow chant, a bit above a humming sound. So, he meant to sing *fore* (be the song leader). He would lead a hymn today. That was good. Kate was glad. Hans had a clear voice that rose and fell like deep, chiming bells, a rich and full baritone. He was a good song leader, not one who stumbled and other men had to come to rescue, the way it was for some who were less talented.

The bundle on her lap began squirming, then tugging at her arms and heaving, before letting loose with a fine howl.

Lifting the flap of her shawl, Kate fumbled to loosen the baby's shawl, wrapped securely about her head, as the howls became more insistent. Shocked to find her beautiful baby's face bathed in sweat, the blanket around her neck already moist with it, Kate hurried to loosen the pins that held the heavy garments too snugly around her.

Frightened, Kate kept her head lowered, as Hester emitted stronger cries, her outrage building at being kept waiting.

Hans's singing stopped. "Can't you feed her?" he asked gently.

"I don't know how I would in this rocking cart. She was a bit too warm, I guess."

"Sit her up. Let her get some air," Hans instructed.

Kate wouldn't think of it and told him so. If a child perspired and then became exposed to frosty air, he or she could catch a cold. But when the indignant child's cries became quite frantic, Hans stopped the mare, told Kate to get her some milk now, because he could hardly see how she could survive under that heavy shawl.

Obediently, Kate tried to feed her the cold cow's milk, sitting beneath a great pin oak in the new grass by the side of the road, but Hester would have none of it. She turned her head and screamed her refusal. Kate lifted her to her shoulder, thumped her back gently, and tried again, to no avail.

Hans was becoming anxious, and the baby continued wailing. Kate wrapped her back into the shawl, stuck her unceremoniously beneath her own, climbed back into the cart with her eyes lowered, and rode the remaining few miles to church services under the fog of her husband's disapproval. There was nothing she could do. Why couldn't he see that?

When they finally reached their destination, Kate was exhausted from clinging to the crying infant, her nerves shattered by feelings of inadequacy. What had happened? Had their life been too perfect? Everything had gone so smoothly, but their first venture to take Hester away had turned into a nightmare.

She turned her head to search Hans's face, alarmed to find his eyes set straight ahead, the brows lowered over them as if he was enduring the misery of the infant all by himself. Did he really love the child so much?

Kate was reduced to carrying the still-crying infant into Amos and Mary Hershberger's well-built house.

Scurrying swiftly, she acknowledged helping hands gratefully, relinquishing Hester into Mamie Troyer's ample, old arms, who clucked and fussed and announced in stentorian tones that this baby was *au-gvocksa* (all tense and tight). Mamie proceeded to unwrap her, every head bending to watch as she lifted the baby.

Kate's dreams of Hester's first entry to church were dashed. Her beautiful child was red and perspiring, her eyes swollen from her painful crying, her little red mouth maneuvering grotesquely as harsh, nerve-jangling noises burst from it steadily.

Hester's beautiful new blue dress was soaked with saliva and perspiration, a dead giveaway about Kate's failure as a mother.

"Too warm!"

"The child is sweating."

"She'll get a cold, sure."

Clucks of pity, disapproval, wonder, whatever the reason, all served their purpose well, adding weight to Kate's utter sense of failure. She should have known better.

They all watched with approval as Mamie grasped the baby's left arm and right leg, bringing them together with a quick solid thump, producing howls of pain and fright. She did the same to the opposite arm and leg, then laid the child on the bare planks of Mary's kitchen table. She began to massage the tiny rib cage and underarms, as the baby's cries increased yet again.

Kate stepped forward anxiously, but Mary Hershberger caught her arm. "Let Mamie alone. She knows what she's doing."

Mamie's fat fingers kept moving up and down, while Hester arched her back and screamed. Just when Kate thought she would go mad, Mamie tugged the blankets, set the baby's arms by her side and wrapped her as tightly as possible, handed her to Kate and told her to "Burp her good."

Hester was limp as a rag doll, her face pale and exhausted, soft rhythmic burps coming up quite regularly. Kate's heart swelled within her as she held Hester close, thinking she might die of a broken heart if she let her loose, even a bit. Poor, poor baby. Precious child.

What a talking, then! These housewives may have been in Pennsylvania, but they spoke German endlessly the minute they were finally in the company of other women who knew the language, hungering to hear and to be heard.

"It was the cart ride. If you take a baby out before six weeks, they get an awful ache. The muscles are growing, and they ache. It's very painful. When I rub along her sides, it loosens them, and the burps can come up. Then the pain goes away," Mamie said, watching Kate's face intently. Kate only nodded, too close to tears to answer.

Barbara Fisher leaned her head to one side and said she'd never seen a prettier little one. That was met with a smile of approval from Mamie, and a bitter, awkward look from Hans's mother, followed by, "She's an Indian."

The women drew in their breaths, stiffened their shoulders, and crossed their arms as Rebecca's uncontested disapproval settled around them, poisoning the atmosphere with her taut words dripping toxins. Mamie gave Rebecca a level took, then said good-naturedly,

"Well, Kate couldn't leave her by the spring to die. That would be murder, wouldn't it?" Murmurs of assent rippled through the kitchen, leaving Rebecca isolated, but only for a moment.

"What do our English neighbors say? 'The only good Indian is a dead one.'"

The women gasped in disbelief and raised their fingers to their mouths. What boldness!

Mamie went right home and told her husband, Obadiah, what Rebecca said right there in the kitchen on a Sabbath morning. Obadiah told John Lantz, the bishop, and he said the statement bordered on hate, and that woman would have to be stopped.

Mamie took a secret glee in seeing Rebecca having to confess her sins in church two weeks later, that spiteful woman, talking like that about her own daughter-in-law, and the Amish being a loving, nonresistant people, at that. It was surely the end times, when a woman spoke such words. The Lord would not tarry very long anymore.

Church services were held in the barn, with straw scattered along the floor, the wooden benches set on top. Pigeons cooed from the rough-hewn rafters that were held together with wooden pegs, and shafts of dusty sunlight shimmered between the slats of a window set up under the eaves.

The horses stomped their feet and rattled their chains, while the slow-moving sound of the German songs rose and fell, as the congregation sang from the *Ausbund*, thick, little songbooks, each book shared by two members throughout the barn. The hymns had been written by Anabaptist prisoners, foreparents of the Amish held captive at Passau on the Danube River in Germany.

Kate sat on a bench alone, her baby settled in the house between two rolled up blankets on Amos and Mary Hershberger's bed. She'd go check on her, if need be, but now, she wanted to remain seated, her voice chiming in with many others, her heart swelling with praise to God, for Hans, for Hester, for her life here in America, for the freedom to worship God the way they chose.

And now she had Hester, a baby of her very own, and her battle to fight the good fight of faith was over. Likely she never would conceive, but that was God's will. It was all right. She had her beloved daughter. And Hans loved her every bit as much as she did.

When John Lantz rose to preach, she was reminded of the ancient patriarchs, Abraham, Moses, all of them. John was tall and wide, with bushy white hair springing into riotous curls, his beard circling his face, a bib of the same curling white hair, wagging up and down as he spoke.

His eyebrows were still dark gray, giving him an austere demeanor, as if the lowering of those bushy brows could decide your fate, godlike. His voice was low, well modulated in the beginning, but as he continued speaking, it rose to an emotional crescendo, instilling into the congregation the need to repent of their sins, that the day of the Lord was fast drawing nigh.

Kate sat, worrying her lower lip with her fingers, thinking how very much she hoped Hester could grow into a healthy little girl yet, before the Lord would return in the clouds with hundreds of thousands of his angels.

She wanted to sew her bright dresses and soft white nightgowns and braid her jet-black hair. She wanted to laugh with her and hear her speak and teach her the ways of the farm and the surrounding forest. But was that carnal thinking? Her own worldly views? She wished she had her mother or her sisters to confide in, but she didn't. They had all remained in Switzerland the day John Zug and his parents boarded the *Charming Nancy* and made the perilous journey across the heaving waters of the Atlantic.

She would write to them of her precious child, and she would receive a letter from her mother months later. She would be in favor of the Indian child, this beautiful baby who would grow with the Lenape nature of wisdom and *faschtendich* (common sense) ways.

Kate had no fear of the Native Americans. She often felt pity for them, without speaking of it to Hans. Deep in her soul, she found the arrogance of the Amish settlers disturbing. They were here first, these forest dwellers, their minds a wellspring of knowledge about so many things, especially the ways of survival. When winter and its bitter allies—wind, snow, and cold—threatened their existence, they survived in wigwams covered with bark, and they survived well. Their knowledge was beyond measure. They valued the land, worshiping the Great Spirit. Who was to say they were heathen? Kate didn't believe they were. The marauding, the murders, and massacres were the only way they knew to protect and keep the land they felt was rightfully their own.

When she felt a tap on her shoulder, she looked up into her young friend Anna Troyer's smiling face. "Your baby is awake," she whispered, then sat down smoothly, a smirk of accomplishment on her face. She had been the one to tell Hans *sei* (Hans's wife), Kate, that the little Indian baby was awake.

Quickly, Kate left the barn, hurried around the side of it, down the grassy slope to the house, where she found Hester cooing and smiling in Enos Buehler's wife, Salome's, arms. "What a pretty child! It takes my breath away," she said, lifting her face to smile sweetly at Kate.

"She is, isn't she? We're guessing she's Lenape."

"Oh, I would say so. She looks like them. Her rounded, high cheekbones, the wide, flat eyes. You are surely blessed."

Eagerly, Kate searched Salome's eyes, for truth, for honesty.

"Do you . . . Are you one of those . . . Do you think it's all right that we have her?" she stammered, uneasily.

"Why, of course. Kate, you couldn't let the dear child perish. Don't you think an Indian girl that was in trouble likely hid the baby for you to find? Who knows? They might be harsh in their punishment of loose girls, so, of course, what else could you do? Surely you believe she's a gift of God."

"We do. We do," Kate said, nodding her head. "But . . ."

"What?" Salome asked.

"My mother-in-law."

"I heard."

Salome clucked her tongue, shook her head, said she wished her much *gaduld* (patience). Kate nodded, but her lower lip was caught in her teeth, her eyes bright with unshed tears.

"Did you sew the dress?"

"Oh yes. It was a work of love. Every stitch was a joy. You can't imagine how it really is, after nine years."

Salome laid a kind hand on Kate's shoulder, gave it a squeeze, and went back to the service, leaving her alone with Hester. She marveled again at her perfect features, the little rosebud mouth, which opened into a smile that melted her heart every time.

Now she would have to grapple with the suspicion of men, or women, and what they thought of her. Of them. Of her and Hans and their decision to keep this little lost Indian baby and raise her in the Amish church. Mostly, they'd been supportive, but still. She'd have to wander among her people with the feelers of a cockroach, waving ahead, searching, checking attitudes, always fearful of a slam, a put-down, a glance of disapproval. Or would she?

Perhaps all she needed to do was hold her head high and be assured, proud of what they had done. So often that was hard to do, the lessons of humility, lack of pride, fear of authority, so skillfully imbedded in her soul, the teachings of the ministers a much-needed discipline. They were necessary, she knew. It was why the Amish stayed free of the worldly ways of excess and pride.

Just sometimes, she wanted to be free of the cross that was hers to bear, the fence that proved to be a two-edged sword. Safety and security, love, a feeling of community; on the other side, the indecision, fear of doing wrong, lack of backbone. Were these ways a safety or a handicap?

At home in front of a crackling fire, Hans lay on the bearskin rug and pulled her down beside him. He apologized for his impatience when Hester cried on the way to church. He stroked her face with his rough hands. He bent to place his lips tenderly on hers and told her he loved her with all his heart.

She returned his love, and far into the night they talked of her fears, her doubts, of Hester being Native American, of his mother's disapproval. She told him of her lack of resolve, withering under his mother's stern words.

He explained to her, then, about his mother. She had not been like other mothers, those of his friends. She was harsh. She punished him with a branch from a willow tree that sang through the air before it sliced into the tender flesh of his bare legs.

He rolled onto his back, his hands crossed on his chest. As he spoke, his voice quivered with the intensity of memories that he had not been able to successfully bury. They were pushed back, perhaps, but still alive, as he spoke of the iron hand his mother wielded over him, and still did.

Kate nodded, loving her husband with a new understanding. This, then, was why he loved Hester with such limitless feelings. He wanted a much better life for Hester than he had had, growing up beneath the stern rebuke of a woman who wasted no time in vaingloryying her children.

When the baby woke to be fed, they bent their heads together, a beautiful silhouette. In the background, a warm, crackling fire, the picture of perfection, a small family whose foundation was communication, love, and trust.

Hester wasted no time. She drank her milk, burped, and returned to the deep sleep of an infant. Her day had been strenuous, traveling to church with her parents for the first time. Kate tucked her in, kissed her cheek, and said a little German children's prayer, asking God to watch over her precious baby daughter.

They slept in front of the fire that night, and long after Hans was asleep, Kate lay on her stomach, staring into the red coals on the hearth. She relived each step of her day at the spring, the mewling cries, the feeling of being watched.

She prayed that God would watch over them, keep them safe from harm, and let the Indians know Hester was safe, all right, and in good care.

She thought of her mother, and the need to speak to her rose so strongly in her breast, she felt as if she would suffocate. "Mam. Oh, my Mam," she whispered, but no one answered. Only the cry of a screech owl reverberated through the surrounding trees, followed by the shrill, undulating reply of his mate.

Instinctively, she reached across Hans's back, wrapped her arms around his strong body, and felt exhaustion enter her mind. Secure in the sturdy log home, she soon fell asleep. A mouse emerged from the hearthstone and delicately lapped up the spilled cow's milk before scurrying back into its nest.

Chapter 3

Kate was puzzled when a summer virus persisted. She'd drunk the salted water from the oats she boiled, the way her mother told her. Unable to keep that down, she'd rolled onto her bed in the middle of the day, wave after wave of nausea sending the room spiraling counter-clockwise as she retched into the stoneware chamber pot by her bedside.

Today, she was looking for wild ginger. Hannah Fisher had told her there was nothing better for summer virus than ginger root steeped in boiling water. She combed the north side of the ridge with Hester in a sling on her back, her black hair visible above it, her bright black eyes following every moving object around her.

When Kate was outside, Hester was always quiet, completely immersed in her surroundings, leaving Kate free to go about hoeing the garden, pulling weeds around the cabin, or whatever she chose to do.

It was hot, much too hot to be walking all across the side of the ridge with a baby on her back. Her head pounded, and dizziness set in. She had the evening meal to think about and all the white laundry to retrieve from the fence, fold, and put away.

The heavy summer leaves stirred lazily above her as she sank to her haunches, squatting to take up a corner of her apron and mop her flowing forehead. Her eyes scanned the forest floor. Mayapples, way past their prime, a few mountain laurels, some dandelion, a few ginseng plants, poison oak, but no ginger plant.

She'd go back. Surely, tomorrow the nausea would abate. This was only the summer stomach woes, the way she'd often experienced. She had probably eaten too many onions with the fried rabbit on Sunday evening when Manasses and Lydia had paid them a visit.

The minute she stepped inside the door of the small log house, she knew she had been sloppy and left milk to sour somewhere. She sincerely hoped there were no blowflies on it. Sniffing, the nausea threatening to gag her, she lifted lids, checked the cupboard for spoiling food, but found none. What smelled so sour?

She sniffed Hester's cradle, lifted the little blanket and pillow and buried her nose in them. But she could not trace the sourness that hung over the interior of her house.

Shrugging her shoulders, she slid her baby off, sniffed her lower dress, then patted her and kissed the top of her head before placing her in the cradle. Immediately, Hester set up a howl of protest, which Kate had learned to ignore, and she soon quieted.

Taking up the poker, she stirred the coals on the hearth, poured water into the iron kettle on its swinging arm, and turned it above the hot coals. She'd boil some beans, adding a bit of salt pork. It was too hot to make a full meal. Hans appreciated cold soup, so she placed raspberries in a crockery bowl, added a dollop of molasses, broke some stale, coarse, brown bread over it, and pushed the bowl to the back of the dry sink. When the beans were finished, she'd add milk to the cold soup, and that would be his supper.

The smell of the molasses brought a fresh wave of nausea, which she stifled by holding her breath. She sank to the wooden settee by the fireplace, surveyed the line of white undergarments and sheets on the fence, and sagged wearily against the wall. She wondered if Hans would offer to bring in the washing.

Surveying the interior of the house, she noticed a few tired-looking cobwebs hanging limply from the ceiling, ashes scattered across the hearth, grease stains on her normally immaculate floors. Perhaps she would die. It had been two weeks, and if anything, the nausea was worse. The house needed a good cleaning, and she had absolutely no energy. It was frightening, suddenly.

There was that sour smell again. Getting up, she began her frantic sniffing, coming up empty-handed, hot, and frustrated. It had to be the hottest summer she could remember.

The beans bubbled in the pot, and she went to the barrel to slice off a bit of salted pork. When she lifted the lid, saliva rushed into her mouth, followed by a hot wetness in the back of her throat. She made a mad, headlong dash for the front door, where Hans found her straining and retching a while later. He put his arm about her waist, led her into the bedroom, and laid her gently on the crackling straw mattress. He said he'd go for the doctor, tonight yet.

No, no, Kate shook her head, desperately not wanting him to spend precious dollars on an unnecessary doctor visit. She assured him she would be fine after she found ginger root and they made tea with it.

Hans lifted Hester from her cradle, cooed and crooned to her, then slid the soft, white undershirt from her shoulders, saying it was too warm to wear anything in this heat. Such a small baby shouldn't be so uncomfortable.

Hester loved her new freedom, kicking and chortling, blowing little spit bubbles and laughing, while Hans stood and gazed down at her perfect little body, the skin a golden-brown hue. He had tears in his eyes when he told Hester that God had been too good to them. They did not deserve this perfectly beautiful child to have for their own.

Tears formed in Kate's own eyes, her overwhelming love for him filling her with an almost spiritual emotion. Hans was everything she ever wanted in a husband and father of her children.

It was her friend Lydia Speicher who finally drummed it through Kate's thick skull. They laughed about the episode for years to come. Kate had gone on her desperate quest for ginger root once more, after a few days of lolling about in the heat, sick, tired, and completely at odds with both Hans and Hester.

Finally, late one afternoon, when it was so hot the whole atmosphere seemed to sizzle, she stumbled on one lone plant. She dug it up as feverishly as a half-crazed man panning for gold nuggets, carried it home, and soon had a cup of the life-saving, fragrant tea.

She took a deep sniff of its fragrance, anticipation stamped on her face, illuminated by the glad light that normally played across her face. But her deep intake of breath turned into a surprised look of disbelief. Before she could swallow, she dashed to the front door and relieved herself of anything she had managed to keep in her stomach.

She would have allowed Hans to bring the doctor, had it not been for Manasses and Lydia's visit. They lived about seven or eight miles to the east along Irish Creek. They had two children, both boys with curly brown hair and wide-set brown eyes, named Homer and Levi.

Lydia was short and thin, with freckles splattered across her nose, as if God had had an afterthought and sprinkled her face with extra decoration, like a fancy cake. Her hair was mousy brown, her eyes the same color, and her nose was flat and wide. To hold more freckles, she told Kate, wryly.

Manasses was called Manny, for short, and he was of average height, with sun-tanned skin, a shock of brown hair, and eyes that were not really a color, just not white like the area around the irises. He couldn't grow a decent, manly beard, only a tuft of hair on his chin and a few discolored straggles along the side of his face, which was the source of endless ribbing from Hans.

When they drove their wagon down to the log barn, Hans jumped up eagerly, but Kate dragged herself to the dry sink to begin washing dishes in cold water, fast, before Lydia saw the dried food on them.

It was all she could do to keep from crying when Lydia walked through the door, but she wiped her hands on her apron, shook hands, and said she was glad to see them.

Lydia peered into her face in the fading light of evening and said Kate looked like something the cat had dragged in. In spite of herself, Kate laughed in short, helpless bursts, then told her she'd been sick for many weeks with an upset stomach. She guessed she'd eaten too many onions.

Lydia said nothing, just found the straw broom in the corner and began a thorough sweeping of the hearth. She scrubbed the planks of the tabletop, still saying very little.

Lydia always talked, always, so Kate asked her a bit timidly if she'd done anything to offend her.

"Not other than being dumb."

"What are you talking about?"

"Katie, you're . . ."

Her voice trailed off, as color suffused her face. She blinked, and more color deepened the blush on her cheeks. She stammered. She looked out the window and sighed.

Finally, Kate asked her if she had a serious disease. Was she going to die?

With a tortured expression, Lydia whispered, very soft and low, "You're in the family way."

Kate sat back in her chair as if she had received a blow. She blushed as red as the wild strawberries that grew along the bank by the barn. "I can't be," she whispered back.

But she was. Hans received Kate's stammered whispers with whoops and uninhibited yells. They had waited almost ten years for this, and now they would have two. Hester would be a bit over a year old when their baby arrived.

Hans helped her with the garden. He helped her pick the peas and beans and then helped to shell them. He planted carrots and beets, more pumpkins and late onions.

Slowly, the nausea subsided, her energy returned, and she tackled her chores with renewed energy.

They dug the carrots, turnips and beets, carefully placing them in the root cellar behind the house. She helped him make hay, hoe corn, and haul manure.

Hester, barely five months old, sat up by herself now, and Hans made a small wooden box for her. They placed her in one corner and adjusted a feather pillow around her. Everywhere they went, Hester bounced along, her brilliant black eyes shining below the thatch of blue-black hair.

When the hot sun shone down unmercifully, Hester never whined or whimpered. She sat bolt upright and viewed her world with eyes that missed nothing. Sometimes it seemed as if her skin absorbed every sight and sound and smell, keeping her fulfilled, occupied simply by watching the horses and birds, or smelling the outdoor scents of honeysuckle, ripe manure, and the sun-kissed earth. She loved to sit in the corn rows, playing with the dirt, sifting it through her little brown fingers.

Kate had watched when she'd taken her first mouthful. An angry expression crossed her face, and she let it all dribble back out. What stuck to her tongue, she swallowed dutifully, and she never tried eating it again.

Hans said she was a sensible child. Later in life, he predicted, she would be gifted with many talents, with the amount of things that kept her interested now. Kate agreed, secretly proud of her beautiful daughter. Then Hans brought another small swatch of homespun fabric home, this time a shade of rose, almost identical to the color of the curtains he'd torn down. She swallowed her anger like a bad tincture of herbs, smiled, and said she was pleased.

Dutifully, she produced another fine Sunday dress, placed the little white linen apron over it, and was glad. She asked Hans, though, why he never bought enough fabric so she could have a new shortgown and skirt.

When he became very upset, blaming her for being someone *behoft* (possessed) with lust of the eyes, she let the matter drop and never brought it up again. She did, however, keep a very small sliver of the fabric and tucked it into the letter she wrote to her mother, asking her if she knew where to purchase something of this shade that was less expensive.

The underarms of her only Sunday shortgown were wearing though, so she patched them, using tiny stitches so no one could tell. It was not unusual to wear the same dress to church for many years. But she felt as if everyone was whispering behind her back about wasting money on the plumage she put on that daughter of hers. Perhaps she was ashamed of Hans's adoration of Hester. Whatever it was, she wasn't comfortable carrying her brilliantly dressed daughter into church, knowing her own frock was in a lamentable state.

But it was a small thing. She decided not to fret or worry about something so insignificant. It was actually nothing.

In the early summer, they whitewashed the interior of the house. Hans mixed lime with water, and they brushed it over the logs and crumbling mortar, bringing a new cleanliness to the walls and a new white light over everything.

Kate's energy was renewed, and she cleaned the furniture with linseed oil, washing all the insides of the drawers, scouring the plank floors with hard lye soap, and loving her house.

She realized how happy it made her to be surrounded by the things she cherished. The woven coverlet on the wooden settee by the fireplace was a nine patch, washed many times, its colors fading to a sort of nondescript sameness, so she set about making another.

She lifted the brown homespun bag from the small attic she could reach by the sturdy ladder against the wall, heaving it over her shoulders as she stood on the top step, her memory serving her well. Every scrap of worn-out clothing went into this bag. She would sew the small pieces together to form a bed covering or a child's coverlet.

She would make a fine coverlet, a small one, to soften her seat on the bent hickory chair she always sat on to rock her baby to sleep. The interior of her house was so white, so clean and new, she would make a colorful coverlet like a bouquet of flowers she'd picked by the spring. Her mind darted rapidly from one pattern to another as she strained to remember the design she'd seen at Amos Hershberger's. It was multi-colored strips.

Could she cut and arrange a variety of strips into a pleasing whole? It seemed a bit daunting, especially now, with all the garden work. She'd have to do it when she found a few minutes now and then, probably mostly in the evening by candlelight. The gardening could not wait the way the bits of colored scraps of material would.

She cut some of the patches that morning though, guilt hampering the sure slices of the scissors, as she cut around the rectangular template made of wood. The blue fabric represented the joy Hester had brought into their lives. Yellow was the sunshine of summer, the warmth that drew the healthy plants up from the earth, fruits ripening, ears of corn maturing, beans hanging in heavy pods from the lush vines twined around the shaggy bark poles set in straight tripods along the rows. There was gratitude in the yellow, too, gratitude for God's sunshine, its warmth and nourishment.

Green was the forest, the mainstay of every settler's existence. The trees, the leaves, the abundant herbs and berries, the wild animals that provided them with food and clothing. The pine trees and mighty oaks provided shelter for all the creatures and enveloped the small log house with their bountiful green embrace, a protection sprung from the earth itself.

Kate frowned at the lack of red. Well, she'd take care of that later. Red signified the red bird's wing, wild raspberry bushes, the holly, and all dots of brilliant, glossy red. She'd dye some of the pale swatches of fabric with pokeberry juice whenever she had time.

The nausea had all but disappeared now, leaving her with an enormous appetite. Everything she had not been able to eat before, she ate now in large quantities. Great piles of beans, sizable slabs of fried meat and eggs, all disappeared from her heavy redware plate, followed by sips of creamy buttermilk or milk laced with molasses.

Hans watched his wife's head bent over her plate, shoveling food into her mouth with quiet efficiency, a sudden urgency to fill the great grasping stomach that seemed to be constantly empty. She developed a bit of a double chin, and her neck and shoulders became rounded, fuller, along with the rest of her.

But she kept the garden weeded, helped in the fields, and whitewashed the small log house, cleaning it until it shone. He had no complaints. If his wife put on a pound here and there, it was no big concern of his. She was a good woman.

Soon the attic would fill up with the harvest, onions heavy and white, braided together by their tops in a long string, mounds of orange pumpkins, turnips, and squash laid out on the floor for the winter's use. Kate grunted a bit as she bent over to pick the yield, Hans opposite her in another row, and his good-natured teasing made her laugh.

Hester was crawling fast now, so quick that Kate could hardly keep up with her, grabbing at the little dress as she came close to baskets of beans, pulling her back from the edge of the chair she always loved to sit on.

Kate's whole world turned into constant color and motion: Hester's bright black eyes, her brown skin, the orange of the pumpkin against the changing leaves of the forest, all red and yellow and green. The whitewashed log walls inside the house brought out the rich, brown hues of the wooden furniture. Kate mixed strong apple cider vinegar with a bit of beef tallow and polished all of it with a bit of soft cloth, rubbing it into the wood grain to produce a luxurious sheen.

In the evening, when the light of the betty lamp shone in the windows, the fire leaping and dancing on the hearth, and Hester sound asleep in her cradle, they sat talking, making plans. Kate's needle wove in and out of her patches, and Hans's voice rose and fell. They were truly content. God had blessed them far beyond measure, allowing them to become parents again, even after the gift of little Hester. They felt unworthy of God's goodness.

Hans worked on a new springhouse, set by the flow of the cold waters that bubbled out of the ground at the base of the ridge, fed by the runoff from the surrounding mountains. Kate was thrilled to think of having a cool place to set her eggs, milk, and cheese.

She watched Hans lift the heavy limestones, his massive shoulders straining at the seams of his shirt, the constant way his hands lifted and cut, fitting the stones tightly, building this sturdy little house that would help keep food cool in summer. The well-placed structure would greatly ease Kate's burden of cooking and preserving.

Manny Speicher came to help when the stone walls became taller than Hans. Together they formed a scaffolding of stumps and planks and lifted the stones onto it, as Hans kept laying the stones to the eaves.

He made a small window at each end, one to the south and one to the north, and then built a sturdy shake roof over the top. The spring flowed through small openings on each end, keeping the stone interior cool and moist.

Hans built a trough made of stone and mortar so that the running water would not upset the heavy crocks filled with milk. They marveled at the occasional buttermilk they could have, no matter how warm the days would become.

Kate's springhouse was the envy of the whole community. More than one housewife was guilty of serving her husband soured milk with his breakfast porridge, raising her eyebrows in practiced meekness, saying sweetly that a springhouse built the way Hans Zug had done would take care of any milk spoilage. They came by the wagonload to view this wonderful springhouse. Kate beamed with pleasure, her full cheeks blooming with color, her blue eyes radiant upon her husband.

Hester sat on Hans's knee, her bright eyes missing nothing, always alert but seldom smiling, although her black eyes twinkled, enhanced by her thatch of straight black hair.

When the November winds swooped down off the ridge and blew the tired, brown leaves to the ground, the beautiful red, yellow, and orange ones came along with them. Hester sat outside, her nose red from the cold, and played in the leaves, crawling among them, sometimes holding so still she was like a stone child. She watched a curious chipmunk scamper close then sit as still as Hester as they eyed each other, neither one showing any fear.

Kate wondered at this. Were Indians trained in the way of the forest, or did these traits flow in their bloodlines, as much a part of them as the color of their skin or the growth of their thick, black hair? Kate had never realized a baby could be so perceptive, so curious, black eyes missing nothing, constantly darting here and there, the unsmiling little mouth beneath them expressionless.

Yes, she was an Indian, and an Indian she would likely remain. That was all right with Hans and Kate. They would take her to church and raise her within the religious tradition they knew would shape her and bring her to God, the Amish way of life instilled in her heart.

Yes, they would dress her modestly and simply, in clothing like that worn by grown women. She would be baptized upon her faith, and all would be well in the end. They were devout, believing that through the blood of Jesus Christ they were redeemed from their sins. They practiced a godly lifestyle and prayed for their sweet baby girl every day.

And now she would have a sister or brother very soon. Kate's heart was alight with anticipation. Hans made a trundle bed, a low, small bed that could be shoved beneath their large bedstead during the day, made of the same sturdy pine boards.

So the cradle stood, awaiting the next little occupant, empty and quiet, the rocking stilled for now.

Chapter 4

They were blessed that there was very little snow on the ground so the doctor could arrive that February.

Hans drove Dot like a madman. The doctor clutched his hat and prayed out loud, his prayers peppered with exclamations of surprise and astonishment that they came out of that gully or over that rock in one piece.

Hans's face was as white as the few inches of snow that dusted the road and surrounding woodland. His eyes bugged from his face in genuine panic, and he leaned forward until his nose almost touched the walloping haunches lunging ahead of him, as if that position would get him back to the house sooner.

Dot was wild-eyed, lathered with white sweat, her sides heaving, when the wagon careened to a stop by the barn. The doctor sat still as Hans launched himself from the wagon, instantly loosening the traces, his hands shaking.

Tugging at his hat brim, the doctor told Hans very courteously that he was, indeed, extremely fortunate to be among the living, let alone steady enough to attend to his wife, and he hoped he would never again have to sit in the same wagon Hans did.

Hans paid him no mind, just waved a hand as if to rid himself of a fly, and asked if he intended to sit in that wagon the remainder of the evening.

Elizabeth Hershberger was already there, the neighborhood matriarch who attended mothers at a time like this. Everyone called her Lissie, a tall, round woman of roughly seventy years, well trained in midwifery, although she usually worked with a doctor, if possible.

Lissie was a widow, Dan having been knocked over by the tree he had felled, miscalculating its crash to the ground. They found him pinned underneath, his skull crushed. Lissie buried her man, took up the reins of the fat brown mules, and kept the farm going with the aid of her two sons.

Lissie was not one to be soft-spoken or humble. Her voice rang out with a deep, bell-like sound. Unlike many Amish women, she knew her own mind and spoke it without fear of being corrected.

"What took you so long?" she asked, as her way of greeting. The doctor was not overly fond of Lissie, having been scolded many times by her tongue-lashings. His nerves were already shot, and he was in no mood to tangle with her self-appointed position as head coach.

"Look, Lissie, if we would have been here before this, we wouldn't be here at all. So keep your nose out of it."

Hester began to cry, this loud exchange from strange people frightening her. Hans scooped her up, kissed her on her soft face, and held her the remainder of the evening until her head drooped against his chest. Then he changed her into the heavy nightgown she wore on winter nights and tucked her into the trundle bed, setting it carefully into the shadows.

Lissie made tea, strong and black. She spread cold biscuits with apple butter and swung the kettle of beans over the fire until the house was filled with the aroma of browning beans.

Dr. Thomas Hess was a gentleman with refined ways. He had graduated from a college of medicine in England, so he did not take kindly to Lissie's slurps and rumbles of appreciation as she tucked into the food.

He watched her large fingers grasp the heavy handle of a cup, lift it to her lips, gulp, and then grimace, her eyes squeezed shut in endurance as she swallowed the hot drink. She dipped her biscuit into the bowl of steaming beans, then opened her mouth wide to shove half the bean-laden biscuit into it, leaving a trail of apple butter on her greasy dress front.

"Now, then, Dr. Hess, why aren't you eating? It's *wunderbar goot*" (wonderful good), she chirped, her small black eyes dancing with pleasure.

Dr. Hess thought of his wife lifting a china teapot to pour tea into a china cup for him, but he didn't mention that. He just said politely that he would have a cup of tea, which was plunked in front of him with more enthusiasm than good manners.

For the second time that evening, Dr. Hess thought he might not live, swallowing the boiling hot tea from the scalding cup. When the pain on his tongue became unbearable, he went outside, scooped up a handful of snow and considered it a great and calming luxury to bury his stinging appendage into it. Lissie chortled to herself at the doctor's discomfiture. The smarter a man was, the less common sense he had. So much for college, if he didn't think a redware cup was hot.

Kate delivered a fine son. Dr. Hess pronounced him "strapping," already able to plow the fields. He was pleased to say that with feeling as Lissie whisked the baby away for his bath.

The doctor puzzled over Hans Zug's expression, or the lack of it, for a long time. Finally, he shrugged his shoulders and let it go. Clearly, something was wrong.

Hans looked at the pale face of his son, the too wide forehead, the swollen eyes, the pouting red mouth, and searched desperately for any inkling that someday he would have hair. There was none. Only a whisper of pale, red down, or was that his imagination? To think that his own flesh and blood, his offspring, would look like this shook him to the core of his being. He always imagined his sons would be handsome. He asked Lissie if there was something wrong with him.

"What do you mean, Hans Zug? Why, of course not. He's the finest, sturdiest baby I've seen in a coon's age. You better not mention one word of this to your wife, or I'll clout you with a wooden spoon. Shame on you."

And Hans was ashamed. He cringed, turned red with embarrassment, and gave Lissie a whole ham instead of giving the doctor the other half, to get back into her good graces. He sincerely hoped she wouldn't speak of this to anyone.

After his son's bath, the baby looked clean, but not much better. Hans watched with a sort of mistrust as Kate held their son, her face shining with a mother's love, cooing and whispering to the baby, saying he was so beautiful. *"So an shay kind"* (Such a beautiful child).

Hans tried to smile and share her joy as he bent over his wife. But his smile was thin and wobbly, his eyes dull with disbelief.

"What do you want to name him?" she asked, her voice soft, her eyes luminous in her wan face.

All Hans could think of was Ham. Wasn't he one of Noah's sons in the Old Testament? He looked like someone who could be named Ham. What he did say was, "It's up to you, Kate."

"Oh, but a father should name his child. Especially his first son. Remember, I named Hester." Kate's voice was soft and quivering with emotion.

Hans couldn't think of anything except Ham, but he didn't say it. Noah was Ham's father, and a man of God with that ark building and all, so he said, "I like the name Noah." He hoped his voice came out reverent and loving, without a trace of Ham in it. He sighed with gratitude when Kate smiled up at him, her eyes full of love, and said that was a good name, a sound and reasonable name from the Bible.

Lissie was pleased with their choice, although she told them they should have named their son after Hans's father, Isaac. But Hans didn't want Lissie to know he wasn't overly fond of his father, who had let his youngest brother Shem have the farm back home in Switzerland.

He looked Lissie square in the eye and said his name was Noah. She shrugged her shoulders and thought she was glad Hans wasn't her husband, with those bugging eyes and pushy demeanor. "You need to name one son after your father, you know that," she said, tartly, packing her things in her square, black bag.

Hans was tired, sleepy, and disagreeable, so he merely asked her why. She said it was the *ordnung* (law) of the church. Hans said he never heard of such a thing, whereupon Lissie lifted her finger and shook it at him, and told him if he wanted to know he could ask John Lantz, the bishop. It was only common sense and good manners, and it brought a blessing to a family to name a son after the father.

Andy Fisher's Ruth was their *maud* (hired helper), arriving before breakfast, a small, narrow-faced girl with brilliant green eyes and a small sliver of red hair showing around her cap. Kate would stay in bed for ten days and be waited on for everything she needed. Ruth was capable, and the household was run smoothly, much to Hans's delight.

He felt sorry for Hester, the poor, dear child, not able to understand any of this, Kate in bed with the new baby that she was so jealous of. She held out her arms and wailed for her mother, but Kate was not allowed to hold her because it would take too much strength.

So Hans spent a lot of time with Hester. He taught her to take her first steps, watching her face as she concentrated on keeping her balance. Her black eyes lit up with the challenge as she wobbled toward her father, giggling gleefully as he swooped her against his chest in a loving embrace when she succeeded in taking a few steps alone.

From her bed, Kate's eyes shone, watching Hans with their daughter. Yes, he was a wonderful father, so good with her, the dear man.

As she fed their son, she held him close, running the palms of her hands across the small, bald head and marveling at his beauty. He was so different from Hester. Of course he was. He was white, and would likely be blond when his hair came in, but he had Kate's blue eyes and a strong nose. This baby was already sturdy and well rounded, his hands and feet large. She envisioned him walking behind the plow, his hands clenched on the wooden handles, his bare feet coming down solidly, crumbling the earth. These hands would wield an axe, fell mighty trees, clear land of his own, continue the way and heritage of the Amish.

Ruth was so good with Hester, entertaining her with stories, twining string around her fingers, and playing "Hide the Thimble," so that Kate's recovery was a time of contentment and bliss.

During the second week, when she got dressed and sat on her rocking chair, resuming light household duties, she was bothered by a niggling doubt. At first she could push it away successfully, but later, as the days marched on, she confessed to herself, it was beginning to be a worry.

Hans's lack of attention to his son loomed above her, a real adversary she had to face. He still had not held him. He very seldom looked at him. Usually the baby was sleeping, but still. Was this normal? He hadn't been this way with Hester. Not at all. He still wasn't. Why wouldn't he hold his son?

Before Kate could control them, thick tears leaked from her closed eyelids, and her chest felt as if it would cave in on her stomach. She simply could not rise above a feeling of deep despair.

Hans found her in the rocking chair, crying. Kate would not say what was wrong, but after Ruth was asleep behind the curtain that was placed at one end of the small house, Kate confided in her husband, haltingly at first, but her voice gained strength as she continued.

Hans was guilty, ashamed, and caught red-handed, possessing terrible thoughts about his newborn son. He begged Kate to forgive him. Kate said of course she would and assured him that Noah would grow hair and his looks would change as he became older. She slept dreamlessly that night, so glad the little talk had changed her worst fear about Hans as a harsh and uncaring father.

The following day, Hans held his son for the first time, and Kate's heart overflowed with joy. He looked down on Noah's sleeping face, smiled, and said, yes, he would be a strong and husky boy some day. Then he didn't pick him up or acknowledge his presence for three days. Kate finally decided to let it go. Perhaps this was more usual behavior than she was aware of.

When company began to arrive on Sunday, Hans hardly let go of Hester. She was always ill at ease around strangers, but when the house became full of visitors, she clung to Hans, her black eyes darting from one face to another, as if surveying the room for her own safety.

Many of the visitors commented on Hans's devotion to Hester and thought it was truly a sign of a caring heart, the way she wasn't even his own child. Kate smiled and nodded, glad Hans loved the little Indian child. When she confided in Lydia about Hans's lack of affection for little Noah, Lydia pooh-poohed the silly notion and said lots of fathers didn't pay much attention to newborn babies.

"They don't know how to hold them. They feel awkward and think they look stupid. They can't feed them, so they act as if they don't even know a baby is in the house. It's normal." She held a finger to her lips, held her head sideways. "I'm sort of surprised, though. He's so good with Hester. I mean, look at him, she never leaves his lap."

Kate nodded and met Lydia's eyes, but neither woman said more about it.

Spring came late and slowly that year. Some of the mountain laurel didn't bloom till June, and many buds froze, so that the pink flowers seemed to be scattered randomly across the bushes, as if they had been forgotten but tacked on at the last minute.

The wind was harsh and the earth cold as Hans and Kate plowed the garden. Hans ran a harrow across the heavy clumps of soil that had rolled away from the plow.

All around them the woodland was coming to life, buds pushing out of branches, small green leaves unfolding under the sun's caresses, wild daffodils popping out of the moist layer of leaves. The weathered log house stood solidly against the backdrop of trees and hills, a cozy home surrounded by rail fences, the shake roof almost black with age now.

Kate had planted a lovely wild flower on either side of the door, and small pine trees dotted the area around the house. The cows had kept the grass down very well, so it was coming up green and smooth. The slope to the barn contained many dandelions and purple violets.

The new springhouse was more picturesque than ever, now that Hans had built an arbor for the wild grapevines. There were glossy leaves and pink buds where he had trimmed the vines, and Kate was looking forward to making wine in crocks. Her mother had always done that at home in Switzerland.

The barnyard was alive with calves, two new lambs, and a white calf named Ruth. Hester toddled everywhere. It was impossible to keep track of her, she was so quick, darting in and out of buildings or the surrounding forest. Like a mouse, Hans said, a little brown mouse. Kate smiled, then laughed out loud. She really did look like a field mouse.

Kate was so busy she did not notice the nausea when it returned. She just knew she wasn't hungry, and not once did it occur to her that another child might be on its way until she began losing her breakfast in the woods behind the house. Wiser now, she didn't undertake a frantic digging for ginger root. Grin and bear it, she told herself.

She didn't tell Hans, afraid of what he might say. She knew he was busy getting the tobacco in. He had no time for his son, who at almost five months, was grabbing at anything he could catch and stuffing it into his mouth. His hair was still not there, as reluctant to grow as Kate had ever seen anything. Hans always spoke to

Noah when he returned from the fields, hot, tired, and overworked, but he seemed reluctant to pick him up even now. Kate paid close attention, her anxiety decreasing whenever Hans would take him up and hold him for a few minutes before a meal was ready. But always Hester was the one he held, whose plate he filled while talking in silly, childish tones. She shrieked with glee, imitating his voice.

When another son arrived, they named him Isaac. He looked very much like Noah, except for a nice amount of brown hair growing mostly along the top of his head.

Lissie was in attendance once more and told Hans this was very nice, naming his son Isaac the way he should. Hans merely said he was glad she approved and left it at that.

He did, however, have to take her home after the *maud* arrived. He did it with the same speed and lack of caring he'd used when driving Dr. Hess the last time. Lissie careened around on the seat, her full cap sliding around on her head, her hip hurting with each teeth-rattling bump over rocks and ditches. She got down stiffly, faced him, and said if they ever needed her again, she'd bring her own horse and wagon, that if he didn't have more sense than he had just demonstrated about how to drive a horse, why then, she'd just drive herself.

Hans was deeply ashamed. He hadn't wanted her to think that way about him. Old bat. Maybe they wouldn't need her for a while.

With each child, Kate seemed to spread out around the hips until she was quite ample. He felt ashamed of the fact that he didn't want his wife to look fat like Mamie Troyer.

Well, at least this son had hair. That was a huge relief.

Kate was so busy she had to employ every skill she could muster to get all her work done. Hans's mother, Rebecca, was pleased they named their second son Isaac, so she made the trek across the hills and ridges quite often to lend a hand wherever Kate needed her, which gave her a boost. She baked sturdy loaves of satisfyingly chewy bread, which they sliced and ate alongside chunks of pork, cooked with some parsley, and salt.

Rebecca said new things were being discovered, different seeds. How would they like to have watermelon? She had planted some, so hopefully, till the end of summer, they would be eating this succulent fruit.

Isaac was a cranky baby, fussing after each feeding. Mamie Troyer treated him, but he remained fussy. Hans said she needed to stop breastfeeding and put him on cow's milk, but Kate resisted. When Hans stomped out to the barn, slamming the door, she began to cry, but not for long.

She lifted her head and decided Isaac was not fussy because of her nursing. He was cranky because that's just how he was. So she fed him, changed his diaper, and told herself that if he preferred crying, that was up to him. Noah was not walking at thirteen months, so Kate's shoulders and arms became strong, enduring many hours of lifting and holding her heavy sons.

Hester was two years old, a happy child and able to entertain herself endlessly outdoors. She ran just for the joy of running, her thin, brown legs propelling her down the slope to the barn at an alarming rate. She could also sit quietly for hours, watching butterflies and bumblebees or listening to the voices of the many kinds of birds singing from the treetops.

That summer she imitated the crow, the cardinal, and the turkeys that gobbled ceaselessly in the evenings behind the house. She began to talk in garbled German. She could not quite master the "r" sound, which always came out as "w."

Hans was completely enamored of his winsome daughter. Although Kate had her moments of wishing he would pay as much attention to the boys, she held her worries inside, bottled up against his anger and denial. It was easier that way. Submission was necessary as a wife, and she had been taught well by her mother. So she let Hans's undivided attention rest on Hester, while she tried hard to make up for his lack of interest in Noah and Isaac, devoting her time and attention to them.

Sometimes meals were a disaster, with Isaac screaming and Noah clumsily shoving great amounts of food all over his face. Hans was always quick to smack his hands, which resulted in great howls of protest and Noah's large mouth spilling food all over the table. Hester sat, her black eyes taking it all in, her mouth giving away no feelings. When Hans turned to smile at her, she did not always smile back. Sometimes she would go around to Noah's chair after the meal was over and wrap her thin brown arms around him, lay her cheek against his back, and close her eyes briefly.

One night after the children were in bed, Kate saw an opening to approach Hans about his lack of fatherly affection. Hans became contrite, ashamed, yet again.

"Have patience with me, dear Kate. I don't mean to be partial to Hester. I really don't. It's just that I feel so much more for her than I do for my sons. Perhaps I was raised that way. Maybe it's normal. I do like my sons. I do. Kate, Hester is just different. Do you think it's because she was abandoned? A poor foundling?"

His face was so earnest, his eyes clear and searching, that Kate's heart melted within her. She put her arms around her husband and loved him. Of course he was sorry. He was doing the best he could.

Their nest egg grew as Hans carefully placed the dollars from his blacksmithing jobs into the jar. He bought more land and planned to build an addition to their small house before winter.

Kate thanked God for a hardworking husband who provided well for them. She put her worries aside, threw herself into her work as never before, and tried to keep away every unsettling thought that entered her mind.

The women of the community didn't know how she could manage so well with three little ones. Her house was clean. Her picturesque garden produced many fine vegetables. Her bread was light. She churned butter with great skill so that the wooden dasher pounded the milk into gobs of butter. Her arms grew strong and muscular, and her figure expanded with the many pats of good, rich butter she spread on thick chunks of brown bread. And Kate did like her ham.

Chapter 5

At Christmas-time, the snow lay deep and heavy, covering the log house with the new addition, burying it up to the windowsills. The snow had come down steadily all night long, and a whole day before that.

Hans stepped out of the house, surveyed the white world, and thought they'd be able to make it to his parents for the *Grishtag Essa* (Christmas dinner), an annual event, long-awaited and looked forward to.

He'd get the bobsled and clean it well with the straw broom. Yes, hitched double, Dot and Daisy could make it. He went to the barn, fed the livestock and polished the harnesses, swept the bobsled, then went to get Kate's opinion.

Her eyes were cloudy with doubt, but at his persistence, she placed bricks in the fireplace and began to dress the children. It would be all right to travel the eight-mile distance as long as the wind did not pick up, and it was too early to tell about that. The snow had just stopped.

Hurriedly, they ate cornmeal mush fried in lard, along with bread and butter. Hans rinsed the dishes while Kate pulled on the warm underclothes she would need to stay comfortable, then dressed in the old linen Sunday short-gown and apron she always wore. She did have a freshly washed linen cap, which looked quite neat, so she tied the strings under her chin, jutting it forward so it fit better.

She dressed Noah in warm undergarments, then placed his linen shirt and vest and knee breeches on him.

Little Isaac still wore a dress, which he would continue to wear until he was two, or close to it. He looked angelic with his bangs cut straight across the forehead and locks of light brown hair hanging below his ears in the traditional "Dutch Boy" haircut.

Noah had some very fine blond hair, but you could still mistake him for being bald from a distance. He was husky, large for his age, and a bit pigeon-toed, but he walked and ran as if he'd been doing it for quite some time.

When everyone was bundled into their outerwear, Kate pulled on her cape, wrapping it around herself, tied a heavy scarf around her head and across her mouth, flung the shawl across her shoulders, and secured it with a straight pin. She put her flat hat on last, pulling the front well past her face.

Hans placed the hot bricks wrapped in cloth at their feet. When they were tucked in below layers of bearskins and coverlets, with the horses hitched to the singletree, they were on their way to *Doddy* (Grandfather) Zug's house.

Kate was unprepared for the winter wind's cruel bite. She bent her head to the spray peppering their faces from low-hanging branches and from the horses' hooves kicking up the powdery snow as well. Chills crept up her spine. She shivered then set her mouth in determination. She would not whine, neither would she complain. It was her wifely duty to abide by the wishes of her husband.

Behind them, Noah was not visible, he was so covered with a heavy layer of robes and skins. Hester, however, had managed to extricate herself from the confines of the heavy covers and sat, her eyes two dark stars of wonderment, peering out over the sides of the bobsled, dodging the spray of snow from the branches, or lifting her face to it, her tongue catching the cold wet particles.

The wind was definitely picking up, and it was only mid-morning. A stab of fear shot through Kate, but she only glanced at Hans, his face resolute beneath the heavy black hat, as he urged the horses forward.

When they arrived at the top of an especially steep incline, Hans pulled back on the reins and said, "Steady, there, Dot. Easy, Daisy."

The bobsled creaked across a few rocks then dipped at a dangerous angle as they started down over them. Kate pushed her feet against the dashboard to stay seated. She clung desperately to little Isaac and prayed to God that he would see them safely through this dangerous trek to her parents'-in-law home.

She was thankful for Hans's skill as a blacksmith, as the horses' haunches backed against the britching, holding the bobsled back, keeping it from careening madly down the rocky incline.

A break in the trees revealed an awesome world of brilliant white, puffs and layers of snow piled on every pine, their jutting, dark green needles accentuating the brilliance of the snow. The sun was obscured by a mass of cold-looking gray and white clouds, and Kate bent her head as a shower of snow blew across her line of vision. There was no doubt in her mind that there would be high winds, and how were they to remain safe? She knew well the roaring of the wind that blew in after a long snowfall, driving great walls of loose, powdery snow ahead of it, creating drifts that could be up to ten feet high.

She swallowed. "Hans," she said, "the wind is picking up."

Hans did not answer. He was occupied with the task of getting his family safely down the treacherous mountain road.

A thin, high wail sounded and increased steadily as Noah was thrown from side to side, sliding under the robes and then out of them.

When Kate could turn, she found Hester on her hands and knees, her black shawl flapping in the strong wind, her voice crooning, comforting her brother. "*Na, na, na, komm,* Noah. *Net heila*" (Don't cry).

Noah heard his sister's voice and calmed down as her mittened hand patted his back. She was not much bigger than he, but she thought of herself as his little mother, taking him under her wing, a two-year-old biddy hen.

Kate's shoulder slammed into Hans's as the wagon swung hard to the right, straightened, and then continued its descent. Steam came from the horses' nostrils in small gray puffs, their exertion showing now in the dark, wet hair around their harnesses.

When they finally found level ground, Kate breathed out as she let the rigid set of her shoulders slump, glad to have navigated that long, steep downhill safely.

The roaring of the wind in the treetops increased now. The snow was only little bits hitting their faces, but as the tree tops lunged and swayed, showers of snow whipped across them, the horses bending their faces along with them, to avoid the stinging.

Hans leaned forward, urging them on, calling loudly. The horses responded by lowering their backs and giving a strong lunge against their heavy collars so that the bobsled whispered through the deep snow.

Whether they hit a rock, or one runner went into a ditch, or one of the horses slipped, Kate could never be sure. She knew only that there was a sharp thud as if the bobsled had slammed against a tree. She heard a resounding crack of wood splitting and felt herself falling sideways, her only thought for Isaac, her sleeping son.

Everything turned into pandemonium after that. Horses whinnied in terror, unable to understand the jutting of the broken singletree that pulled their heavy collars taut to their sweating neck muscles.

Hans cried out as he lost his grip on the leather reins, although he managed to cling to the seat of the bobsled as it turned over on its side. Kate cried out hoarsely once, then remained silent as she lay in the deep fluffy whiteness. Noah screamed and kept on screaming as he was dumped into the snow, his wide, red mouth filled with it. He choked, coughed, and then resumed screaming.

Hester flew off the bobsled, landed in deep snow, sat up, and blinked. She watched Hans leap and flounder through the snow, his face red, his mouth open, screeching and threatening as the bewildered horses thrashed and kicked in their traces. They panicked as they became thoroughly entangled, their eyes rolling.

Hans yelled and yelled. Kate lay in the snow, her shoulder sending out red-hot stabs of pain. She gritted her teeth against it, willing herself to stay conscious as the cold, white, whirling world spun around her. Isaac, wakened by his rude dive into the snow, cried loudly, matching his brother's screams.

Hester blinked again. No sound emerged from her mouth. She lifted herself to her feet, waded through the snow to comfort Noah, and then went to her mother. Bending her head, she touched Kate's face. *"Mam?"*

Kate struggled to sit up. The children needed her. She had to rouse herself. Leaving little Isaac crying in the snow, she managed to push herself onto her side with one hand. Her shoulder was fiery with pain. She was able to move her fingers, as well as bend and turn her elbow, so she figured her arm and hand were all right.

A heavy wall of snow came roaring through the trees, the massive trunks creaking and bending. Kate struggled to see Hans and the fleeing horses then bent her attention to her throbbing shoulder.

She concluded that nothing was broken. She was likely bruised, the joint having taken the brunt of her weight as she fell off the bobsled. She would be all right. Gritting her teeth against the pain, she bent to retrieve poor little Isaac, his teeth chattering with cold and fright. She held him against her body beneath the heavy shawl, hunching her head to the flying snow, then searching the wild, cold, unrelenting winds for her remaining two children. Hester was visible in her little black shawl and hat as she crouched over Noah, who was still crying out in terrified howls.

"Hester!"

Her word was whipped away by the wind. Kate realized in that instant that their situation was dire. She fought down the fear that threatened to take her common sense away and replace it with stupidity, tempting her to try walking through the snow and the drifts that would certainly and rapidly form.

Hans would calm the team. She watched as the broken bobsled lurched, lifted, and then fell over and over, as the kicking, galloping horses drew it steadily away from them. Hans cried out as he plunged clumsily after the frantic animals.

They had to have the horses. Could they possibly get to *Doddy's* house without them?

Kate turned her head to view the long, steep hill they had just traversed, inch by dangerous inch, and now here they were on level ground, but with a useless bobsled.

Thank goodness, Noah stopped screaming, calming under Hester's motherly words. Only the wind, the retreating sounds of the galloping team of horses dragging the overturned bobsled, and Hans's cries brought Kate harshly to her senses. They were alone.

Kate calculated the distance back to the house. Somewhere between two and three miles. Between here and there was the long incline. She had two babies and a two-year-old. There was her painful shoulder. She had nothing but the wagon robes and the deerskins. They would freeze here. Hans needed to take care of the team. She would have to provide for the children.

Laying Isaac carefully in the snow, she moved her left shoulder gingerly, telling herself the pain was, indeed, subsiding.

Hester stood in the whirling whiteness, her black eyes peering from beneath her hat's rim, watching her mother, saying nothing, waiting to hear what she would say.

"Hester, can you walk home with me?" Kate asked, her words catching in little gasps of pain.

Hester blinked. "*Ya.*"

So Kate made a sled of sorts by gathering two corners of the wagon robe together and then laying the babies on it. She shushed Noah, bunched the corners of the robe in one hand, and then bent to its weight, walking briskly as she struggled through the snow.

She assured herself that Hans would know she was heading back to the farm. She had to. It was the only rational thing to do. They never should have started out in the first place. Anger at Hans washed over her. Jealousy stabbed her heart. Tears of rage and weakness boiled up from her pain, thinking of Hans's undying love for his mother. Skinny, meticulous, ill-tempered, old . . .

Kate caught herself, guilt stopping the flow of Adam's nature that she knew caused these thoughts. She knew how much she resented Rebecca too much of the time.

Her anger propelled her straight up the hill, her babies' yowling and bouncing only adding to her strength. She was glad for her strong legs and wide backside, her powerful shoulders, her muscles tempered like a man's from the lifting of her sturdy sons, the washing, the gardening, the cleaning.

She stopped to catch her breath, swiping a wet, mittened hand across her running nose, her streaming eyes.

"Mein Gott, vergebe mich meine Sinde" (My God, forgive my sins), she whispered.

Her thoughts were of the devil, she knew, and he must be overcome by the power of Jesus Christ, she knew, too. And so she did her utmost to repent, her inner spiritual struggle matching her strides, hampered by the incline and the snow.

"Hester, are you coming?" she called back to the small form, struggling to place her footprints in those of her mother, the dragging blankets making it much easier for her to walk.

"Ya."

Hester's voice was calm, unafraid. She was simply going about her duty, following her mother back to the house. She had to place her feet carefully, but she could do it.

Love for her beautiful little daughter welled up in Kate as she leaned forward, pulling her sons steadily up the incline, picking her way carefully among the rocks and through the ruts where rivers of rain had furrowed deep ditches down each side.

"Do you want to sit on the blanket awhile?" Kate asked, turning to Hester.

"*Nay.* I can walk."

"Are your legs tired?"

"*Nay.*"

"Can we go on?"

"*Ya.*"

Hester scooped up snow with her mittens, brought it to her mouth, and took big mouthfuls. The child was thirsty, Kate realized. How did she know enough to eat the snow to slake her thirst? For the hundredth time, she marveled at the child's common sense, the way she knew things far beyond her years.

There was no time to contemplate these things, she had to get her babies home. Their cries of terror had turned into pitiful whimpers, sniffles, and an occasional cough, so Hester plowed on.

The bare branches of the trees were increasingly whipped about by the force of the wind, the snow thick and whirling around them. Kate was not as frightened as she had been when they were going in the opposite direction. She knew exactly where she was and the distance she had to cover. Her shoulder had settled into a dull, pulsating pain, bearable now, and she knew she would make it home.

When Hester lagged behind, Kate stopped, rolled her sons more tightly in their cocoon of deerskin, and then kept on going. Her hands were numb with the cold, her toes like blocks of ice, but she had no time to worry about that now.

Chickadees fluttered by the wayside, crows cawed overhead. A red bird called from a bush nearby, and Kate did not know Hester stopped walking until she turned to see, her daughter now a small black dot a hundred yards away.

"Hester!" she called, impatient.

The call of the red bird was repeated, over and over as Hester resumed her little steps through the snow, her eyes alight, snapping brilliantly beneath her flat hat.

"*Rote birdy*" (Red bird), she announced.

Over and over, she repeated the call.

"Aren't you cold?"

"*Nay.*"

When a particularly strong gust of wind whipped the snow into a fast-moving white cloud, enveloping them inside, Hester merely sat down and buried her face in her shawl. She didn't look up until the stinging snow had slowed, then she pushed herself to her feet and looked at Kate, as if to say, "All right, let's go."

Long before the small, gray house came into view, Kate dreamed of it, longed for it, felt as if she would never lift the heavy iron latch and stumble through the door.

At first, when the house came into view, Kate could see only the walls, and then just a part of them was visible. The roof held a layer of drifting snow; the windows were frosted with snow flung against them. She felt a little crazy, as if the cabin had changed in appearance, having turned into a half-buried cave, cold and white and wet with snow.

When she lifted the latch with frozen mittens clinging to her cold fingers, she heaved the burden of blankets and babies through the opening and collapsed beside the makeshift sled after closing the door behind Hester, who stomped the snow off her boots, imitating Hans.

She breathed fast, then got to her feet and went to the fireplace. She uncovered the red coals, digging around in them with the poker. She added a few small sticks of wood and went to attend to her shivering, half-frozen sons. Hester walked to the fire, removed her mittens, held her hands to the warmth, and imitated the call of the red bird once more. She lifted her face to Kate and smiled the sweetest, calmest little grin she had ever seen.

Kate bent, grabbed her daughter and smothered her in kisses. "My sweet, darling little Hester. You did so good. I love you so much. You are the very best daughter I have."

Hester giggled, then turned to place both palms against her mother's cheeks inside the dripping hat. She placed her lips reverently on Kate's, a solemn vow of love.

Somehow, as long as she lived, Kate would remember this.

Hans recovered the team, his lungs on fire from yelling, drawing on every ounce of his strength as he plowed through the snow and roaring wind.

Dot, the intelligent horse, regained her sense of calm first, which helped Daisy slow her headlong plunge through the snow. The bouncing sled hampered their progress, so Hans was able to catch up with them after less than half a mile. He had to spend considerable time freeing the still-struggling horses from the broken sled. He cut his hands and pinched his fingers, but with heroic effort, he eventually freed the heaving, sweat-soaked animals from the terrifying confines of twisted harness and bouncing sled.

He stroked Dot's neck, praised her and calmed her down, then looped the reins across her neck and flung himself on her back, leading Daisy.

He figured he'd find his wife and children huddled beneath the blankets. He planned on continuing the trek to his parents' house on horseback, which might have been better in the beginning anyway. He was shocked to find no trace of his family. He sat on the horse's back, peered through the whirling whiteness, and did not know what to make of the situation.

Where had she gone? She couldn't carry three children. Then he saw the indentation, the wide path through the blowing snow, all but obscured in some places. What was wrong with her? She couldn't return home.

He peered up the steep hill they had just slid down and thought he'd find her, that they'd resume their journey to his parents' house. His mouth watered, thinking of the wild plum pudding, the roast turkey and stewed rabbit, the potpie made with squirrel, the applesauce and cream drizzled over the berry pie.

The whole way home, his ill temper worsened. Kate never heard him put the horses in the barn. She didn't know he was at home until he burst through the door, lifting the latch in the same second, a heavy, clunking sound that made her jump.

"Kate."

"Yes?"

"Why did you come home?"

"What was I supposed to do? I couldn't sit in the snow with two babies. And Hester."

"We could have ridden the horses to my parents' house, Kate. You know that. I'm disappointed in you."

Kate hung her head. "I'm sorry."

"I want to go."

"But . . ."

Kate floundered. She lifted her eyes to the window, the now whirling whiteness never letting up.

"Hans, I don't feel it is wise to take these young children out in this blizzard. God has spared us this time. If we were foolhardy enough to try again, he might not."

Slowly, Hans's anger abated, and he shrugged off his steaming coat. Going to sit by the fire, he acknowledged Kate's words with a nod of his head, but barely.

Kate kept more thoughts to herself as she bathed both sons in very warm water, gave them chamomile tea, and dressed them in heavy flannel nightgowns before putting them to bed.

Silence hung invisible, a spirit of martyrdom on Hans's part, a deep shame on Kate's. How much of her wrong decision had come from her hidden jealousy of his mother? For it had been a wrong decision, if Hans, her husband, had wanted to go.

She made fried mush and *fishly*, the best cut of deer meat fried in lard, steaming hot and crispy, a pot of bean soup with *rivels,* the flour and egg dumplings thick and heavy in the scalding milk to cheer him, but he said he was not hungry. Instead, he watched Kate lean over her large bowl of soup, spooning it into her mouth with studied intensity. He felt an emotion close to disgust, but he read his German *Schrift* (Scripture) to resist it.

Only Hester could elevate his dark mood, playfully grabbing his shirt and hanging on like an agile little squirrel.

Kate washed dishes, listened to their play, a smile on her face. Yes, God had sent the darling girl into their lives to fulfill them. Already she was weaving her special magic in the family, a little mother to Noah, a ray of sunshine to Hans, a blessing to Kate, who needed her now, more than ever, as the familiar nausea welled up yet again.

Chapter 6

By the time Elizabeth was born, Noah was a hefty two-year-old, and Isaac had turned one.

Elizabeth was called Lissie, after the midwife who attended the birth. Never pronounced "Lizzie," in the refined manner of the English, she was known as "Lissie," with the German pronunciation. A fair child with a thatch of thin brown hair and her mother's blue eyes, she was welcomed into the family with gladness.

Hans held her, became more familiar with her than he had with his newborn sons, but it wasn't long until he largely ignored her.

Hester was three years old, almost four, although Kate and Hans never knew the exact date of her birth. They calculated she may have been six weeks, perhaps a month old, when Kate found her at the spring. So on the first of March they celebrated her birthday with a sweet cake made of molasses and brown sugar.

Little Isaac had come down with an alarming fever and cough after Kate's trek through the snow. Onion poultices and Lissie Hershberger's knowledge pulled him through. He remained sickly throughout that summer, crying endlessly with wheezing little breaths from his damaged lungs. Finally, at summer's end, Mamie Troyer made a tincture of herbs learned from an Indian grandmother who was traveling through, and he became stronger.

Noah, however, ate ceaselessly, developing a fine physique at a very young age, although his hair was still thin and very blond. He followed Hans about the farm wherever he could and did not think anything was amiss if Hans kept him at bay, barely noticing or speaking to him, rarely acknowledging him and often smacking him. He learned to wait his turn for food, to stay out of Hans's way, never to speak unless he was spoken to, and to sleep when he was put to bed.

With his mother, he could be more lively, ask more questions, be more playful. He never thought much about it that Hester was always granted favors and never spanked. It was simply the way of it, through a child's eyes, his life accepted without question. He loved the dark-eyed Indian child and was too young to know she was anything but his older sister.

By the time Rebecca arrived, Lissie was a little over a year and a half old, and Hester was already learning her numbers. From her bed, Kate taught Hester the alphabet, nursing little Rebecca as the *maud*, Ruth, went about running the household smoothly.

Lissie Hershberger, however, returned to visit with Kate when Hans was out shoeing horses. She brought a box containing pennyroyal tea for Kate to drink and a determination that Kate needed to hear what she had to say. The varicose veins in Kate's legs were not *goot,* and she needed to look after herself.

Lissie sat in the hickory rocker, drank cup after cup of peppermint tea, held little Lissie, and told Kate she had a beautiful family, she really did, but now she needed to take care of herself. She asked where Hester was. Kate told her she went with Hans to shoe horses. Lissie squinted her eyes, pressed her lips in a straight line of disapproval, and asked why Hans didn't take Noah. Kate lowered her head as a small blush crept across her tired features. "Noah gets in Hans's way," she said. "He's too small."

"Hmph!" Lissie snorted, which set little Lissie to giggling, reaching up to touch Lissie's face. "That's no excuse. Kate, I have to say this. Either you love your husband beyond all reason, or you're just plain dumb. That Hester of yours is spoiled beyond control. Does she ever get punished for anything she does? It's unnatural the way all of you dote on her. Believe me, your harvest will come with these poor, needy boys. Oh, don't talk, Kate. Let me finish. I've been here at all the births, and nothing ever changes. Hester gets five times the amount of love and attention the rest of the children do, and you don't notice at all. That Hester will bring you down, you mark my words."

Kate dropped her eyes and kept them lowered as wave after wave of color chased over her features. She plucked at the woven coverlet on the bed with work-worn fingers, pleating it nervously. Finally, she sighed, heavily.

"All right, Lissie. If you promise not to speak of this, I'll talk. No, I'm not dumb. Yes, I know Hans is partial to Hester. He always was, but I figure there's nothing I can do to change that, and to punish Hester for his unfairness will only make the situation worse. He is my husband, and I have promised to obey him. His will is my will, Lissie."

"Well, good for you."

The words were short and hard, pellets of mockery now. Kate watched her fingers methodically pleating the coverlet, as if her own hands did not belong to her.

"All I can say is, be careful with that child."

Kate nodded.

The subject was dropped, conversation flowed to easier subjects, and they spoke of community news and the band of Lenape Indians who was traveling through the area and had stopped to trade furs at the trading post on Northkill Creek.

"You know, they are peaceable people, the Lenape. I don't believe they'll ever make much trouble for us, except perhaps if we push them out of their land. Too much of that going on as it is." Lissie spoke her thoughts out loud. "I'll make dinner for you, before I leave," she said, suddenly, getting up and asking what Kate was hungry for.

Kate was grateful and said she would love a good pot of deer stew—fresh venison, onions and carrots, thickened with cornmeal, just a bit—to eat with bread and molasses.

Lissie rumbled and buzzed around the house, teased the children, complimented the housekeeping, and then brought Kate a bowl of the fragrant stew. She filled one for herself and sat beside Kate's bed to eat it. Ruth fed the children. The house smelled wonderful when Hans stepped through the door, Hester's hand clutched firmly in his own. Seeing Lissie, the smile on his face became crooked, then disappeared entirely, as he let go of Hester's hand.

Hester went to sit beside Noah to peer into his bowl. She took a bite of his bread, licked the molasses off her lips, then took another bite, a large one. When Noah protested loudly, Hans gripped his shoulder and gave it a shake.

"Let Hester have some, Noah."

So Noah watched silently as Hester finished his bread and molasses. Isaac dropped his spoon, yelled loudly about it, and was given a smart rap on his shoulder from Hans. By that time, Lissie was visibly shaken, but, wise woman that she was, kept spooning up her stew, her eyes lowered.

Hans filled a bowl of stew for himself and one for Hester, then asked everyone to bow their heads in silent prayer. Lissie shot him a look of disrespect, yet she set her bowl on the small table beside Kate's bed and bowed her head. But she didn't pray, pretty sure the prayer wouldn't be heard under these circumstances, when she felt like a teakettle ready to explode from the buildup of steam.

Isaac and Rebecca came to visit, clearly pleased, their faces wreathed in smiles at the arrival of the little namesake. She was short and plump, measuring only nineteen inches long, her eyes big and blue, her skin pink and healthy. Rebecca was so pleased, she unwrapped the baby, counted her fingers and toes, then, alarmed, quickly counted them again.

Kate watched the consternation on her mother-in-law's face.

"She . . . Wait a minute."

Then, quietly, a mere whisper, "She has six fingers on one hand, Hans." She said this to Hans, not Kate, as if he could do something about it if she told him first.

Hans moved swiftly to his mother's side. He looked, his lips moving softly, his brows lowered.

"Yes, there are six."

Kate didn't care if she had seven fingers on one hand, she was a dear baby, another girl, and her love only expanded and wrapped itself about this newborn, same as all the others.

Hans's eyes found Kate's, accusing, begging her to fix it. He certainly did not want a disfigured child. She would be *fa-shput* (mocked). "Can you do something?" he asked quietly.

Her face white, Kate shrugged, holding the baby tightly to her breast as if to reassure herself they could not take her away because she had six fingers. Who would notice?

Rebecca would not hold the baby after her discovery, after seeing the extra finger. She had decided that Rebecca was, indeed, disfigured, unclean, as if she had leprosy.

The remainder of the evening crawled by, stilted, miserable. Kate wept after Hans's parents left, but quietly, so he wouldn't see.

After the children were put to bed, Ruth cleaned the kitchen and retired to her bedroom, quietly whispering a polite goodnight. Hans asked her how she enjoyed the new addition. Ruth blushed and said it was nice to have her own room.

He had built the addition because of his forethought, his wanting to provide well for his growing family. He had even built a second stone chimney for that time when they could have a small stove from England, the way wealthier families had. He had also constructed a long cupboard against the wall to hold the children's clothes, another well-thought-out plan on his part.

Kate had so many things to be thankful for, how could she fret if Hans showed a bit of partiality among the children? Kate let her loyalty to Hans edge out Lissie's warning, bolstered by her resentment, too, that Lissie had intruded into their private lives.

Lots of families lived with unequally divided love. Kate remembered that her sister Fannie, a year younger than herself, was most certainly favored by their mother as her skilled fingers produced one work of embroidery after another. Sometimes you had to accept life for what it was and not what you wanted it to be.

Hans came to Kate's bed and lay down beside her. Quietly, he held her hand, his thumb caressing the back of it over and over.

"Kate," he said softly, "I really want to know if there's nothing to be done about the extra finger. What caused something like that in the first place?" His voice quivered like a little boy's, and Kate turned her head to watch her husband's face. There was real fear in his eyes when he turned toward her.

"Is God punishing us for something we have done, that our babies are not perfect?"

"What do you mean, Hans?"

The firelight played across her husband's features, creating a dancing yellow light in his eyes, changing their color and expression, fascinating her.

"I feel I have sinned, that our baby has six fingers."

"Why?"

"I don't know. Sometimes I have impure thoughts."

"Oh, Hans, confess to God. He will forgive if you are truly contrite."

"I don't know why I carry this burden of guilt, but I do."

"If it helps, you can confess to the church. I'm sure John would help you with your confession."

"Oh no, no. I can't do that. It's only fleeting. It's not that bad. Sometimes it seems as if it raises itself, and I can't stop the thoughts that go through my head."

"Pray about it, Hans. Ask God to help you."

"I will."

When he leaned across the baby to kiss her, an involuntary shudder passed through her, and she turned her face away, his lips reaching the formal presentation of her cheek.

When Hans rolled on his side and slept, Kate's eyes remained wide open, her thoughts racing, unable to sleep. Why would Hans have this trouble? Was it Ruth, the hired girl? She'd have to keep an eye on her, for sure, but she'd never noticed one single flirtatious move from the dear, shy girl. She was so hardworking, bless her heart.

Kate's thoughts traveled across the community, the young women and girls, none of them holding the least bit of suspicion even for a second. Oh, well, perhaps it was only a passing thing. Hans was young, and the devil strode about like a lion, seeking whom he may devour, she reasoned. She would be sure to perform all her wifely duties well, obey him in everything, and God would bless them.

Sometimes she could hardly grasp the fact they had been childless all that time. Nine and a half years. And now she was thirty-five years old and had five children. If this continued, she'd have five more by the time she was forty. My, oh.

She hid a smile now. Poor Hans. Why did he think that sixth finger was so awful? His parents were given to myths and old wives' talk entirely too much. Rebecca had told her once that when the moon was full, people lost their minds much easier, and that bad skin came from eating grapes before they were ripe.

She'd ask Lissie. She'd know.

And Lissie did know. She laughed out loud, said she must be getting old. How did she miss that extra finger?

Well, it was no problem whatsoever. She plied the limp finger gingerly, testing its strength, then took a length of string and tied it firmly at the base, saying it would fall off in a few weeks.

Kate nodded. She knew it would not cause the baby pain, and Hans would be relieved of his burden of guilt. The poor man, he worked so hard to support all of them; he certainly did not need the added load of wrongdoing.

When Baby Rebecca was six weeks old, summer was upon them once more. Kate was rested and energetic and threw herself into the work of cleaning her house thoroughly. She sent the children outside to play, then opened the windows, shaved strong lye soap into buckets of steaming water, and scrubbed and swept and polished and waxed until the house shone with cleanliness. It was their turn to have church in two weeks, and Kate was in a frenzy of activity. No one was going to come to their farm and find anything unkempt or slovenly. Not the barn, surrounding fields, the garden, or the house.

Hester and Noah pulled weeds, crawling around the rows of beans and corn, throwing weeds into the wooden bucket Kate gave them. They worked all morning, stopping only to imitate the calls of birds or to watch a timid deer walk across the field with its tiny fawn.

Hans praised Hester's efforts warmly, then tousled Noah's hair with the palm of his hand. Kate's heart ached to see Noah's face light up by this one infrequent gesture, almost an afterthought, but it was a crumb of blessing Noah grasped eagerly. His father had touched him, and it was a benediction, a feeling that was almost holy in a way only little boys know.

Hester was pleased for Noah as well. She was always glad when Hans was nice to the boys, her heart pure and unselfish, the way she'd been since the day she arrived.

As Lissie had predicted, the extra finger on Rebecca's hand lay in the cradle one morning, leaving a funny looking spot on her hand. Kate took up the tiny finger, buried it in the woods behind the house, put a salve on the place where the finger had been, and never spoke of it to anyone after that.

When the first cart drove around the turn in the road and came to church services at Hans Zug's farm, the men's practiced eyes appreciated the amount of forest Hans had cleaned since last time they'd had services, the green of the cornfields, the size of the tobacco plants.

The women gazed at Kate's garden and wondered aloud to their husbands how that busy woman got all her work done the way she did. Did she get up at four o'clock every single morning? She wasn't getting any thinner, said the more mean-spirited ones. Those who held a generosity of spirit were quick to praise, asking Kate, indeed, how did she do it?

Kate blushed and became quite pink and flustered. She said her children were good and helped in the garden, which sounded dumb to her own ears, but she hardly knew what else to say, since praise of any kind was a bit foreign. Not that that was Hans's fault. Of course she knew he appreciated her efforts most of the time.

Hester appeared especially pretty, wearing a new dress in a light shade of green, setting off the caramel hue of her skin. Her eyes were darker than ever, the dress that was buttoned around her neck giving her skin an almost olive hue.

Old Mamie Troyer watched the Indian child and clucked internally, her expression giving nothing away. Why wouldn't Lissie and Rebecca have a dress of the same color? Or Kate, for that matter? Perhaps Hester had an indulging aunt or cousin who presented her with these brilliant shades.

None of it was any of her business, so she would let it alone. That was best. Her eyes followed the graceful, fawnlike movements of the child, caught the glistening blue of her black hair, and thought if she was Kate, she'd pull that white cap front further over her hair. But maybe it was Kate herself who dressed her in that finery.

The sun shone warmly, and the green leaves of the trees dappled the earth as the women walked solemnly to the barn, where Hans had spread the clean straw and set the wooden benches. The barn below was also as clean as a whistle, without a trace of manure anywhere.

Silently, the women filed in, their heads bent, eyes lowered in submission, and sat down, spreading their skirts smoothly across their laps, setting their bare feet neatly on the floor. They never crossed their legs or bounced their knees or feet. This was the Lord's Sabbath, and they were to respect it as such.

When the strains of a man's baritone reached their ears, they waited respectfully until the first line was finished, then joined in, their high soprano voices blending well with the men's deeper voices.

The summer breezes played with the golden straw, as Hans sat with his sons by the opened doorway. Flies buzzed about, a bumblebee droned by, a butterfly made its crazy way along, wings fluttering as it veered left and right.

Hester was making her way to her father between the benches, sliding her bare feet along in the slippery yellow straw. Her eyes caught the butterfly's movement, following it until it was out of sight. It was only then that she completed her walk to Hans, who pushed Noah over to make room for Hester close to him. He bent his head and smiled at her, receiving her smile in return. Isaac leaned forward, smiling at his father, but the smile Hans gave Hester never reached Isaac, disappearing as Hans focused on Hester. Isaac sat back, sighed, kicked his bare heels below the bench, clasped his hands, and looked for something else to hold his interest.

Rebecca was crying, so Kate took Lissie's hand and walked to the house beneath the waving maple trees overhead. The slow, undulating chant of the German words swirled about her, filling her heart with gratitude for this warm day, the sunshine, the fair weather, and the added blessing of having services in their barn, the mothers making their way back and forth to the house with crying babies.

God was in his heaven, as Hans would say, sending his love in the form of nature, the wonders of it abounding everywhere she looked.

Rebecca had cried herself into a red-faced screaming frenzy, so Kate was at the cradle in a few long strides, raising her to her shoulder with the blanket trailing after her, patting and crooning until the baby quieted. She sat down on the rocking chair to feed her. Looking around the house, she was glad the walls were whitewashed, the furniture polished, the floors clean and gleaming, her expertise at housekeeping so evident.

Her close friend Sarah emerged from the bedroom and said it would be wonderful to have a new addition put on her house. Kate was fortunate to have a hard-working man like Hans. Sarah spoke wistfully, her fear of being overheard evident in the slant of her eyes, the discreet touch of her hand to her mouth.

Kate let all the blessings of her life soak into her heart, saturating it with a bounty of gratitude. She loved Hans with all her heart, his four sweet children she had borne, and adorable Hester, the jewel in Hans's crown. If his love and devotion was a bit lopsided, she could overlook it, no matter what that suspicious Lissie tried to instill in her, whittling away at every bit of faith she had in her hardworking husband.

And so she smiled at Sarah, acknowledged her praise with a thankful heart, and assured her friend that, in time, she would have a larger home as well. Sarah's eyes shone warmly, her smile genuine, but with a veil of sadness that alarmed Kate. It was transparent, but barely. Kate looked deeply into Sarah's eyes, lifting her eyebrows in question. But Sarah shook her head, pulled her upper lip down to catch it with her lower one, drawing a curtain of privacy in front of herself as she did so.

Kate had to be satisfied with the puzzlement she carried with her in the coming weeks.

Chapter 7

It was only a few months over a year later that Solomon came into their lives, a red-faced, squalling son who tipped Lissie Hershberger's scales at ten pounds, three ounces. His head was large and well rounded, slick as the new moon. He began his crying within the first hour, and it hardly ever came to an end day or night, his hoarse cries stopping only when he fell asleep. It was those short naps that restored Kate's sanity.

Rebecca remained small and thin, a sickly child who lost her appetite easily and was prone to high fevers. So when the winter winds slammed against the little gray house, shaking it to its teeth, Kate stirred up the fire on the hearth and added more logs, keeping fear and panic at bay by telling herself the fever was coming down now.

For days, she'd lain, her little Rebecca, the fever causing her to cry out with chills, feeling as if she were frozen. Then she'd kick and scream when the heat from her fever became unbearable.

Kate washed her little body with cool vinegar water and fed her echinacea and garlic. She soaked strips of elm bark in boiling water and gave her the cooled liquid, but nothing seemed to help.

Solomon kept on fussing and crying, sometimes reverting to short gasping screams, his face turning purple with the noise.

Kate held her mouth in a thin line as she moved through the small house from one to the other. The rest of the children played around her, sometimes squabbling, but she could usually nip the uprising in the bud by a firm twist of an ear or a pinch of forearm flesh between her strong fingers.

Hans was away much of the time, shoeing horses. Kate wondered if that was really what he was doing, but she reasoned that Solomon's crying was very hard on Hans, that his nerves simply couldn't take it. The poor man seemed not to be able to put up with such a racket, and her own ministrations were simply not enough to make Solomon stop crying. She would need to redouble her efforts, to make Hans's time in the house with his family more pleasant.

Hester was a big help now at five years of age, growing taller, her jet black hair as straight and thick as a horse's mane. Kate wet her hair down, drew it back, braided it into severe braids, and then coiled the braids around the back of her head as tightly as possible. She unwound and combed her hair only once a week.

Her eyes were large, if anything a bit elongated like almonds, her nose tiny and flat, with delicate nostrils, her mouth wide and full, her skin a beautiful brown hue. Everyone noticed Hester, including visitors to the Amish church. Some of them stared, others gasped, and then felt ashamed at their lack of good manners. Kate was accustomed to this and found it mildly humorous, sometimes a bit disconcerting, but she never felt afraid. What harm could come to her beautiful child? For that was all she was, a child.

That evening when Hans came home, he went straight to Solomon's cradle, picked him up, and held him. He looked into his face and told Kate he was changing his looks. He believed he resembled her more and more.

Kate was so pleased. She made sure the ham was done to his liking, fried in the cast iron skillet, then steamed in a bit of water to soften it. She sliced cabbage and cooked it until it was meltingly soft, made hominy from the dried corn, and blushed to the roots of her hair when he grabbed her in a darkened corner of the kitchen and planted a wet kiss on her face. "My *gute frau*" (good wife), he chortled, warbling jubilantly.

To what did she owe this attention? She felt elevated, lifted out of the daily cares and rituals of her ordinary life, and thought she could do anything with that kind of praise.

Rebecca's fever came down that evening. Kate held the shockingly thin body, stroking the brown hair away from her fevered brow, and sang, softly.

Oh, Gott Vater, in Himmelreich,
Un deine gute preisen.

Hans hummed from his seat by the fireplace, smiled at Noah when he recited the German bedtime prayer, tucked Hester's hand in his, and put the children to bed. Kate felt as if she had a visitation from God himself.

The harsh winds of winter moaned and shrieked around the eaves. It slapped loose a shake on the roof until it made a buzzing sound as Kate lay beside Hans, sleepless. Between them, little Solomon lay, snoring softly. He had just been fed, and she should have lifted him for a burp, but it was too warm and cozy under the covers. She'd let him burp on a remnant of cloth, where she'd laid him on his stomach.

From the wooden trundle bed, the sound of thin, fast breathing chilled her through and through. The breathing was Rebecca's, her fever in its second week now, and Kate wanted Dr. Hess. She no longer had the audacity or good faith or whatever you wanted to call it to think that all these remedies she'd tried would heal her now.

The tip of her nose stung, the prelude to quiet sobbing. She could not bear to think of losing one of her babies. Not one. They were her whole life. She gave them all her love. Her day's work was centered around her little ones. They were, pure and simple, a part of her.

But Hans would have to agree about the doctor. She dreaded approaching him, with all the good humor he'd been displaying, splashing it about the small log house with abandon, coloring their world with new and vibrant hues. It would cost money, but she believed the amount Hans had had significantly increased now.

Rebecca's fast breathing was accompanied by a hoarse rattle. Terror filled Kate's chest. Outside, the wind flung twigs and leaves against the small six-paned windows.

Kate shivered and then left the warmth of the bed to check on Rebecca.

The sick child was so hot, she was flinging her arms about. Kate drew back, gasping, then stumbled to the bed, grasped Hans's shoulder and shook, clenching her nails into his muscled arms, whispering, "Hans! Hans!"

He sat up, his brown hair disheveled, his eyes swelled with sleep, his face shiny with night sweat and unwashed skin. "Hans! Please. It's Rebecca. She's very sick. What should we do?"

Hans put a palm to the side, pressed down to lift himself up and away from the bed, pushing little Solomon into the straw mattress. He began grunting, snuffling, and then crying, which soon escalated to shrieks of fright.

"Ach." Hans got out of bed, pulled on his everyday knee breeches, bleary-eyed, his brain still foggy with sleep. He passed a hand across his eyes, rubbing the sleep from them, and said to the crying infant, "Here, here. Hush!"

They let him cry as they hovered over Rebecca, the same silhouette as years ago when Hester entered their lives, and everything had been like a dream, too good to be true.

Now with each passing year, a new baby had entered their lives, leaving them no time for silliness or games or lazy afternoons spent by the creek. Too often, if they had time to give relaxed attention to their children, it went primarily to their one foundling, Hester.

When Hans saw his wife's tears, sliding down her cheeks, he was stung into action. "I'll go," was all he said. Kate lifted her eyes to his with raw gratitude.

"Oh, *denke* (thank you), Hans," she whispered.

A small form appeared in the doorway, then padded noiselessly across the floor, and climbed up on the bed, tugging efficiently at Solomon's blanket.

"Sh. Sh. *Net heila*" (Don't cry). Hester sat on the bed, her legs dangling over the side, her arms wrapped around the crying baby. She lifted one hand and allowed the baby to suckle on her finger, which quieted him immediately.

Hans said goodbye, a thick form in his heavy overcoat, a scarf tied across his head to cover his ears, his heavy black hat set firmly on top.

"Take the wagon," Hester said.

"Certainly."

How long he had been gone when Rebecca went into *die gichtra* (seizures) Kate did not know. She screamed in fright when the small body convulsed, the soft, pliant form becoming stiff as a board, the back arching, the head thrown back as her blue eyes turned up in her head.

Hester sat holding Solomon, her black eyes alive, dancing in the firelight, erect, unmoving, waiting to see what her mother would do.

"No, no, no, no," Kate moaned softly, her mother's heart unable to grasp what her head knew with uncanny intuition was to be.

How many hours, how many minutes? Was it only seconds until her little tongue curled back into her throat and shut off the tiny passage behind it? Her fever had been too high, the infection raging unchecked through her lungs and then into her bloodstream, taking her life.

When Rebecca choked, Kate cried out again. With superhuman effort, she tried to save her little daughter, but there was no use. She was gone.

Gone to a better place. A little angel in heaven. A flower in the Master's bouquet. All of these comforting phrases pushed themselves into her mind and then were sent away by her own refusal to accept the fact that Rebecca had died.

Oh, she had willed her to live. She'd done everything. She'd had Lissie Hershberger more than once, tried all of her herbs and tinctures, the foul-smelling concoctions that spread their vile odor through the house, and nothing helped.

When Hans returned with the doctor, he found his wife on the floor on her hands and knees, rocking back and forth, her eyes squeezed shut as a high, keening sound rose and fell from between her clenched jaws.

Hans went to her but drew back before he could touch her, raising terrified eyes to the doctor. The good doctor assessed the situation by the dim light of the dying fire and shook his head, his mouth grim. Bending, he touched her back. "Kate."

The word cut through Kate's grieving, opening the possibility that she might live rather than die with Rebecca. She had never felt such despair. A great yawning abyss had been before her, beckoning to her. It had been easier to think of simply slipping away into it than to keep fighting.

The doctor helped her up and onto the other side of the bed. He gave her a double dose of laudanum before turning to Hans and the body of the child.

"Hm." His experienced hands felt along little Rebecca's throat, her limbs, her stomach. He realized the suffocation was brought on by her convulsions. It was not unusual. Children died from "the fevers" or "lung fever," as the condition was frequently called.

This baby had never been as hardy as the rest of the family. She'd been pale since the day she was born, her cry a thin, mewling sound like a newborn kitten.

Baby Solomon was in good hands, Dr. Hess knew. He was more concerned about Kate. Sometimes these women who bore a child every year seemed strong and capable, fulfilling their duties without one word of complaint. But they were extremely fragile on the inside, and a sudden shock, a terrifying incident, changed them forever. Dr. Hess said none of this to Hans. He believed Kate was strong, a fighter. She'd come back.

Hans had no tears. Grief was written all over his face as he bent low, talked to the Indian child, then took Solomon from her and laid him gently in the cradle.

He went back to Hester and talked in soft tones, pointing to Rebecca, lifeless and still, laid down tenderly by her mother. Then he took Hester up in his arms and buried his face in her thin shoulder. Soon hoarse sobs began, a manly sound of grieving the doctor had heard many times. It never failed to chill him.

He watched as the little Indian girl's arms went around her father's neck, her little hands patting his thick shoulders. *"Do net heila, Dat,"* (Do not weep, Dad) she said, for all the world like a capable grandmother.

The doctor finally concluded that Hans derived condolence from his small daughter as he held her, the grieving child clinging to her father for her own support. It was, indeed, something to see.

Word spread through the community after Hans rode to tell his parents, who sent their son, John, to other Amish families.

Hans Zug's little one-year-old Rebecca had died of *lunga feva* (lung fever), and Kate wasn't good, were the furtive whispers, the knowing rolling of the eyes. This would get the best of her.

The doctor left a large brown bottle of laudanum, with the precise instructions of a dedicated doctor, more worried than his professional manner allowed.

The wagons began to arrive, Isaac and Rebecca first, dressed somberly in brown from head to toe. Rebecca's eyes remained dry, but her mouth twitched and her chin quivered for just a moment. She felt as if this was a bad omen, her very own namesake, Rebecca, dying like this. God was calling loudly, and she needed to heed his voice.

Isaac's kind blue eyes filled with tears, and he shook his head up and down, saying the young child was *goot opp* (well off). She would not have to go through this sad world with its many trials and temptations.

Rebecca asked Hans why they hadn't sent for her. He said Lissie Hershberger had been there twice.

"Piffle!" Rebecca snorted.

Hans looked sharply at his mother.

"What does fat Lissie know?"

Hans lifted his shoulders and then let them fall.

When Solomon began wailing, Rebecca took him from the cradle, and handed him to Kate, shaking her awake with powerful hands.

"Your baby needs you," she said, sharply.

Kate pulled herself up, shamefaced, then looked at her mother-in-law with eyes that were chillingly empty. She reached for Solomon, fed him as if each movement was too hard to accomplish, keeping her eyes dry and giving nothing away.

They came to help, close friends as well as those who were acquaintances, all sharing the common bond of being Amish and attending the same church services. The depth of friendship didn't matter at a time like this. A child had died, linking them all together within the *bund der lieve* (bond of love).

The neighbors who weren't Amish came and the friendly Indians, the Lenape from the trading post on Northkill Creek. They brought gifts of beads and tobacco. The Shawnee were less confident than the Lenape, not as comfortable in the presence of the Amish, but they came, too.

People cleaned the house and the barn as well. They set up the little brown, wooden coffin on sawhorses. The women sewed a tiny linen dress.

It was Kate's duty to dress the lifeless body of her child. She accomplished this stone-faced and rigid, her eyes dry, with the help of her mother-in-law, Rebecca, who sobbed and cried, alternating between hiccups and nose-blowing.

Noah and Isaac stayed in the background, out of the way, not making any noise, barely whispering. They ate when they were told and sat down where they were told to sit, watching everyone with large eyes that did not seem to understand what was going on around them.

Hester helped with the care of baby Solomon, watching the people coming to the house or leaving it. She offered to find kitchen utensils or cloths for cleaning up, anything she could do to be helpful, amazing the women of the church with her grown-up wisdom.

Lissie Hershberger sat in a corner with a huge slice of apple pie (she hadn't time for dinner before she came) and wagged her large head from side to side.

"See iss an chide kind" (She is a sensible child).

She licked the pewter spoon clean, then asked who made the apple pie. No one seemed to know, so she polished off the whole slice and sent for another, making no excuses except to say she hadn't had apples for too long. How can you make apple pies without apples? Hm? You can't.

No one laughed, or smiled, for this was the day before a funeral, a quiet, holy time, but a few hands were put up quietly, gently placed across mouths that twitched up at the corners.

They dug the small grave with pickaxes and shovels, the frozen, stony soil reluctant to give the child a resting place. Brawny men of the community hacked away at it, inside the rail fence where twenty-five bodies lay buried in their wooden coffins, returning to the dust from which they were formed, and God the judge of their souls.

Funerals were not uncommon. It was the way of it. Folks took sick and died for various reasons. Snakebites, lockjaw, childbirth, whooping cough, accidents, many maladies. That was life in the 1700s.

They cooked a sizable slab of pork, sliced yellow and white, strong-flavored cheese. They fixed carrots and grated cabbage, seasoning it with vinegar and store-bought sugar. They cooked dried apples, plump and full, to be eaten after the meal.

Mamie Troyer said those prunes put her to mind of the *auferstehung* (resurrection). Dried, dead, and dusty-looking, but the minute they were boiled, they returned to life, plump, juicy-looking, and quite tasty.

Lissie Hershberger choked on her hot, black tea, and said Mamie better stop saying those unholy things. It wasn't funny. This was a funeral.

Then they sat together like two fat, black hens, their faces drawn and somber, with due respect to the *hinna losseny* (the ones remaining). But their eyes twinkled and sparkled every time they thought of what Mamie had said about the prunes.

Kate washed and dressed in her best shortgown, skirt and apron. She pulled her cap well over her head and tied the wide, white strings beneath her chin. Then she dutifully received the grieving members of the community and was comforted by them. But she remained strangely dry-eyed, compliant, agreeable, and without emotion of her own.

The graveyard was situated on top of a rise, on a plot of land that was only partially cleared. Sturdy pine trees swayed in the bitter cold, the bare branches of the oak and maple trees creaked and bent by its force.

As Kate stood, hearing the sighing sound of the wind through the pine needles, a wrenching sadness gripped her soul. Her tears began to flow, a warm steady stream that welled up in her eyes and dripped steadily off her chin, falling on her black shawl and splattering on the frozen earth, a baptism of the Pennsylvania soil with tears of a mother's sorrow.

Hans stepped closer to her when he saw her tears, and she drew comfort from his solid presence. She leaned back slightly against him.

They set the house to rights, packed the food away, and resumed their lives as best they could.

Baby Solomon quit his endless crying. He sat up and noticed the world around him, and even smiled at Hester. A restful atmosphere fell across the weathered little house in the woods.

Three more babies were born, in the next four years. Daniel, John, and Barbara. Hester was nine years old when Barbara arrived in June of 1754. She was a capable little maid, used to hard work at this tender age.

Her arms were round with muscles, her legs strong and slender, as lean as a willow. She rode any horse on the farm without a saddle or a bridle. She just flung a rope around its nose, tied it with her own special knot, and was off.

Noah was her best friend, with Isaac coming in second. The three were inseparable, skilled in many ways for as young as they were.

With seven children to feed and clothe, Hans and Kate remained constantly busy, working from dawn till dusk, the children working side by side with their parents as much as possible.

Kate was nearing forty, and she carried her spreading hips and midsection with a certain sense of submission. She accepted all childbearing as a duty, her God-given ability to fill Hans's quiver with arrows. Children were a heritage of the Lord, a blessing, truly.

Hans accepted his wife, grateful for her understanding of him. He indulged her appetite for ham and eggs and great bowls of thick porridge. She loved buttermilk when they had some, aged cheese, drizzles of milk over fruit pie, and homemade bread. She fried cornmeal mush in lard, spread the thick, greasy slices with apple butter, and ate slice after slice, sometimes frying another panfull while she washed dishes in the wooden tub that hung on the wall by the dry sink.

Rebecca eyed her daughter-in-law's burgeoning figure, drew her mouth down, and tightened her grip on the disapproval that threatened to escape. Why couldn't she control her appetite? When Hester was older, she'd be ashamed of her mother. She watched the beautiful child grow tall, muscular, and slender and noticed the innocence of her devotion to her two brothers who were not her brothers at all. Rebecca wondered how long it could last.

Hester was not just beautiful, she shone from within with a goodness, a purity of heart. Love flowed from her, unhampered, the generosity of her spirit endearing her to each member of the Amish community.

"Hans Zug's *glay Indian maedly*" (little Indian girl), they all called her. They watched her light-footed comings and goings, unable to hide how much she charmed and captivated all who knew her.

CHAPTER 8

ON THE TENTH DAY OF AUGUST, WHEN HESTER was ten years old, Hans decided it was time the children had some schooling, and he set about enrolling them in the *Englishe schule* (English, or non-Amish classes). It was a miserable little clapboard hovel five and a half miles away, with old Theodore Crane as head schoolmaster.

Many of the children were Amish, with a few half-Indians, and two or three rowdy sixteen-year-olds. Crane kept his school with a rigid eye and disciplined with unrelenting harshness. He had to. If he didn't, the boys would throw him out and thrash him within an inch of his life.

When Hester, Noah, and Isaac met Theodore Crane, they were dressed primly in clean Amish clothes dyed with walnuts. The boys held their broadfall knee breeches up by a strip of sturdy rawhide when they were too thin around the middle to keep them up otherwise. Their straw hats were yellow, made with fresh straw that summer. Kate made all her family's straw hats, soaking the straw in water until it was pliable enough to be braided, shaped, and sewn together.

Hester's hair was pulled back so tightly, her eyes were raised up at the corners, giving her a slightly foreign look. Her dress was dyed a light purple, her brown legs and bare feet emerging from beneath the hem.

Hans knocked on the door of the school, and Theodore opened it from inside, the latch wobbling to one side after he let go of the knob.

To Hans, it seemed incongruous that there was a knob on that wooden door, broken and muddied as it was by children's boots. But he said nothing about it or the broken windows and stick siding that was warping away from the wall behind it. Instead, he said, "Theodore? I am Hans Zug."

Theodore's bushy black eyebrows shot straight up, his Adams apple rose high and immediately plunged much lower. "How do you do, Mister Zug?" he asked in a high-pitched voice that scared both boys. But Hester was so mesmerized by the bushy eyebrows, she didn't notice the voice.

Hans said he was fine and hoped Theodore was the same. These were his three children, Hester, Noah, and Isaac.

Whereupon, Theodore Crane's eyebrows rose and fell, his Adam's apple bobbed from under his chin to below his tightly buttoned shirt collar, and he squeaked like a mole. "Oy! Oy!"

He was looking at Hester. "This one is not yours."

"Yes," said Hans. "She is ours."

"But not . . . um, you know, your own."

"Yes, she is our own."

Up shot the eyebrows. He hooked a forefinger across his very prominent nose, and a wise rumbling came from somewhere near the vicinity of his throat. The subject was never spoken of again, not once, although Theodore Crane surmised plenty, thought more, but kept his mouth closed.

He tipped his rail-thin body from his heels to his toes and back again, still rumbling in his throat, his narrow, green eyes still surveying Hester. A full-blooded Lenape if he ever saw one.

"Well, do come inside. Please do." He stepped aside and swung both hands to usher them in, still rumbling and clicking his heels.

Hans was appalled at the dark, odorous interior of the classroom. The floorboards were rotting, the old cast iron stove rusty, the desks merely hard, splintering, wooden benches. Field mice scampered across the filthy, leaf-strewn floor. The teacher's desk was more like a box pegged together with wooden pins than a desk.

"How many students are enrolled?"

"This year, if your three come, we'll have twenty-nine."

"That many?"

"Oh, yes."

"Don't you think the school needs a few repairs?"

"Well, yes, but the parents think not. There's no money."

"Would you accept help if we came?"

"We?"

"The Amish."

"If you promise not to convert me. I don't hold with your principles."

Hans Zug found that humorous. It was not the Amish way to try and persuade other people to conform to their ways. They believed they had enough to do, staying on the straight and narrow themselves.

Hans told Theodore this and made a true friend, right there in the middle of the dilapidated schoolhouse.

So a work bee was called for the following Thursday. Theodore Crane had never seen anything like it. The wagonloads of people with little heads sticking out all over was downright heartening. He didn't know these Pennsylvania woods held so many people.

After the first five minutes, he gave up his impeccable manners. He had his hand shaken so hard his teeth rattled, while clammy palms slapped his thin shoulders with the force of a sledgehammer, until he sincerely hoped he'd just met the last hearty Amish man.

The women started a roaring fire, roasted sausages, and then served them with thick slices of bread. One woman brought a wooden crate lined with a tablecloth that was stained with grease and asked him if wanted a fatcake.

He didn't know what a fatcake was, so he said, Yes, he would try one. It was round with a hole in the middle, lighter than a small cake, and coated on the outside with a sort of sugary glaze. He found it delicious and told a woman named Elizabeth, who very much resembled a fatcake herself. He would not like to pay for all the fabric it would take to make a dress for her, but then, he wouldn't have to by the looks of things. They all had husbands.

They whitewashed the walls, scoured the floor, fixed the siding, built long tables in front of every bench, added four new windows, and then sanded and rubbed the stove with lard to keep it from rusting.

Theodore ate a roasted sausage and two fatcakes, marveling at these women's ability to cook, or however they made those fatcakes. He met many of the children who would be coming to his school. At one point he stood and called for everyone's attention.

"I want to say thank you for all you have done here tonight. I hope we will have a successful school year. I look forward to working with you." His eyebrows rose and fell at an alarming rate but never simultaneously. He tipped forward and backward so fast, everyone seemed ready to spring to his assistance if he should happen to tip over.

Lissie Hershberger was quite taken with him, telling the other women he was *sodda schnuck* (sort of cute). Much clucking and eye-rolling followed that remark, but Lissie was quite unabashed. She went over to Theodore and struck up a most interesting conversation, telling him all about little Hester, found by the spring.

Theodore nodded and nodded, rocked on his heels, and stroked his chin with long, thin fingers. "Yes, yes. She was found. Yes, I agree. Hm. Yes, obviously, someone wanted Kate Zug to take the baby. Yes . . . I would say an unspoken pact was made, wouldn't you? Oh, yes. And she's such a winsome child."

Hester sat on her haunches, her purple skirt tucked modestly around her legs, cooking a sausage and staring at the fire. The night was warm and humid, too hot to be sitting so close to the fire, but she was hungry. Noah had wanted her last sausage.

She didn't like this school. She didn't like all these people, but she didn't know what to do about it. Her father was making them go to school, so she was reasonably sure she'd have to obey. She didn't trust that tipping schoolmaster with the dipping eyebrows. She wanted to tell him to hold still, but she guessed she'd better get used to him.

Hester sighed, her eyes flat and expressionless. Why did she have to learn about books? It was worthless, as far as she could tell. She could ride any horse, muck out the stables better than Noah, weed the garden, do the washing.

She could imitate every bird call, knew every bird's own distinctive call, could tell a frog species just by listening—a high trill, a low garrump, a fast whirring sound. She could milk a cow and catch chickens, easily. Even roosters. She was able to change Barbara's diaper and feed Daniel. What else did she need to know? And why?

Far away across the ridge, she heard the yipping of a coyote, the thin, high wail of a distant wolf. The moon was sliced thin, the new moon, when the night was very dark and the whip-poor-wills called best. When the moon was full, their cry was a bit furtive, afraid. Those birds were afraid of their own shadow, silly things. The high call of an elk, bugling frantically, turned the men's heads.

"Harrich mol sell" (Listen to that)! shouted Aaron Speicher.

Whoops of elation followed, smiles widened, beards wagged as the men's adrenaline flowed, reminiscing, recounting tales of the hunt for these magnificent creatures.

Bats dove and swerved through the trees. A night hawk set up its plaintive screech.

"Screech owl."

"No, no. Not a screech owl!" Noah shouted.

Hester grinned in the shadows, her eyes expressionless. Good boy. Not a screech owl.

"Is, too!"

"Nope."

"Yes, it is."

"No. I said no. It's a night hawk."

"Here. Here." Hans hurried over, lifted Noah by one arm, and conveyed him to the wagon, reminding him not to argue. It was not polite, especially for children, who should be seen and not heard, especially in a crowd.

Theodore Crane viewed this scene with hopeful eyes.

Sure enough, the last week in September found Hester, Noah, and Isaac on their way to school, their bare brown feet moving swiftly along the path that led to the newly renovated classroom.

Hester carried a round wooden pail containing the bread and butter for their lunch. The boys were dressed in linen shirts, long-sleeved, and homespun knee breeches, also Sunday ones, kept for church services but assigned for school use now.

Hester's hair shone in the sun's rays that pushed between the brilliant foliage, the large bun twisted on to the back of her head and secured with hairpins only suggesting the amount of straight black hair on her head.

Her usual good humor was not in evidence, her brows lowered, her eyes expressionless, her mouth a straight, firm slash in her dark face. Her brothers had to scramble to keep up with her. They paced off the five miles in quick footsteps without any words.

Hester did not want to go. Kate had done something highly unusual that morning, chastising Hester's disobedience with a firm slap on the side of her head when she refused to allow the comb to rake out the snarls as she did her hair for school.

It was the first in a long time that Hester had displayed any sort of self-will or rebellion. An alarm was set off in Kate by the violent jerk of Hester's head, the flat eyes that hummed with silent defiance. Kate stood her ground, however, admonishing Hester with strong words and sending her out the door with motherly warnings, words of wisdom, and no pity. These things had to be nipped in the bud.

Theodore Crane presided over his twenty-nine students with a good balance of authority and friendship. His eyebrows raised and lowered busily according to his words.

Enrolling was simple. Each child stood, stated his or her name, birth date, and age, then sat down, either blushing, blinking, or showing some sign of discomfort.

When it was Hester's turn, she stood, announced her name, "Hester Zug," her age, "ten," and then stopped, still as a stone, her eyes boring into the opposite wall, black with defeat.

She had no birthday. Kate had never spoken of it.

The silence stretched like a rubber band, taut, dangerous.

Theodore Crane waited, then swallowed. What to do?

Instantly, he thought of Lissie Hershberger's kind words. This girl had no idea at ten years old? He was angry at Hans and Kate suddenly. Why hadn't they provided this girl with a birth date?

What he said, was, "That will do." His Adam's apple rose and fell as he swallowed again, moved on to the next pupil, and vowed to have a word with Hans Zug.

But it was too late. The damage had been done. The two sixteen-year-olds, Joash and Obadiah, had found a delightful new plaything, the angry Indian girl with no birthday. They teased her without mercy, conjuring up myths and old wives' tales of how she appeared at Hans Zug's house.

Hester stood, her head bent, the purple dress billowing behind her where the black apron parted, her sleeves too short, thin arms contracting at the wrists as she clenched and unclenched her capable fingers. That was her only movement, the ripple of purple, the leaves overhead rustling as the early autumn breeze moved them about.

"Your Mam found you, huh? That's because a ghost left you there."

Raucous laughter followed, the smaller boys tittering behind their hands. "*Schpence* (ghost)! *Schpence!*" they yelled, looking eagerly for the big boys' approval.

Where was Theodore Crane when all this was going on so close to the classroom? He was, in fact, tutoring young Isaac Zug, who had to stay in for recess and go over some of the numbers that he always wrote backward.

The sounds of yelling and calling were all commonplace, hovering on the edge of Crane's knowing, but not penetrating it, so the merciless ribbing continued.

When the bell rang, they all went to their seats and sat obediently.

Hester sat down, bent her head to her black slate, lifted the dusty white chalk, posed it above the slate, and waited for instruction, showing no outward sign that anything out of the ordinary had taken place.

The numbers and letters required of her all swam together in a hopeless mish-mash, a sort of vegetable soup of undecipherable shapes and lines that made absolutely no sense.

It took her a few weeks to remember the letters in her name. She could not grasp the concept of using letters to form simple words or doing addition problems. All numbers cavorted around in her head like mayflies, and she could never quite grasp them correctly.

Now the teasing included a new name. "*Dum kopf* (dumbhead). She can't spell, she can't write, that's because she's not quite right!"

Over and over the children continued their brutal chant, and as children will do when something cruel gets started, especially when it's led by the "big" leaders of the playground, the children who felt kindness toward Hester couldn't bring themselves to stop the cruelty, not wanting to be unpopular.

Noah and Isaac played with the little ones and knew vaguely that their sister was being teased, but they figured she was capable of taking it. They thought it was all in fun, and there was no harm in it.

When Hester became withdrawn, Kate reasoned it was due to her dislike of school. She went about the never-ending job of being a mother to her brood, cooking, cleaning, washing, and helping Hans in the fields. Hester's moods became no more than an annoying thought.

So, Hester took matters into her own hands. She roamed the surrounding forest, looking for the perfect branch that was sturdy yet pliant enough to cut and shape. She climbed trees, took Hans's hatchet, and whacked away at a suitable branch, only to have it split down the side, making it useless.

It was months until she finally finished her weapon. The hardest part was procuring a long length of rubber for the part of her slingshot that would launch the rock. Rubber was rare, a precious commodity, but she knew Hans had a small square of it stored away in the chest where he kept his horseshoeing supplies. So she waited for the chance.

The teasing had quieted, somewhat, from a novelty to an occasional uprising from two or three of the more mean-spirited children who thrived on hurting their classmates. Hester brushed it off like bothersome horseflies.

It was the ones who'd started it, Joash and Obadiah, whom she remembered. In her mind, sixteen-year-old boys who are almost men and who resort to bullying a ten-year-old girl need to be put back a notch.

One morning, she told Noah and Isaac to go ahead, that she needed to heed a call from nature. They went on to school without their sister, talking animatedly, innocent of anything out of the ordinary.

Hester slipped into the woods, took a running leap at a low branch her sharp eyes had discovered a week beforehand, caught it deftly with both hands, and swung herself up into the tree. Her purple dress billowed up and out, her bare feet latched onto the rough bark like a squirrel.

A small grunt, and she was up to the next branch, her hands and feet quick and sure. She took the slingshot from the large pocket sewn into the seam of her dress and draped it around her neck.

She stopped. Her dark eyes peered through the brownish-red foliage of the white oak tree. Unsatisfied with her vantage point, she moved quickly to the opposite side of the tree, her eyes moving from side to side, evaluating the distance and the clearest view.

Lifting the small homemade slingshot, she reached into her pocket for the largest, smoothest stone. She rolled it between her thumb and forefinger, savoring the perfection of it. She knew her aim was uncanny, completely without fault. She'd practiced behind the barn for weeks, sliding the slingshot into her pocket whenever footsteps approached.

Her breathing was steady, her muscles bunched, rigid as iron, her feet wrapped about the thin branch as she squatted, her back leaning against an adjoining branch. A group of children approached, walking fast, low words rising to Hester's ears, but she made no move to acknowledge them. A horse and wagon followed, rumbling by beneath the tree. Still she waited.

Then she spied both forms strolling into view, stalling for time, wanting to be the last ones into the schoolroom, to see what Theodore Crane would make of it.

Joash wore a brown straw hat, which made it more difficult as a target, so she chose Obadiah's instead. Skillfully, she fitted a smooth stone into the strip of rubber, drew back, and let it fly, picking Obadiah's light-colored straw hat expertly off his head and setting it neatly in the tall, dry grass beside the road, where it swung on the grass tops, then slithered from view.

"*Voss in die velt*" (What in the world)? Obadiah stopped and lifted his face, his mouth open in astonishment. Before he could retrieve his hat, a stone knocked Joash's hat neatly off his head.

"*Voss gate aw*" (What's going on)?

Shaken, their faces blanched now, they bent to retrieve their hats, only to be hit simultaneously on their backs by hard objects that caused them to cry out, each grabbing at the spot that was already smarting.

When a high-pitched ghostly yodel followed, an otherworldly, weird quality in the awful sound, they scrambled around on their hands and knees, grabbed their hats, and with a wild-eyed glance at the treetops, took off running, unable to resist a few backward glances as the high, undulating wail continued.

When Hester saw a knot of boys in the schoolyard, listening with rapt attention and large, scared eyes as Obadiah and Joash gesticulated with their hands, she turned away, her eyes flat and expressionless.

When the teasing stopped, she said nothing. When she heard Obadiah say there was an old legend about a ghost in the hollow where they had their hats knocked off, her mouth twitched.

For months, the men discussed this happening at church and every other gathering. Always, for a long time afterward, they lifted the reins, brought them down on their surprised horses' rumps, and moved through that hollow at a smart clip, keeping their eyes straight ahead as they rumbled past the haunted tree.

Hester never turned when she felt Obadiah's and Joash's eyes boring into the back of her head.

Chapter 9

That she was an Indian became more evident as time went on, Kate thought to herself, watching her eldest daughter at twelve years of age. The high cheekbones, the flat nose. Her profile was striking, the full view of her face breathtaking, as she blossomed into the first fringes of womanhood.

She was still a girl, a child, and yet there was a difference. She moved with a supple grace, her footfalls without sound. She moved through doors, opening them only wide enough to allow her slim body to slip through, as if opening them wider would allow too much wasted space.

She often seemed to experience the house as an uncomfortable place of detention, causing her to become restless, often pacing from window to window and back again.

With the horses, she was phenomenal, showing no fear and much patience. She exercised a skillful authority that usurped Hans's own expertise. That was why she often accompanied her father on his horseshoeing forays, able to assist with the mean-spirited ones.

On this day in early summer, Hans had asked Kate if it was all right to take Hester, but Kate had demurred, saying the blackberries were ripe, and they needed all they could get to make jam. Hans protested, becoming quite upset, but Kate refused to budge. The family numbered ten now, after the births of Menno and six-week-old Emma.

In the rocker by the hearth, Kate rocked the baby, the chair almost completely hidden by her voluminous skirts, spreading over her ample hips and long, thick legs. Her swollen feet protruded from beneath the heavy skirt, her soiled black apron reaching only a bit below the knees. Her arms were thick and capable, her shoulders fleshy and soft, a home to the dear babies God had been kind enough to allow them to have. That was a thought she still clung to, grasping it with greedy fingers as she completely panicked at the thought that kept trying to push its way into her knowing.

Her life was often a bit more than she could handle. She tried steadily to tip the scales toward accepting children as good blessings, at least they were supposed to be.

Kate struggled. She loved a clean house. She liked her washing done on time, the whites as white as possible. For that, she scrubbed the laundry in water that was almost unbearably hot, using a knife to scrape cakes of strong lye soap with a vengeance.

She carefully folded and put away the wind-blown wash as soon as it was dry. She liked to have a weed-free garden, the walk and floors of the house swept.

But when the babies came every year, the workload increased tenfold. The pounds on her tall frame kept adding on until, when she came to the age of forty, her bones creaked in the morning, her back hurt by evening, and still the babies cried. The weeds multiplied in the garden, and Hans could hardly keep up with the farm and all the horseshoeing.

Kate slung little Emma across her back in a large cloth tied around her shoulders. She told all the children to come along, to gather up the wooden pails by the spring-house, and to climb the ridge behind the house with her.

Hester helped with the little ones, carrying Menno piggyback, her strides effortless, until she pulled far ahead of everyone else.

Kate grabbed a young locust tree, lowered her head, and gasped for breath, the pain in her chest suddenly smothering her. She coughed and wheezed and put a hand to her throat. She watched the little ones cavorting about the low grass like energetic rabbits and remembered wistfully the time when she, too, frolicked so effortlessly.

Quite unexpectedly, an unexplainable rage gripped her. She lifted her head and screeched at Hester in a thin, whining sound of reprisal. "Hester! Stop! You're going too fast, and you don't wait on the little ones!"

Impatient, Hester turned without saying anything, her eyes flat, dark slits. Menno was asleep on her back.

Mopping her streaming forehead with the edge of her dark apron, Kate saw her young daughter looking like an Indian princess—haughty, superior, capable—and the first nibble of jealousy crept into her heart, a subtle invasion, a harbinger of maladies.

Oh, she looked astounding, this child who was no longer the small baby she had found. Her hair was like the wing of a raven. She had perfect form, the ability to climb any mountain or tree, ride any horse, and impress Hans with all of it.

Of course, it was Hester who led them to the black raspberries. They were even better than the blackberries. At the edge of a natural clearing, the bushes grew in such great abundance, it was difficult to remain calm.

The children squealed in delight and were soon covered in purple stains as they tore the berries off the prickly bushes and stuffed them into their mouths. They savored the sweet juice on their tongues, forgetting their steady diet of turnips, cabbage, carrots, deer meat, and pork.

They filled every pail heaping full. Then Hester took off her apron and filled it with the succulent berries. Bees flew lazily by, sated with the sweet juice, and butterflies hovered over the vast growth, sipping their own portion of summer's bounty.

Noah stopped, lifting his face as three crows wheeled across the sky, their raucous cries a warning to his trained ears. At the same moment, Hester pointed, mute.

A black bear and her cubs.

Hester and Noah acted in one accord, herding the children silently, efficiently, out of the clearing.

"Mam, you must come." Noah's voice was a whisper but with much urgency, a tone that Kate completely missed. Loudly, she said, "This bucket isn't full yet."

Noah held a finger to his lips, grabbed the baby from her sling, and ran into the safety of the woods where Hester had herded the remainder of the family.

Intent on filling the one pail to the brim, Kate turned back to the bushes, her wide back to the heavy black brute that was now raised up on its hind legs, its nose snuffling, sniffing the wind. Its small brown eyes rolled from left to right, searching for the intruder with the strange smell.

Kate turned at the cawing of the crows, subconsciously aware that it was never a good omen. At the same time, the bear dropped on all fours and moved toward the trespasser in her berry patch. Kate turned and froze. The black bulk was moving fast in its lopsided, shuffling gait, the hulking body propelled by the bear's desperation to save her cubs.

A high wail of despair tore from Kate's lips, and she raised her arms up over her face, instinctively shielding herself from the black onslaught. The mother bear hit her with terrific force. Its stinking hot breath was the only thing preceding the slashing, red hot, ripping sensation as four sharp teeth embedded themselves in the soft white flesh of Kate's shoulder, shredding the homespun fabric with ease.

She didn't know if she was screaming or the bear or her cubs. She only knew that a blood-curdling bellow went on and on as she lay, waiting for the subsequent bites and her death. She knew the end was here as she cried out in the German language of her forebears. She remembered her parents in Switzerland and the loss she realized when she left them, knowing she would never see them again.

"Mein Gott, ich bitte dich, hilf mihr" (My God, I beg you, help me)!

She begged for mercy, at the same moment she accepted her fate.

"Dein villa geshay, auf erden vie im Himmel" (Yet, oh blessed Lord, your will be done on earth as it is in heaven).

The screaming went on, the wild howling accompanied by thumps, someone beating, beating.

Kate knew the bear had gone when an eerie quiet hung over the clearing. She lay on her side, her bloodied shoulder on the ground. Slowly, she rolled on her back and grimaced as she struggled to sit up.

Immediately, Hester was there, her dark eyes taking in everything—the shredded dress, the punctured shoulder, the dark blood pumping out of it, slowly running down her arm and across her dress front.

"*Komm*" (Come). Hester spoke calmly as she helped her mother to her feet. They both knew the importance of getting to the house as quickly as possible. To save her mother the added burden, Hester transported baby Emma in the sling and carried two pails, while Noah and Isaac brought the remaining berries, the other children between them, their eyes wide with fear.

No one complained or lagged behind, and few words were spoken as they made their way off the mountain. Often Noah looked back or to the left, then to the right, keenly aware of his surroundings as Hester took the lead. She strode swiftly down the steep incline, scrambling over rocks and between trees, her only objective to get her family back to the safety of the house.

They poulticed Kate's bleeding shoulder with ground red pepper, eliminating the heavy flow of blood almost immediately.

Noah slung his powerful body across the back of the swiftest roan and rode headlong to Lissie Hershberger's house. She was in her garden, busily tying up her pole beans, hot, red-faced, and ill humored. She sincerely hoped that crazy rider was not someone needing assistance. She was dead tired and so sleepy her whole head felt fuzzy. Midwifery wasn't easy, and she wasn't young anymore.

Hans Zug's Noah. What did he want?

He told her, breathlessly, shaking the blond hair away from his face. Lissie gave herself up right then and there, but she couldn't help grumbling to herself, imagining that fat Kate, so greedy for berries to make all that jam to put on her many slices of bread. Her own fault.

Ach no, she reasoned. Forgive me, *Herr Jesu.* I have sinned.

Lissie settled the cloak of love securely about her shoulders, buttoned it well with the virtue of duty, hitched up her own horse, and drove recklessly to Hans Zug's, her leather case of tinctures and salves rattling along on the back seat of her wagon.

She entered the house amid crying babies and wide-eyed little ones. Kate was propped up on pillows, grim-faced and pale.

"*Voss hot gevva*" (What gives)?

Kate blinked, then ground out through tight lips, "A mother bear. Picking raspberries."

Lissie peered over her round, gold spectacles and lifted the thick square of cloth.

She clucked like a hen, sucked her teeth, and said, "*Eye, yei, yei.*"

Kate lifted worried eyes and asked if she'd be all right.

"Oh, *ya, ya.* But she got you good. It's a wonder she didn't finish you off."

"She would have, but for Hester."

Lissie stood still.

"Hester?"

"*Ya.*"

"What did she do?"

"Oh, she screamed and carried on."

"She banged on the bear with a big branch, kept it right up, yelling the whole time," Isaac offered, his eyes bright with excitement.

Lissie turned to Hester, who sat on the wooden rocker holding the baby, dipping a cloth into warm milk, satisfying its constant need to be fed for now.

Hester ducked her head, and Lissie was presented with the sheen of black hair.

"Hester! My, oh," Lissie said.

Hester volunteered nothing, so Lissie turned to her bandaging. She washed the wound with hot water and lye soap, then laid comfrey leaves over it and held them tight with clean cloths, watching as Kate's lips compressed, gritting her teeth as Lissie pressed the remedy against her skin. She'd be fine, Lissie knew. This woman was strong.

"All right?"

Kate nodded.

Lissie knew her remedies. Chickweed salve and a clean compress with strips tied around her chest and beneath her arms, comfrey tea, and comfrey leaves to help with infection.

Lissie marveled at Kate's size. My goodness, she was a lump. Now who would take care of all those raspberries, with her laid up from that bear chomp?

"There you go, Kate. Now don't do anything for at least a week. You could tear those puncture wounds, and you don't want to start up the bleeding. Do you need help putting away the raspberries?"

Kate tried to smile, but it turned into a grimace. "Hester can."

"By herself?"

"I think so."

From her seat on the rocking chair, Hester raised her head. Lissie watched the dark eyes glisten in the noon light, slide away from her mother's face, then move back again. This time, a new and darker light shone from those mesmerizing eyes, and Lissie stiffened, her small blue eyes going rapidly from Kate's face to Hester's.

Was there *ztvie dracht* (divisions)?

Turning to Hester, Lissie raised her eyebrows.

"You look tired. You have things to do. I'll manage," Hester spoke quietly.

Lissie looked dubiously at the little, dark-skinned girl, at the nine children surrounding her, the weary Kate, the six pails of raspberries, the apron thrown in the corner with dark purple juice leaking out of its bulk, spreading a purple stain across the scrubbed oak floor. And Lissie made up her mind. She'd stay.

Hester placed the sleeping Emma in the cradle by the hearth, sliced a loaf of sourdough bread, spread it with wild pear butter, and sat the children in rows on the benches pulled up on each side of the long plank table.

Lissie poured cups of spearmint tea and laced it with molasses. The children ate hungrily, and then the littlest ones were put to bed for their naps. Kate fell asleep, snoring softly.

Noah and Isaac went down to the barn to finish cleaning the cow stables. Lissie set to work.

Hester was a fast learner. She washed the berries and put them to cook in the large cast iron pot.

Lissie tried to get Hester to talk, in the manner of mother and daughter. She soon discovered that Hester was not comfortable with too many questions. Yes, she got along well with her mother. Yes, she enjoyed the babies. Yes, she worked hard. Yes, she liked it.

Finally, Lissie's round form shook with laughter. "Can't you say anything except yes?"

Hester's head dipped, but her eyes sparkled, and when she raised her head, Lissie felt as if an angel had visited her. When she finally looked Lissie full in the face and smiled a full, wide smile, her eyes danced with humor.

Where would this young girl's destiny take her? She was, indeed, a special girl, a gift of God for Hans and Kate. But after nine children in ten years, did they remember? Or was Hester turning into an unpaid servant?

She mentioned Hans, and Hester's face lit up.

"Dat likes me. He's very nice to me. He buys me things special. He tells me to hide it from the others. Especially Noah and Isaac."

Lissie's eyes narrowed. She stopped stirring the raspberries. "He does?"

Hester nodded happily.

"Look!"

She ran to the adjoining bedroom, and Lissie heard the scraping of a box on the wooden floor. Hester returned with a necklace of turquoise stones, draping it across her fingers, lifting them to move the exquisite lights of blue green. "Isn't it beautiful?" she whispered.

"But it's jewelry. From Indians. We Amish don't believe in adornment of the body. Hester, Hans should not have given it to you."

"Oh, it's just for pretty. To keep. I have to put it in my box under the bed."

Lissie nodded, her eyes wary. Well, suspicious or not, real Christian love would accept and believe the child's story, so she did, for at least five minutes. Then she blurted out, "But he didn't ask you to wear the forbidden jewelry?"

Hester shook her head, her eyes averted.

When she looked up, Lissie's eyes questioned the shaking of her head, but again, Hester's eyes were flat and expressionless, so Lissie shrugged it off once more and changed the subject.

Hester, however, enthused by the rare peek into her dearest thoughts, told Lissie how Hans had draped the necklace about her neck, just to see what a true Indian looked like. "He doesn't *schput* (mock) my dark skin, the way some others do. He is a very good father. He is kind."

Lissie lifted the heavy square of muslin, bulging with steam and hot cooked raspberries, and squeezed so hard the juice burst out of the cloth. She burned her fingers and whistled.

"*Häse*" (Hot)! she chortled.

Hester laughed out loud, a sound like the tinkling of cold spring water tumbling over mossy stones.

Lissie realized why the sound shocked her. Hester rarely laughed, and certainly not out loud.

They added precious coarse sugar to the steaming raspberry juice, then set it to boil in the big pot over the low burning embers in the fireplace, filling the whole house with its summery fragrance.

Lissie set about mixing lard and brown flour, wetting it with vinegar water, her capable hands kneading and mixing. She thumped the wooden rolling pin across the lump of dough under Hester's watchful eye.

Not one bit of the raspberries went to waste. Lissie poured the pulpy mush out of the muslin square, added a bit of sugar, and thickened it with more flour. Then she dumped the mixture into the waiting pie crusts, slapped another rolled pastry on top, and set the pies on the table while she got the brick oven going.

Not too far away from the back door, Hans had built a bake oven for his wife. The low building was large enough to contain a sizable brick oven with a cast iron door built into the opening and room for a roaring fire. A large wooden paddle hung on a hook beside the oven. When the fire had died down, and the coals had been raked out of the oven, Kate placed pies and bread on this thick paddle, inserted it into the vast interior, or slid it beneath them when they were done baking and pulled them back out.

The bake oven was not in the kitchen because of the heat in the summertime. Kate was as proud of Hans's craftsmanship of the oven as she was of the springhouse he had built.

With the addition built onto the house and the many acres Hans had cleared through the years, the little gray house and weathered barn were turning into a farm, a place where hard work and skilled traits were in evidence.

Kate lay in her bed enduring the pain, half listening to Lissie Hershberger and Hester. When Hester laughed out loud, Kate strained to see, catching a glimpse of their bent heads, Hester voicing her admiration of Hans.

Wearily, Kate closed her eyes and let her head roll back and sink mercifully into the softness of the feather pillow. That bothersome old agitation about Hans's admiration of Hester was too wearying for words. Lissie didn't need to be nosing into their life this way. It really was none of her concern. But here Kate was, unable to work, Lissie's capable hands *fa-sarking* (caring for) all the raspberries, and she was having contentious, selfish thoughts. She was ashamed. She fell asleep with humility coasting through her dreams.

Hans listened to the children's tale of adventuresome raspberry picking and fussed over his bedridden wife, his face filled with loving concern. Kate gazed into Hans's face, his round cheeks gleaming in the light of the fire, and let the love she felt for him hover between them as her eyes stayed on his.

Yes, he was a loving husband, a good provider, a man clever with his tools, building her a bake oven and springhouse, so why would she fret about *kindish* things like a small bauble he gave to Hester?

Lissie was out at the bake oven wielding the heavy wooden paddle. She removed the piping hot raspberry pies, muttering her grievances to herself, and mumbled her way into the house in time to see the loving exchange between husband and wife. Guilt-ridden, she decided to drop her suspicions then, considering her thoughts nothing but evil surmising, a horrid sin.

Hester tucked the turquoise necklace into the wooden box beneath her bed and felt confident that she had made a friend, a trustworthy one, at that.

CHAPTER 10

KATE'S SHOULDER BECAME SWOLLEN AND streaked with fiery fingers of infection. She lay in bed, miserable and soaked in perspiration as the raging fever tormented her.

Hans brought Dr. Hess. He lanced some of the most infected parts of her shoulder, wrote instructions for the care of it, and left, leaving Hans pacing the floor, his head thrust forward, his hands clasped behind his back.

He was worried about Kate. How could he manage with ten children if something happened to her? Would she be laid to rest beside little Rebecca in the damp earth of that lonely, forsaken graveyard?

He shivered, the shadows around him becoming living things, raking at him with dark, transparent claws.

His breathing became labored. Beads of sweat formed above his lips. He stopped pacing. The suffocating shadows immediately clambered over him with nerve-wracking accuracy. A roaring began in his ears. He stopped the sound with forefingers pushed against them.

Lunging against the door, he fell out onto the pathway in the cool night and lowered himself to a stump in the yard, trembling. He turned, slid to his knees, lifted his hands in prayerful supplication, and begged his God for mercy. *"Mein Gott, Mein Heiland!"*

Tears rained down his face as he prayed for Kate's deliverance. When he opened his eyes, the twinkling white of the stars blurred with the silvery leaves that were bathed in moonlight. The low-lying dark barn rose in stark contrast to the surrounding fields. He thought of the growing herd of cows, the pigs. Who would milk them? Who would make butter and cheese? Who would make bacon and sausage?

Kate's worth rose above him, leaving him reeling with the need to keep his wife alive, and so he prayed on, far into the night until he was completely spent.

The robins set up a raucous chirping before the sun had even begun its ascent over the mountaintop. Hester closed the door of the log house quietly behind her, padding noiselessly on bare feet down to the barn. She stopped to listen to the saucy chirping of the robins, smiled to herself, and moved on. Ambitious birds. They always got the worm first, waking up before anyone else.

"Guten morgen" (Good morning)! Hans greeted her cheerfully. She nodded at her father, a smile parting her lips, as she found his direct gaze.

"Hester, if it's not too much for you, I guess you'll have to milk the two cows your mother normally does," he said, leaning against a rough-hewn post as his eyes surveyed her face.

"How is she?"

"Not good, I'm afraid."

Hester nodded, alarmed at the pain in her father's voice. She was spare with words, as well as emotion, so she chose to leave it at that. She reached for the wooden bucket hanging from a nail in the barn, next to the cows' stalls.

She supposed she could ask Dat if Mam would live, but he didn't know the answer. No one did. So she became very quiet within herself, sat down on the dirty stool beside Meg, the Brown Swiss cow, and began to milk.

She pulled and squeezed, her strong brown fingers capable of producing jets of warm, creamy milk into the wooden bucket. But by the time the third cow was milked, she wasn't sure if she could ever open or close her fingers properly again. She rubbed one hand over the other, her face pinched with exhaustion, her mind jumbled with Noah's inability to milk. And Isaac's for that matter.

When Hans met her at the barn door, she asked him why she had to milk alone.

"I milked two. Why can't Noah?"

"He's too young."

"He needs to get up early and learn to milk if Mam isn't well."

Hans was surprised at Hester being so outspoken, finding it a bit unsettling. Well, the boys weren't capable like Hester. Besides, he enjoyed the peace and solitude while milking. Hester was quiet and soft-spoken, and those boys would be yakking on about their *dumb heita* (foolishness), disturbing his morning. He didn't need them in the barn.

Hester had never cooked breakfast by herself. She came into the kitchen hungry, her fingers dulled by pain, her mother a large form beneath the coverlet, and baby Emma screaming from the cradle. Menno, awakened by the baby's cries of hunger, let loose with a loud yell of indignation. For a moment, Hester was overwhelmed with inadequacy, a tiny form in the face of a huge, unscalable cliff.

She looked around, her eyes large in her brown face, her dress hanging loosely on her thin frame, tendrils of straight, black hair draped over her forehead and into her eyes.

The house was in disarray. A greasy white tablecloth hung sideways on the plank table, unwashed dishes scattered over it. The redware jar with lilies of the valley that Barbara had picked a fortnight ago was perched precariously on the edge, half full of murky brown water, the small white flowers drooping and half-dead. The floor was strewn with bits of string and corncobs, wooden spools that were empty of thread, colorful pieces of cloth, hay, mud, and dirt.

A rancid odor came from a redware plate in the middle of the table. Hester picked it up and shooed the blowflies from it. Slimy yellow maggots had already hatched from their eggs where the half-cooked rabbit had begun to spoil.

She took the smelly mess to the door, opened it, stepped out and away from the house, and flung the spoiled food angrily into a briar patch. Let the vultures find it.

She stood very still, lifting her eyes to the rising sun. She let her gaze wander across the beautiful green ridges that fell away on each side of her, over the sturdy, gray, log house, and the barn below it, the stone springhouse, split-rail fences, the lush pasture with grazing cows behind it. The sky was lavender, the rosy-hued sunrise turning into a heavenly color.

She turned to the sun, the yellow orb warm on her skin. The Creator made the sun, the land, and her. She felt a part of the waving grass at her feet, the moving leaves over her head. She was here. This was her home. She couldn't separate herself from the forest or the sky or the sun. God had made it all, set her here with this family. They were hers.

Taking a deep breath, she lifted her face to the sun, letting the pores of her skin absorb its warmth, receiving its strength. The rustling of the leaves from the great oak tree whispered its resilience against drought and storms and hordes of insects. The morning breeze lifted loose strands of her hair, caressing her smooth brown forehead, and she felt the breath of her Creator. She would be strong. She would do her best. In the face of all the obstacles, she would be able.

In the house, she changed the baby's cloth diaper, swaddled her in a warm blanket, and then set Isaac to work feeding her. In clipped words, she ordered Noah down to the barn, telling him he should have been down there since five when she went. He cast her a red-faced look of shame, but she already had her back turned, retrieving the heavy, cast iron pot from its hook.

She wrinkled her nose at the residue of burnt beans, then carried the pot outside and sloshed tepid water into it from the bucket on the bench beside the door. Better let that soak. She'd watched Mam soak burned beans.

Daniel and John were awake and already quarreling, their long nightshirts stained from too many nights of being worn and too few washings. Their hair was stiff and tangled, their eyes heavy with sleep and the inability to understand.

"Solomon, get the boys' knee breeches," Hester called, from her station by the fireplace.

"Where's Mam?" he asked.

"Asleep."

"Why?"

"She's sick."

Climbing to the top cupboard on a kitchen chair, Hester got down her mother's recipe from the pile she kept there, then snorted, a balled up fist on each hip when she realized she could not read the recipe. Well, she'd watched Mam.

Taking up the clean, cast iron pot, she filled it half full of water, added a handful of salt, hung it on the heavy, black hook, and swung it over the fire. Grabbing the heavy poker, she stirred up the coals and barked a command to Isaac, who laid the baby in her cradle, where immediately she set up an awful howling. Unsure what to do, Isaac hesitated but was immediately pressed to a choice by Hester's second set of orders. She wanted wood for the fire. She wanted it now.

He dumped the wood on the glowing ashes, which sent up a shower of sparks. But Hester chose to ignore that as she sliced bread on the dry sink.

She put Lissie to work cleaning the dirty dishes from the soiled tablecloth, telling her to shake the cloth, replace it with a clean one, and set the table with clean, redware plates. She put down redware cups and a spoon with each plate, then placed a pat of butter on a small plate in the middle. The breakfast table was set.

Hester stopped, hearing her mother's soft cries. Swiftly, she went to her and bent low, listening. Her anxious wails were punctuated by hiccups, her ramblings unintelligible. Hester placed a hand on Kate's forehead, then drew back, catching her lower lip in her teeth, surprised by a sharp intake of breath.

Her mother would die. Already her festering wounds were odorous.

Hester ran with the speed of the wind, breaking into the cow stable where she found Dat, who looked up, surprised.

"You must come. Mam is very . . . she's burning hot."

With an exclamation of dismay, Hans let the pitchfork in his hands fall to the floor with a dull thud. He followed Hester from the barn, then flung himself by his wife's bedside, groans of despair wobbling from his loose, heavy lips.

"The doctor. The doctor!"

Hester looked at her father sharply. It was not proper for a girl to ride, but she had no choice. Her mother would die.

Lifting agonized eyes, Hans said, "Noah. Go."

Noah, terrified, shook his head. "I don't know the way."

"You have to go."

Hans was wailing, his teeth bared, as his lips drew back in unaccustomed fear.

Hester mulled the way in her mind, the forks in the path, the ford across the river. Already her heart pounded, knowing she would be the one to go. Hans couldn't. His beloved Kate might die in his absence.

She pulled on a pair of Noah's patched knee breeches, whistled for Rudy, the blue roan, caught him easily, and slipped the halter on his head and the bridle with the smallest bit attached to it. Then she stood aside, grasped a handful of the coarse mane, and flung herself up onto his back.

Rudy lifted his head, wheeled, and was out of the barnyard through the gap in the rail fence and onto the road that led to the doctor's house in Irish Creek.

Dust rose in little puffs as Rudy's hooves thundered down the grass-covered road. Deep ruts were cut into the road where spring thunderstorms had poured buckets of rain on the hilly landscape, sending gushes of muddy water down every incline. Rudy was surefooted, but Hester kept a watchful eye for especially deep and treacherous grooves, ducking her head, her face against the flying mane whenever a low branch loomed ahead of her.

The first fork in the road was a surprise, but she knew enough to stay left, and they thundered on. A small branch, like a whip, caught her forehead. She felt the sharp sting but let it go. When she put her hand up, her fingers came away sticky with blood that seeped from the wound.

The trees were thinning now, just as the road turned to the left yet again. When it headed steadily downhill, she knew they were close to the river. She remembered the boatman at the ford the last time she'd come to the trading post with her father.

When the road leveled off and Rudy's hooves sank deeper into the sandy soil, she caught a glimpse of the sparkling water, sunlight glinting from its wavelets, the water dark green, gray, and brown all at the same time.

She pulled back steadily on the reins, her dark eyes peering ahead into the unknown, a troubling scene that was the river and its ford, a large raft, a rope, and a boatman with a long wooden pole. A woman alone was never good, and she was only a girl. She'd heard Hans speak to Kate about this ford and the questionable characters that regularly took too much money from honest travelers, or worse.

She had no time to decide her plan or the action she would take if the boatman was dishonest. She had no money. She had forgotten the coins she'd need, overcome as she was by wanting to save her mother.

At a trot now, Rudy broke through the line of trees, Hester low on his back, her eyes downcast. She had seen the boatman and was fully aware of his flaming red hair, his youth. She could only try.

She pulled Rudy to a stop. His nostrils quivered, his sides heaved, sweat stained his odd, bluish-gray, cream-colored flank.

The youth was tall, thin, and dressed in a clean linen shirt and knee breeches. His feet were brown and bare. His face was dark-skinned, his freckles barely visible, his eyes green. His head looked as if it was on fire, his hair was so red.

He looked up, said, "Har."

Hester said nothing. She sat still as a stone, her black eyes watching his green ones.

It gave him the creeps, so he said, "Har," once more.

She nodded her head, then continued to stare.

He jerked his thumb in the general direction of the river. "You want across?"

"Yes."

"Five cents."

"I don't have money."

"Then yer gonna haf to swim." Rudy snorted, turned his head at the small tug from Hester's hand, and started down the embankment to the waving grasses at the water's edge.

"Hey! I didn't mean it."

"Say what you mean."

The youth watched as she turned her horse again, then slid off with the ease of long practice. She was just a slip of a thing. Couldn't be older than fourteen. Maybe even thirteen.

"You shouldn't be by yerself."

"My mother is very sick. I'm going for the doctor."

The youth whistled. "That's a long way off."

"So."

"Why don't you go to Trader Joe's? Indians all over the place."

"I'm not going for an Indian."

"Why not?"

"I want Doctor Hess."

"You're an Indian, ain't you?"

"I'm an Amish Indian."

"A who?"

"Take me across."

"S' wrong with yer ma?"

"She's . . . She was . . . She has wounds. They're festering. She has a fever."

"You don't need a doctor. You need Uhma. She's a herb healer. Sort of like a witch."

Hester looked at him, wide-eyed, her face revealing nothing.

"Did you already have the doctor?"

Hester nodded.

"I figured."

The youth stood looking across the water, then turned and looked back the way she had come. He seemed to be considering something. He looked at Hester finally.

"Look. Is your ma dying?"

Hester shrugged her shoulders, her eyes flat, giving away nothing.

"Can you stay here and let me take your horse?"

"No!" The sound was an angry outburst, a vehement refusal.

"Then you're going to have to let me up on your horse's back. I can't give you directions. I have to take you to Uhma's house."

"Your mother?"

That question showed the crack in her steely resolve, and he said quickly, "No. Everyone calls her Uhma. She's an old, old Indian woman that mixes herbs and stuff. If your ma was bit and has a fever, ain't much Doc Hess is gonna do, trust me."

He watched the young girl's face. Nothing changed in it. Her eyes didn't blink or her lips part or anything at all. Her answer was merely a dipping of her head, the glossy black hair visible instead of her face. Was she Indian or wasn't she? She sure was pretty, he thought, but odder than a two-headed calf.

"Come," she said, suddenly.

In one swift movement, quicker than he had ever seen anyone mount a horse, she swung up on her horse's back, looking down at him. He met her black eyes, a question in his, and she nodded. He had to grab a handful of the horse's mane, but she sat firm as he flung himself up, his left arm raking across her middle.

He pointed to the narrow trail following the river, and she goaded Rudy into action, his hooves pounding the wet sandy earth with dull thunks as they sped along the river bottom, skirting willow trees, honeysuckle vines, and great arches of raspberry and blackberry bushes hanging across the trail.

Blue jays screamed their hoarse cries as they flew out of their way. Fat groundhogs sat up, listening, then lowered themselves and waddled out of sight at their approach. Turtles sunning themselves on half-submerged logs slid silently into brackish water, and frogs briefly stopped their endless croaking, starting back up again after they passed.

The road led up from the river bottom into dense forests of pines and briars so thick, the road became only a trail. Jagged rocks protruded from the pine needles, and the pines thinned to a few dead, old trees, charred from some long-ago forest fire. Seedlings sprang up everywhere, the sunlight filtered through the dead trees giving them life.

The trail became steeper with rocks jutting out over it. Hester slowed Rudy, afraid of the sharp edges. She lifted her head. She heard water. She remained silent, thinking the youth would speak if she needed to know something.

Rudy continued climbing up the trail at a fast walk. They rounded a bend, and Rudy lowered his head to pick his way carefully as the trail turned steeply down.

The sound of water became more apparent, a sloshing, tumbling sound. Birds called, a myriad of sounds that surpassed anything she'd ever heard. It seemed as if hundreds of birds were warbling or singing, whistling and calling, all at once. The trees around them were alive with the colorful songsters.

Emotion that had no name rose in Hester's chest. The plaintive calls and whistles evoked the nameless call of the Creator. He was alive and had made her and the life around her. He had formed the youth with the flaming hair that sat so close behind her. She felt bound to a great and Higher Spirit, a power far beyond her years.

The trees thinned once more, the trail smoothed out, and the light became brighter with shafts of sunlight piercing the branches. Hester breathed deeply. The dry summer smell of the forest had changed to a rich, wet smell, the way a quick thundershower in summer gave out a clean scent.

Suddenly, they broke through the trees into a natural glade where strong sunlight poured through the gap in the forest. Hester quenched a gasp of pure astonishment.

The youth behind her said, "Stop your horse."

Mute, she pulled steadily on the reins, remaining seated, unable to move. She had never seen or experienced any place of beauty such as this. An outcropping of limestone created a shelf high up the side of a steep cliff. Pure, clean, silver water tumbled off the rocks and splashed against more stone before it fell into a deep pool, so clear it was the same color as the trees and the sky and the earth beneath it.

Great masses of dark green ferns moved restlessly, either by the breeze or the droplets of water that sprayed endlessly from the moving water. Lilies, orange, yellow, and white, grew in abundance, great colorful clusters of them everywhere she looked.

Hester was aware of the youth's hand lightly on her waist. "I guess you still remember yer ma."

Shaken by the strong feelings, the response to all this beauty, Hester could only nod and slip quickly from her horse's back. She was brought back to the moment by his voice. "See that goat? It's Uhma's. Best tie yer horse."

Hester dropped the reins. Patting Rudy's neck she said, "He'll stay."

She caught the sunlight in the youth's green eyes and was amazed to find they were exactly the same color as the deep pool of water where the ferns grew out over.

Chapter 11

"Follow me."

Obediently, she fell in behind him. His quick footsteps led her along the outskirts of the glade.

The white goat grazing by the pool lifted its head, chewing rapidly before bleating its high-pitched sound.

Hester laughed out loud. "Silly goat." Her voice was a caress, that of a lover of animals. Her laugh was a waterfall, a human tinkling sound of spring water, but more refreshing. He'd never heard any sound of laughter like that, ever.

They rounded the falls, becoming silent as the power of the water stilled them. Another bower of rocks and ferns, a few young trees, and they came upon a wooden hovel tucked beneath a pine tree so large it seemed to reach all the way to the sun. It was mostly made of bark with a round top that was all one piece. Moss grew over it in some places to the north like an old tree. Plants were growing everywhere. Vegetables in sunny areas—beans and corn, squash and pumpkin. Many different flowering plants tumbled over and about one another in colorful profusion. More goats were tethered close to the peculiar little house.

As they approached, the youth called out. Instantly, a white head appeared at the door, the face beneath it as brown and craggy as the bark surrounding the door. Two white braids hung on each side of the face, the black eyes hooded by layers of loose skin, wrinkle upon wrinkle folding themselves beside the eyes, up the side of them and down along the cheeks. A shift hung loosely on the narrow shoulders, but the hips were wide, the skirt hanging in gathers over the width of the old woman.

She did not smile. She spoke only in broken English, her speech soft, as if it came from deep in her throat. "You." That was her way of greeting.

Her black eyes examined Hester with the intensity of a magnifying glass. She spoke another language very fast, then came over to Hester and touched her hair, her face. A strong grassy odor enveloped Hester, like when a pitchfork lifted newly mown hay that had been rained on and partially dried.

"Lenape," she kept repeating, nodding her head, her tongue clicking against the roof of her mouth.

The youth watched Uhma, looked at Hester, and waited. Finally, he stated his purpose.

"What bite?" Uhma asked, her black eyes boring into Hester's.

"Bear. Mother bear. A black one."

"Ooo. Ooo." Pursing her lips, she nodded, then disappeared into the bark-encrusted hovel.

The youth told Hester that meant she knew why the infection was there and what had caused it. She would know the mixture of herbs, the medicine they would need.

"I have no money," Hester said, quietly.

"She won't take any."

Hester nodded.

They waited. Silence hung over the peaceful little area except for the songs of birds and the distant waterfall. So many scents wafted through the air, intensified by the misty wetness of the falling water.

Uhma's return brought the bleating of the littlest goat, and she turned, scolding, chiding, in another language.

She handed them a package, a small one, wrapped in skin and tied with string. Her sharp eyes confronted Hester, boldly telling her to stay still and listen.

"This." She pointed to the package. "This. Steep in boiling water. Pack on bite. Hot. Change every four hour."

Producing another package, she held it up. "This. Steep in boiling water. Give to drink. Every hour. All day long."

"What is it?" the youth asked.

In answer, Uhma shook her head, solemnly. "I die, packages die with me."

She straightened, her eyes seeing faraway, further than the mere earth and trees and sky. "The Lenape. Common people. There is no separate. The land and the people are one. No longer. I die. I go soon to my Creator. I have been here awhile, now soon I go. I have knowledge. It go, too. Too many new worlds come. One foot in old, one in new. Not good. Now go. Heal girl's mother."

Hester put out her hand in the manner of the Amish to shake Uhma's hand, a way of thanksgiving, of gratitude, "Thank you. *Denke schöen.*"

Uhma's hand was cool and calloused, the skin paper-thin between them, her grip firm and sure. Her eyes kindled with an ancient recognition of her people, her lips parted in a smile. "You Lenape girl. I die, you come."

She swung her hand in the direction of her little hut, the goats and herbs, the falling water. "You come. Get wisdom. I write."

Her black eyes shone, the wrinkles deepening around them. Hester felt as if she had been given a blessing, just like the way the bishop, John Lantz, would say so lovingly, *"Ich vinch da saya"* (I wish for you a blessing).

A current of understanding passed between them, fully understood by Uhma, still innocent and unaware by Hester. *We are one people, one culture, the same blood flows in our veins, no matter what the white men try to take from us. We had a proud heritage, we are one with the land.*

When their axes bite into the trees of our forest, they bite into our souls. Our heartbeats are one with the Creator, our responsibility the care of the earth.

Young Lenape girl, your blood will be Indian forever. Destiny can take you where it chooses, but your Indian heritage will remain. Go in peace.

The return trip found the youth reluctant to let go of her. He tacked it up to his long days of loneliness as a boatman, shrugged his young shoulders, and tried not to think more about it. But her black hair that blew in wisps across his face was a sensation that stayed with him during the remainder of his time at the river. He slid off the horse with an acute sense of loss. She sat straight, keeping her eyes on the trail ahead, not moving a muscle.

"Thank you," she whispered.

"Will you be coming by again?"

She shook her head."I am not allowed to speak to outsiders. Especially men."

"Yes. Well."

He wanted to keep her there, so he reached out to stroke Rudy's neck, who promptly lowered his head and nuzzled his shirt front. "You like horses?"

She nodded.

"Do you go to school?"

She nodded again.

"You don't know my name, and I don't know yours."

She became very still.

"I'm Padriac Lee. Paddy."

"Paddy is a girl's name."

"It's Irish."

"Oh."

"What's yours?'

She hesitated. Her mother would not be happy, knowing she spoke to Padriac Lee. "Hester Zug."

"Zug? Boy, you are Amish. Only people around with that name."

She hesitated. She was not used to sharing her feelings or her background and certainly not the fact that she was so different from her family.

"Are you an Indian?"

She shrugged her shoulders.

"You're a Lenape. They're good people, most of them. Same as the Amish."

She smiled.

"I have to let you go."

The overwhelming need to go with her, to protect her, was completely mystifying. He wanted to fling himself up on that horse, put his arms around her, and keep her safe for the rest of his life.

He touched the leg of her trousers and looked up at her. "Goodbye, Hester."

She nodded. Her eyes shone darkly as she lifted the reins. Rudy sprang into a gallop immediately, kicking up little clumps of sandy loam, leaving deep footprints in the earth and in Paddy's heart. The remainder of the day, he sat on an old wooden crate, his chin in his cupped hands, and stared across the water, her black eyes etched on the back of every object he saw.

When Hester returned, Kate had roused from her stupor, but the fever still raged, the infection still foul-smelling.

Hans met her at the door, the afternoon sun full in his face, his skin greasy and unwashed, his eyes intense with fear and worry.

"Where's the doctor?" he pleaded, anxiety edged in his voice.

"I didn't go to the doctor."

He raved and ranted. He tore at his hair with both hands on either side of his head, lifted his face to the ceiling and cried like a baby. He scolded Hester. He lifted his hand to smack her face, but couldn't bring himself to do it. The children cried, Noah walked to the barn, grim-faced, the look in his eyes much older than his years.

Hester calmly prepared the poultice and the tea, moving about the whitewashed rooms, talking to Hans quietly. Under her voice, he regained his sense of direction, wiped his streaming face, and set about helping Hester with her administrations.

Far into the night, they fed Kate the strong tea by the spoonful. They changed the poultices and lowered their faces to sniff the wounds, afraid to hope there was a difference.

Toward morning, when the sky was darkest, just before the light streaked the dark clouds of night, Kate began to cough, slightly at first, then with more effort. Hans was alone, Hester lying by the fireplace, her eyelids refusing to stay open.

At Hans's cry of alarm she scrambled to her feet, aware of her surroundings in an instant. She heard Kate coughing, then retching miserably, the strain tearing at her wounds.

When morning broke, Hans went to milk the cows. Hester changed the poultice once more, placing a hand on her mother's wide forehead. She was streaming with sweat. It beaded on her pale upper lip and ran from her forehead, soaking the nightdress she wore, the sheets beneath her, and the coverlet spread over her.

The breathing was very soft, almost indistinct, as her chest rose and fell evenly, her eyes closed as still as death. Through the fog of her weariness, Hester wondered if indeed she would die in spite of the night's vigil, the endless hours of spooning the tea into her mouth.

How patient Kate had been! So obedient, forcing herself to swallow when it took all of her strength to open her mouth. A new, stronger love for her mother welled from Hester's young heart, cementing the bond between a mother and her foundling. Perhaps they were not of the same blood, but heartstrings can be inseparable.

Hester replaced the bitter herbs every four hours steadily. She spooned tea endlessly into Kate's obedient mouth. She continued to perspire, then slide away into a sleep so deep Hans cried out for Hester to come. Had she died? Was this really the moment when he would need to give up his beloved wife?

All during that day and into the night, Kate slept. Toward morning, she began coughing again. Hester lay on her coverlet by the fireplace, hearing the rasping sound as if it was too far away, too unbearable to bother with. So it was Hans who bent his head to hear Kate's words.

"I want water."

Joy pulsed in his veins as he brought her a glass of cold water from the springhouse, stumbling over tufts of grass and his own shoes, bent over, scuttling, muttering to himself like a man possessed, unable to grasp the realization that God had, indeed, heard his pleading.

Kate's recovery was slow, but in a week's time, she sat on the hickory rocker, much thinner, weak and pale. As she held little Emma, her white face took on a shining gratitude.

Hester threw herself into the work, doing her best at the numerous tasks that needed to be done every day. Kate spoke in quiet tones, instructing Hester. How hot the water should be for the washing, how to smooth the wrinkles out of them before folding them and putting them away, how to bake the bread, boil the cornmeal mush.

The weeds in the garden took over, and Noah and Isaac were sent to pull them. They worked together as a team, and life went on. Visitors arrived, wagon loads of curious well-wishers bearing covered dishes of fruit-breads and nut cakes, *schnitz und knepp* (ham, apples, and dumplings).

Kate sat, wan, youthful-looking, almost beautiful, her blue eyes bearing an inner light of gratitude that had not been there before. Hans hovered over his wife in gentle servitude, bringing her a drink of water, a handkerchief, eager to do her bidding.

Hans's parents came, Isaac and Rebecca Zug, wanting to know more about the rumors that circulated through the community. Some said an Indian woman had cast a spell. Others said it was *hexary* (witchcraft).

Still others said Hans had prayed. A real miracle. *Unser Jesu* healed her.

Lissie Hershberger said Dr. Hess gave her enough laudanum that she slept it off, the infection.

So they came, talked and talked and talked, formed their own opinions, and went away *unglauvich* (unbelieving). Hans spoke plenty, his face red with effort, his beefy hands spread wide for emphasis. He showed them the herbs in the deer leather parcels, asked Hester to tell her story. Hester refused.

The air in the log house was stale and stuffy with the scent of mens' puffed up knowledge, their opinions permeating the very oxygen with their foolishness. The wagging beards, the wobbling chins, the endless soliloquizing, surmising, backbiting about the old Indian woman. Some said they heard she lived and moved as one with the earth and its Creator, a witch.

Hester stayed still, silent as a rock, her large black eyes moving restlessly from face to face. When Rebecca laid the tablecloth on the long plank table to serve the food people had brought, her mouth was stern with rebuke. Hans and Kate sat up to the table, ate the good food obediently, and didn't address the subject.

They ate the *schnitz und knepp*. Rebecca piled the plates high with the boiled ham cooked in dried apples and dropped dumplings over the sweet and salty ham and apples, an old Amish favorite. Rebecca, watching her son ladle in huge mouthfuls and chew with great enjoyment, his cheeks round and rosy, was pleased. Here was her favorite son, his wife healed by his prayers, his children around him, his quiver full of good, strong arrows, able, sturdy workers who would be a great help as he journeyed on his way to prosperity.

She served the *schpeck und bona* (ham and green beans) with a flourish, basking in Hans's lavish praise. The cobbler and walnut cake came next, with a heavy redware pitcher of milk to drizzle over the mound of sweet baked goods.

The children squealed in appreciation. Kate smiled and ate small portions, remembering to praise her mother-in-law's cooking skills. Hester ate, aware of the change in atmosphere as the visitors took their arguments smelling of rotten sulphur out of the house. Isaac and Rebecca, too, had voiced differing opinions, but they had chosen to drop the subject, "letting each man to his own thinking," which was right and had cleaned up the air.

After the good meal, they asked Hester to tell her story. Hester shook her head no. Kate watched her eldest daughter and knew that Hester would never reveal the secret of the old Indian woman. She would rather die. Hester was an Indian in so many ways, and no one could change that.

Hans tried, at the milking in the morning. He leaned over the back of the cow she was milking and implored her to tell him so he could thank the old woman.

Hester pictured the silver, splashing falls, the ferns and the goats, and recalled the scent of the pure water. But she knew hordes of mocking people would search for her with their scornful curiosity, and she shuddered.

"No," she said. "No."

Hans promised her a trip to the trading post. Perhaps to town. Would she like to go to town, buy a new dress?

The answer was the same. "No."

He told her she was a disobedient child. What if Kate took sick again and needed herbs?

"Then I'll go," she said into the bucket of milk at her feet.

"Look at me." It was a command.

The steady milking stopped. Obediently, she raised her head. Her father's eyes held a new expression.

"Disobedience is not allowed in this household, Hester. 'Spare the rod and spoil the child,' our Lord says."

She lowered her head, resuming milking as if she hadn't heard him.

"Hester."

"What?"

"You are openly disobeying your father." The words were a taunt, a bold announcement cushioned by something that allowed for a seed of rebellion.

"Tell me."

"I said, no."

Still, Hans leaned on the cow, and Hester bent to her task. By now, her hands had become accustomed to the hard work of extracting milk from the cow's udder. Milk came down in thick, heavy streams, creating dense foam close to the top of the pail, muffling the sound of the jets of milk. Hester's hands stripped the last of the milk from the cow's udder. She held very still, her head bent, hoping her father would leave.

He didn't.

"How did you find the Indian woman?"

With the speed of lightning, Hester was on her feet. Frightened, the cow lifted her right foot, kicking the bucket of warm, creamy milk to its side, sending a gushing stream all over the straw-covered floor of the stable. Rivulets of milk carried pieces of straw into the corner.

Hans jumped back, the fury in Hester's black eyes as lethal as the whirring of a disturbed rattlesnake's warning. "I told you no."

Her voice was barely raised above a whisper, but Hans felt as if an arrow had pierced his chest. He slunk out of the cow stable without looking back. Hester retrieved the filthy milking stool and straw-covered pail, patted the next cow and sat down to milk, steady as a rock, her eyes holding no recognizable emotion. Enough was enough. Obedience was one thing, betrayal another.

Kate sensed the change almost immediately and wondered what had occurred that Hans watched Hester with a certain meekness.

She asked Hester.

Hester looked up from her dishwashing, dried her hands on her apron, and came to sit at her mother's feet, elegantly folding herself onto the tiny wooden stool. She lifted dark liquid eyes to Kate's blue ones and waited.

Kate lifted her eyebrows.

"I wouldn't tell him where I got the herbs."

"Why can't you tell us, Hester?"

She told her mother the real reason. Kate received the words, nodding her head. Quick tears sprang to her eyes as her foundling described the place of beauty, the old woman's words, the awareness of the kinship she felt with Uhma.

Kate recognized the spirit of belonging and was humbled. Would they need to give her back someday? The thought was unbearable. This was her beautiful daughter whom God had entrusted to her care! Afraid to mention the frightening subject, Kate smiled, marveling at Hester's words. She kept hidden the fear of her ever leaving and returning to her people.

From that day, Hester felt a real kinship with her mother. Something so genuine, it clothed her with a sense of belonging, as though it was a valuable garment worn beneath her Amish dress, lightening her days. She had a home, a mother, a place where she was needed and wanted. She loved the constant work, she learned many things, and her days were filled with purpose.

She kept a wary eye out for Hans, however, unable to forget his threats and the way he had purposefully goaded her to anger, inciting that rich fury that had possessed her. No matter how hard Hans tried to change things, Hester's childish trust had vanished like the straw carried away by the streams of spilled milk.

CHAPTER 12

IN THE FALL, KATE HAD STILL NOT REGAINED HER usual strength. Hans had a talk with Theodore Crane, the schoolmaster, and they agreed that Hester would no longer attend school. She was needed at home.

Almost thirteen years old, she was unable to read very much of anything. She could only decipher easy addition and subtraction. And that was the extent of her schooling.

Noah and Isaac begged to be allowed to go to school, however, eagerly moving ahead of their classes in every subject. Book-learning was a wonder to them, and Kate said that was straight from Hans and his mother, Rebecca.

On Saturday, Kate said she was tired of the deer meat and salt pork. Wouldn't a mess of brown trout be a wonderful supper? So Hester, Noah, Isaac, and Lissie carried their poles to the tumbling waters of Maiden Creek.

It was a warm kind of day for autumn. The leaves hung in great bunches of red, gold, orange, and yellow, undisturbed by even the gentlest breeze. The air was golden and dusty, thick with the scent of goldenrod, fiery with sumac.

Little puffs of dust rose from their brown bare feet as they walked briskly along the path that led from the road to the creek bottom.

Lissie had learned to whistle and kept up one annoying trill after another, swinging her fishing rod into the tall grasses by the path, sending shivers of dust and seeds from them. She imitated a cardinal, then the call of a crow, finally settling on the lullaby Kate sang to baby Emma.

"Lissie, shut up," Isaac growled.

"We're not allowed to say that," Lissie countered.

"Well, be quiet then."

Hester's thoughts were far away, wondering how far Maiden Creek flowed until it reached the river. She only remembered the red-haired youth sometimes—when she didn't want to. But she couldn't keep his presence from pushing its way into her mind.

She wanted to forget him. What a name—Paddy! It seemed like a dog's name. Or maybe a doll's. And his red hair! She wondered if he was still shuttling people across the river. He had been kind to her.

She wondered how many English people knew about the old Indian woman.

Her thoughts were interrupted by a singing sound, loud and off-key, a sort of rambling chant.

"*Yugli vill net beer shiddla*
Beer vella net fall.
Yugli vill net hundli schlowa,
Hundli vill net schtecka chawa."

"That's not right!" Isaac screeched, swinging his fishing pole in her direction.

"Is too! *Yugli* would not shake the pear tree, and the pears wouldn't fall."

"The dog and the stick aren't supposed to be yet."

"How am I supposed to know?" Lissie fell behind, pouting.

She certainly had the right name, that Lissie, Hester thought. She was every bit as independent as Lissie Hershberger and about as outspoken.

Lissie Hershberger had visited the house quite often after Kate's near death. She lay no stock in the Indian woman's herbs, saying she'd have come out of that fever all right without those stinking weeds. Everything the Amish needed to know they'd brought with them from Switzerland. They certainly did not need some heathen savage to tell them what to do.

Hester had shriveled up deep within herself, remaining quiet as she went about her work, wondering how grown-ups thought about and understood these things. She shrugged her shoulders as she remembered Lissie Hershberger's generosity while her mother was so ill. Lissie gave her that impression, but Hester didn't want to carry it too far. It was better to stay quiet, or soon she would be just like the visitors, her mouth going and going and going, her own knowledge held high for everyone to examine, quickly looking like foolishness. Yes, the Amish were her people, and they had brought many fine recipes and lots of wisdom with them when they crossed the Atlantic Ocean.

Lissie Hershberger had butchered two nasty geese that tried to chase her down at the barnyard. She had gone to the stone water trough to give her old horse a drink and spied these two geese coming at her like two devils with black eyes, hissing and honking worse than a *schpence.* She vowed to rid Hans Zug's barnyard of his evil fowl.

She told Hans it was she or the geese, and if he planned on keeping the geese, why then, he'd just have to *fa-sark* his own sick wife. Hans had shrugged, gone off to sharpen his axe, and caught the geese with his long, steel hook. Lissie heated the water over a roaring fire and stuck the flopping carcasses into the boiling water, plunging them up and down in it over and over. She chortled to herself about how they would never slam into her leg again, their beaks strong enough to break a limb. Here she was now, safe, but with a nasty bruise swelling on the thick part of her leg behind the knee.

Unfashtendich, that's what.

She butchered those geese, cut the meat into pieces, and rubbed them with garlic. Then she rubbed them with a salt, pepper, and ginger mixture and put them in the large crock in the springhouse till the next day, when she'd set them to boil with parsley from the garden.

She made a gravy with the broth, put *knepp* on top of the meat, and served it all on a huge platter she got down from the top of the cupboard. It was called *Gaenseklein*, or goose with gravy in English. It was so good that Hester could almost stop feeling sorry for the fate that had befallen the poor things. You had to understand geese, that was the thing. They were only protecting the barnyard, same as the black bear with her cubs. Animals had a territory they claimed as their own, a natural order of things, and when human beings stumbled onto it, they could get hurt, if they weren't watchful.

Lissie started in again, now, on her way to the creek, singing the annoying song, whacking at the grass with her fishing pole.

"I'm going to catch the biggest trout," she yelled, when everyone chose to ignore her obnoxious singing.

Hester smiled to herself and turned to watch as Lissie poked the tip of her fishing pole into Noah's back.

"Ow!" Noah whirled and was off. Lissie screeched worse than a coyote as she ran to save herself from her brother's clutches.

Isaac went ahead, not bothering to find out what the end result would be. But Hester stopped, turning to watch. Lissie was sturdy, but no match for Noah's tall muscular legs. He caught her in due time, whirled her around, and knocked her to the ground where she yowled like a cat.

Dust-covered, but her face shining with glee, she bounded to her feet, slapped her hands together, sending dust flying everywhere, and squealed, "Hoo-hee!"

Hester dug a fat earthworm from the bucket at her feet, wove its slimy, wriggling length in and out of the hook, and set it flying across the water of the creek. She hoped to land it exactly in the middle of the shaded pool beneath the willow tree around the bend where the creek widened.

These trout were finicky. It seemed as if they didn't want any bait unless it was close to the surface, so Hester was perfecting a way of drawing the wriggling worm toward herself. She kept the bait moving, which was sure to attract the trout in less time.

Lissie still hummed the *Yugli* song, nodding her head in time to the imagined beats, weaving the hook on the end of her line into the wriggling worm.

Noah and Isaac had gone farther downstream, hoping to get away from Lissie's constant yodeling, who seemed blissfully unaware that she was causing anyone a disturbance.

They eventually caught the trout, six large, fat ones, just waiting to be cleaned. Over the fire in a kettle they would go, dredged with butter and spices, until flaky white chunks of meat fell off the white, pliant bones.

The return trip was uneventful, except for sighting a snapping turtle sunning himself on a flat rock, then silently disappearing before they had a chance to catch him. Turtle soup was "awful good," as Lissie put it. Carrots and leeks cooked in a brown broth with the turtle meat was just awful good.

They reached the barnyard, dusty, with the fish flopping from Noah's tired arms. They met Hans, who was walking behind two horses, his straw hat pulled low.

"What's going on?" he asked, without a smile.

"Mam sent us fishing. She was hungry for a mess of trout."

"Oh, she was? Well, what about the corn picking? She didn't say anything about that, heh?"

"No." Noah was red-faced, nervous. Isaac stood still.

"The next time you go fishing, ask me first. I spent all afternoon picking corn by myself, which is not necessary. I have big boys to be picking corn with me, not wandering off fishing like that."

Hester's and Lissie's eyes were held to the ground and their bare toes, anywhere more comfortable than Dat's eyes boring into them, accusing them all of laziness.

The trout were prepared by Mam's own hand, perfectly done over the fire in the hearth in just a short period of time and then laid on a bed of watercress. They ate the fish along with a big pot of bean soup. For Saturday night, this was a wonderful supper. Normally it was just bean soup.

Everyone had to have their bath on Saturday night in the gigantic wooden washtub behind the makeshift blanket Kate strung across a corner of the room. Church clothes had to be laid out and the wrinkles smoothed away so that in the morning, the chores, breakfast, and getting dressed could all be done, and they could still get to church on time.

Kate was extremely weary, so she allowed the girls to wash the dishes as she sat cuddling baby Emma, hoping to have more energy when it was time to bathe the little ones. She remembered, wistfully, the days when she could work hard from sunup to sundown, without as much as a sore muscle. Now, by mid-forenoon she was tired out.

She looked up, surprised to see her husband in the house at this time on a Saturday night.

"Girls." His voice was stern.

Lissie turned, her eyebrows raised, her sturdy body poised, as she tapped the dishcloth against her side. Hester chose to ignore him, washing dishes steadily, her back turned.

"Hester, are you listening?"

In answer, she stopped washing dishes, her back straight, her eyes boring into the log wall ahead of her.

"Hester!" The shout was a command.

From her seat by the hickory rocker, Kate's grip tightened, her eyes flew to her husband's face. What was this?

Hester turned, her chin lifted in defiance, her black eyes pools of nothing.

Kate shivered and held the soothing body of her baby closer.

"When I speak to you, I expect you to listen. I don't want you riding horses anymore. Not you or Lissie. It's not proper, wearing the boys' trousers. Do you understand what I am saying?"

Lissie's eyes flew to Hester's face, which seemed etched in stone, then back to her father's clouded eyes.

"Dat! You can't do that!" The protest was out before Hester had a chance to retrieve it. Too late. The damage was done, and she awaited her fate as Hans's eyes clouded over.

Hester spoke quickly.

"What is your reason, Dat?"

"If you had never learned to ride, you could not have gone to the old Indian woman that day. Now you are caught in her ways. They are not God's ways."

Accustomed to having her father on her side, Hester felt confused, as if directions about how to proceed were eluding her, leaving her scrambling wildly for a foothold in a world gone dark.

"But the herbs healed Mam!"

Hester's words broke from her, driven by desperation. Life without riding Rudy was as unthinkable as breathing without air. An impossibility.

"It was not the herbs that healed her, and you know it. I prayed long into the night, and God answered."

Hester's heart jumped and took off racing, draining the blood from her face. Her nostrils flared, her eyes dilated as she drew to her full height. "You. You do not know that."

Kate rose in one swift movement when she saw Hans raise his large hand and draw it back. She stood between them, wobbling a bit on legs suddenly gone weak.

"Hans, don't do something you'll be sorry for later. I beg you. What has gotten into you?"

Kate began crying weakly, a soft sound like a kitten. Hans lowered his hand, strode from the house with footfalls like booms from a cannon, slamming the door until the windowpanes rattled in their wooden frames.

Much later that night, Kate lay awake. Resolve flooded her open eyes. Reaching across, she shook Hans's shoulder, hard, until he awakened.

"Hans."

"What is it, Kate?"

"Hans, what has gotten into you? Hester was always your favorite. So much so, that I was afraid it wasn't natural. She is not of your flesh and blood, or mine. But she never did wrong, my husband. Now she does nothing right. This is very hard for her."

"She defies me, refusing to name the Indian woman or her whereabouts."

"Why do you need to know if you don't believe the herbs healed me?"

"She's going to go back, that's why. She'll get mixed up in those old remedies that are nothing but witchcraft."

"When we found Hester, we saved her life. It is up to her, now, to choose what she wants. We cannot force her to stay or force her to go. If the ways of her people are what she chooses, that is her decision."

"But her soul will be lost. She'll burn in hell. She has to remain here among the Amish where she can learn from the ministers how to live a devout religious life. The Indians are heathen."

"Are they, Hans? Are they?"

In minute detail, she told her husband what Hester had described to her about the old Indian woman and warned him of the error of his ways.

"Hans, if you love me, you'll see that she needs to be set free, to decide what she really wants. Please."

Hans lay on his back, his breathing deep and easy, his mind in turmoil. How could he?

He loved Hester as a beloved daughter. He needed her beauty. How could he set her free to go? The only way he knew was to remove all earthy obstacles and expect her to obey. He would lay down rigid rules and see to it that she followed his expectations.

He felt the divide between him and Kate, a chasm, growing even as she spoke, her hands restlessly caressing his chest, her words whispered close to his ear.

Ah, but this precious foundling, so beloved, her price above gold, suddenly growing into a young woman with a mind of her own, the thing that frightened him most.

And now, his own wife was caving in to these heresies. What was wrong with her? Yes, she had been healed, but by his prayers alone.

The corn turned dry and brown; the ears hung heavily from the rustling stalks. Temperatures plummeted. The winds whispered of frost. They carried the cabbage and turnips into the mound of earth that had been dug by Hans's own hands and finished with a sturdy, wooden doorframe.

The carrots stayed in the ground, their tops covered with straw. When Kate needed a carrot or two, she'd send the children to the garden to uncover them.

The pigs were fat, waiting on colder weather. Then Hans would bring his rifle to his shoulder, aim, and fire, while the children were still in their beds.

Kate did the housecleaning scrupulously. Not a windowpane, a coverlet or a floor, went unwashed. She emptied the straw ticks, washed their covers, and filled them with fresh straw. She made new pillows and stuffed them with feathers from the geese they had eaten after one had bitten Lissie Hershberger's leg, although Kate thought the bruise was not a bite, just more like a hefty tweak.

She and Hester disposed of every spider or ant in their path, making sure that the insects' homes were destroyed. They scoured the floors white with lye soap, then buffed them to a dark sheen with linseed oil.

Hans brought home a calendar from the blacksmith shop in Berksville, and Kate hung it proudly by the kitchen table. Next to it was the clock, its wood wiped clean until it shone.

Hester worked side by side with Kate, accepting her admonishments to give herself up to Hans's wishes.

Hester spent hours down at the barn cleaning the stables and caressing her beloved horse's face. Not once did she fling herself up on his back, her obedience to her father intact.

Kate had told her many times that obedience meant sacrifice, but that there was a blessing in it, even if it was hard. Hester nodded and understood, yet she struggled with many ill feelings toward Hans's increasingly rigid rules.

Noah and Isaac continued to ride Rudy especially, their best horse, which was almost more than Hester could bear. Still, she remained obedient and true to her mother.

At butchering time, when two lifeless hogs hung from the rafters, the snow lay heavy on the ground, and the wind whipped around the corners of the barn. Hans stood with his father, Isaac, heating water in great iron kettles over a roaring wood fire. They scraped the hogs clean, then cut them into pieces—hams, ribs, and *seida schpeck,* the meat that would be cured for bacon and other trimmings for making sausage.

All day, Rebecca and Hester worked, seasoning and grinding, cooking and canning. The boys tended fires while Hester cleaned the entrails, the casing that would be used for sausage. This had always been her job, and she became accustomed to it, gamely scraping the casings clean.

Lissie was put to work alongside her. She entered the forebay in the barn as if she was going to her execution, martyrdom shrouding her face, her eyes liquid with self-pity.

"It stinks."

"Yes."

"I'm not going to do this, you know."

"You are."

"Who said?"

"Dat."

"He won't know if I don't help, if you don't tell him."

"Here." Lifting a trailing, grayish mass, Hester held it out to Lissie, telling her to lay it down, take the blunt edge of the knife, and scrape out the whitish substance that clung to the inside, explaining how they would fill it with ground, seasoned meat.

Lissie watched, holding her nose, and pronounced the whole process unfit. She jumped to rigid attention, however, when Hans came over, his face red from the heat, to ask Hester how it was going.

"Good," she answered without lifting her head.

"Lissie." The word was a command.

Dutifully, Lissie faced her father, found his gaze, and said, "Fine."

"Good, good."

Isaac hurried past, carrying a large, bloody portion of meat. Lissie swallowed and set to work immediately afterward, the sight of her saintly grandfather spurring her into action.

When Rebecca came to the barn to season the sausage meat, all eyes turned to her.

"Where's Mam? Where is Kate?"

Rebecca shook her head, her lips compressed, and Kate was forgotten.

Hester knew. She'd heard her being sick again. It had not frightened her at the time, but as her mother's full figure continued to decrease and the color in her face diminish, Hester knew the time was coming when she would need more strength than she had.

She bent over the entrails of the hogs and scraped with a vengeance, her strong brown arms rippling with young muscle. She set her mouth in a straight line, as tightly guarded against the sprout of rebellion and dislike of her father as a cast iron key turned in a lock.

The love she had felt for him was a thing of the past, which she remembered only fleetingly. When had the tide turned? When she was no longer a child and had developed a mind of her own. It had all started with the herbs in the brown packages.

Chapter 13

When Hester was fourteen years old, Kate died in childbirth at the age of forty-four.

The day was gray with rain coming down in slanted, cold sheets, reflecting the misery of the huddled family, hovering about with empty faces, unable to grasp what was before their eyes.

Hans lifted his face to the rain and could not understand God's ways. The little ones cried, snuffling into Hester's shoulder, clinging to her skirts, and whining like little lost lambs.

Noah and Isaac shed solemn tears, even while they squared their shoulders, shoved their hands deep into their pockets, and tried their best to look manly. But tears of grief swam across their eyes, ran over, and coursed down their cheeks, falling on their linen shirts. They blew their noses, blinked, and were finished.

Hester moved about the house as if in a dream. Nothing seemed real. Everything was without clarity. A fog of disbelief left her feeling lethargic, as if nothing mattered. Her dark eyes glistened with unshed tears.

She had cried before. Kate had told her, as her body wasted away, the once ample arms becoming thinner as the months wore on, that she would try her best. But deep inside, she felt as if God was telling her she needed more strength than she could find.

"Perhaps my time has come, Hester. I'm counting on you, though, to keep the family together, if . . . if something should happen to me."

"Mam, don't."

But Kate had pushed on, speaking words like slaps from her hand, words Hester could not bear. She had tried, but she failed to hold back the premature sorrow.

A sadness so heavy lay over the graveyard, crushing Hans, even as the sun shone down on them the day of the burial. Kate and her unborn child were lowered into the wet earth beside the tiny gravestone inscribed with "Rebecca Zug. Daughter of Hans and Catherine Zug."

The community rallied around them, powerful in their kindness, bringing food and labor and sympathy. Love flowed among them, binding them together with its strong ties, and Hester was comforted by these gentle well-wishers who wanted only the best for her.

That she had so little schooling was something they took into consideration, but Hester refused to budge. School held no promise for her. Memories of being mocked formed like clouds on her inward horizon, and she remained obstinate about going back.

Baby Emma was one year old and cried incessantly for her mother. Barbara and Menno wandered around without understanding, and Hester took them under her wing like a fledgling mother hen.

Hans refused to eat or drink, saying he needed to fast and pray, which Hester respected. She eyed him with a new reverence and was thankful she had shown so much obedience. For Hans blamed himself for his wife's untimely death. He had prayed for her life now, and God had not heard him. He was sure his sins were piled around his head, and he sat in the proverbial sackcloth and ashes, repenting of his misdeeds for three days.

He'd charged John Lantz too much to shoe his two mares, and him a bishop and a man of God. He was caught in avarice.

He'd tasted the whiskey at little Reuben Hershberger's house, becoming quite merry, if it came right down to it. He had taken strong drink and guilt rattled his very soul.

He had not listened to the quiet voice of his wife, when she tried to persuade him of the goodness of the old woman and her herbs. He had gone right ahead and despised her all he wanted and was beset by the sin of hatred.

Oh, the list went on and on until he smote his breast, lifted his eyes to the heavens, and implored God to be merciful to him, a sinner. He grieved with many sighs and silent tears. He stood with bent head as kindly men expressed their sympathy. His future loomed before him, frightful with the inadequacy of being without his Kate.

Hester cooked and cleaned, washed and mended. Her grandmother Rebecca came and advised her about rearing the children. Lissie Hershberger hitched up her doddering old horse and stopped by every day for almost a month, helping Hester by sewing clothes, darning socks, churning butter, tending the lamps.

Hester was a fast learner, and although the cornmeal mush burned sometimes, and the beans were undercooked, she forged ahead with every duty Kate had always done.

With Lissie's help, she folded Kate's things and stored them in the attic. Lissie urged Hans to write to Kate's parents in Switzerland, explaining her death, telling them about her life beforehand. John took the letter to the trading post and came home with tales of the Indians who were gathered there, coming in for supplies, saying the winter would be long and hard.

Hester's eyes glinted in the firelight as chills crept across her arms and jangled their way up her spine. She thought of the acorns piled on the forest floor. The muskrats' heavy coats. The early flocks of blackbirds and geese flying low and fast. She wanted to go to the trading post. She wanted to see if the old Indian woman would be safe if the winter was too harsh.

All these thoughts she kept hidden away as she turned her lithe form from the fireplace to the bake oven to the table to the shelves, providing food for the always hungry children, their stomachs growling before each mealtime. Lissie was a help in her ten-year-old way, which sometimes was worse than no help at all. But Lissie could make Hester laugh. Out loud, too. And that was worth something.

On the morning of the first storm, no sunrise was visible, only a heavy white hoarfrost that clung to every blade of grass, crunching beneath Hester's brown leather boots as she made her way to the barn. She knew there would not be enough eggs to go around, but if she stirred them well and added milk, along with some stale, torn bread, the mixture would set up well if she cooked it over the fire. She'd make fresh bread as often as she could, too. They had some maple syrup to pour over it, which Hans was especially fond of.

When she returned to the house, she hung her heavy black shawl on the hook by the door. She was surprised to see Lissie standing by the fire, spreading her hands to its warmth, grumbling to herself.

"What?" Hester asked, a smile already forming.

"I froze in my bed. Mam always put extra coverlets on. You didn't do it."

"I don't know where they are."

"I don't either."

Hans strode into the kitchen, shivering, and went straight to the fireplace, holding his hands to the fire beside Lissie.

"Good morning, Lissie. Why are you up so early?"

"I'm cold. I almost froze in my bed."

"Hester, haven't you *fa-sarked* the extra coverlets?"

It was the way the question was spoken that rankled her. As if she was expected to know everything and carry it out unfailingly.

"No."

"Do you know where they are?"

"Yes."

Hans watched Hester's face, her black eyes giving away nothing. If anything, she was becoming even more beautiful, her face losing its childish roundness, replaced by more chiseled cheekbones. She was tall, now, he guessed at least five and a half feet, her body shapely beneath the loose dress, the black apron tied about her slim waist.

She wore a kerchief too much of the time, but he didn't know how to approach her about that. Again, for the hundredth time, he wished for Kate's wisdom and foresight.

Winter roared in across the Pennsylvania mountain ranges, bold and brash, reaching across the land with fingers of ice and snow, winds lashing the bare branches without mercy. Snow piled in tightly packed drifts, blown against the buildings by furious winds. The cows, horses, and sheep that were unable to be housed in a barn or shed died of the cold that winter.

Farmers built lean-tos, temporary sheds to give their animals a break from the endless wind that drove snow and bits of ice from every branch and raised bit of land. The snow pooled into the hollows, densely packed, so that many a team of horses floundered up to their collars in snow, unable to draw their sled or wagon an inch farther. Red-faced men carried shovels so they could loosen the frightened horses, freezing their ears in the process.

Finally, toward the beginning of January, they admitted defeat. They had no church services for more than a month. No one went to visit anyone else, except for a few hardy teenagers who possessed snowshoes. They brought tales of emaciated deer, unable to move about and starving, all over the mountain.

For Hester, one day blurred into the next, an endless stream of days punctuated by nightfall when she tumbled into her bed, weary and heartsick, the endless responsibility of nine children too heavy on her young shoulders.

Hans brooded. Some days he sat, a great hulking figure, by the fire, staring into it with somber eyes, his spirits so low he could barely lift his head. Noah and Isaac accepted this, even flourished in the face of their father's silence. They had never been used to having a father who cared about them much.

Hans did what was necessary, providing their clothes and food, instructing them in the ways of the farm, but supplying no emotional support. It was Hester he cared about, just as he always had. Now, although he was sternly dictatorial to her, he still watched her with brooding eyes, trying to imprison her with his will, looking out for her welfare in his own way.

Meanwhile, Noah and Isaac grew mentally and emotionally by relying on and reacting to each other. They shared and spoke together about everything. The barn rang with their merry words, chiding, teasing, laughing, and jousting harmlessly, two boys who loved life and each other. They never hated Hester for what she was to Hans. It was just the way of it, a part of life.

The longer the snow piled around the house, the further Hans declined into his pit of grief. He missed Kate's presence so keenly, it was a knife between his shoulder blades, a constant hurting, a deep, dark thing that followed him wherever he went. He tried valiantly to shake this unspeakable misery. He prayed long and loud, his voice raised to the rafters of the barn as he implored God to help him. He tried to conjure Kate's face, but it was only when he dreamed of her that he found a miniscule amount of solace.

One storm followed another, days without end, it seemed to him. Was the end near? Had God lost patience with the sins of the world and said it was enough?

Whether encased in the small, dark house, shoveling his way down to the barn, to the outdoor privy and the bake oven, or carrying wood from the adjoining shed, his spirits steadily worsened until his face became slack. His rounded jowls hung in limp folds. His cornmeal mush went untouched.

Hester saw all this, her large dark eyes observant. It stirred up fear, this unnamed malaise. Hans didn't care enough to scold her anymore. He didn't care about anything.

Increasingly, Noah and Isaac shouldered more of the workload, their faces calm as they carried wood, milked cows, mucked out the stables, carried water, and shoveled snow. School was out of the question, so they studied the books they had available, mostly in German. They learned to read fluently and discussed the Bible endlessly like two youthful prophets, their blond heads bent together in front of the fire.

Little Barbara and Menno clung to Hester, and her arms encircled them, her heart open to the lonely children who remembered their mother but were too young to understand what death meant.

Baby Emma simply crawled into Hester's arms, sighed, and from that day on, claimed her as her mother.

Solomon, Daniel, and John understood Mam's departure. They had a view of heaven, placed their mother in it, and were comforted. They ate the food set before them, accepted Hester as their mother, and went about living their lives the way children do. When they quarreled, Hans shook himself out of his black reverie long enough to mete out due punishment, then returned to brooding.

Sickness entered the house like a gray specter, stealthy, frightening, demanding more from Hester than she had thought possible.

She strung a makeshift clothesline across one corner of the kitchen. It was always pegged with white clothes, either sheets or pillowcases, and long rectangular pieces of muslin that had been smeared with strong, odorous salves and then wrapped around swelling glands, now washed clean.

So many of Kate's words were seared into Hester's memory as she cared for the sick children. Cleanliness was important for a sickbed. Lye soap had the power to wipe away the residue of disease. Kate wasn't sure how, but it made a difference, she always said. Onion and mustard poultices worked well for the croup. Often Hester thought wistfully of the Indian woman and the stored knowledge in that head crowned with white hair.

What would she do when Menno was red with heat from the awful fevers that ravaged his thin body? Which herb of the forest had the magical power to fight the fever? Hester felt sure that somewhere, all over the land God had created, there were remedies used by her people. The ancient old woman's people. Hester's own people.

She wondered during that long winter who her people really were. She had never been an Indian. She was only born one. The only Indian she had ever met was the old woman. She had experienced a fierce kinship, a need to defend the old woman. She'd felt in awe of the beautiful place and wanted to know everything she spoke of. But she felt no sense of belonging.

Here was her home. The Amish way of life was her way. It was all she knew. And yet, she wondered. Someday she would go to the trading post. There were always Indians there. Someday she would meet one or two. Perhaps someone her own age who could speak English. Who knew her own mother and father. Maybe her mother had died in childbirth like Kate.

And so her thoughts went on and on as she stirred yet another load of clothes in the boiling hot water, lifted them, rinsed them, and turned them into twisted ropes, squeezing the water from them before pegging them to the line across the corner of the room.

Baby Emma toddled through the water that had pooled around the clothes, where bits of wood chips, straw, and ashes were turning dark as the water ran in little rivulets.

Grabbing a piece of heavy toweling, Hester swiped at the puddles, then opened the door to shake out the wood chips. For only a moment, she breathed deeply the gray-white purity of the snow and the storm. Bits of snow and ice hit her brown face, but she lifted her eyes, reveling in the cold and startling power of the wind.

Behind her, Solomon coughed a rasping croak, followed by a whine for *vossa, vossa* (water). A sharp reprimand from Hans followed. When she turned, after settling the latch securely, she felt his dark eyes on her, angry and displeased. Keeping her head low, her face averted, she brought Solomon a drink of good cold water from the springhouse. She patted his shoulder as he lay back, his blue eyes so much like Kate's, watching her face intently.

"Why did you stand there with the door open, letting in all that cold?" Hans asked.

Hester chose not to answer him. Whatever her reply was, it would be the wrong one, she knew.

"Answer me."

"I was watching the storm."

"And letting in the cold."

"Yes."

"You're old enough to know better."

"Yes."

It was the answer he wanted. Total servitude. Absolute obedience. Compliance. A deep bowing to his will. When she acknowledged her own stupidity, he was satisfied. Anything else would only have been met with more sparring, a hopeless exchange of words, gone awry without a smidgen of common sense.

And so he brooded, staring into the fire, lifting his eyes only momentarily to absorb the one thing that kept him grounded, his appreciation of Hester's beauty. For he still loved her as he had loved the young Indian child. Only now he was intimidated by her. She was growing away from him, and the experience left him rife with hopelessness, inadequate and afraid.

She moved about the room like a princess. Her figure was tall and perfectly proportioned, her neck long and slender, her face a display of emotion as she bent over

Barbara with her long, slender fingers, healing, soothing. Her eyes were large with a fringe of heavy lashes shading them. Her eyebrows were like the wing of a raven in the distance. Her nose was small and straight but wide at the top, built out between the perfection of her eyes, different from the Swiss and German faces Hans was accustomed to. Her mouth was full, wide, and in absolute symmetry with her eyes, the chin beneath small and round.

He needed to speak to her of her soul. In a year or so, she would be expected to become a member of the church. How could she, if he was certain she couldn't read very much? How much did she really understand? This weighed heavily on Hans's heart, as the storm blew itself out, leaving the sky blue for only a short period of time. The wind returned in an awesome display of furious clouds, spewing forth a blast of frigid winds that gathered in the north and swept over Pennsylvania.

The sturdy log house shook and shivered in the winds' power. The gray shake shingles tore loose on the barn, and snow sifted down onto the backs of the animals, melting slowly, marking their hides with dark streaks. Hester set wooden buckets when yet another drip appeared in the house, until Hans roused himself and set about making more shingles. He placed a ladder against both buildings and set their roofs to rights.

When Hester overcooked the dried beans, leaving the soup thick and mushy and the bread a paste, he let her know in soft-spoken tones that she had better be more watchful of the time when she set the beans to soak.

She agreed, her eyes hooded, giving nothing away. When the bread was not kneaded long enough, he mentioned it immediately. When it crumbled away from the freshly churned butter, he did not hesitate to speak of it as well.

Hester didn't always understand the ways of bread. Sometimes she could knead the heavy brown dough until her shoulders ached, and it would not rise or turn out light and spongy. Other times, she gave it a few good rolls, patted it, put it to rise, and it turned out light and chewy, in perfect harmony with the tasty butter. But she said nothing to Hans, only to Lissie, who looked up from the sock she was darning, her blue eyes sizzling with indignation, and said if Dat didn't like his bread the way Hester made it, then she guessed he needed to make it himself. Hester laughed out loud, a sound heard infrequently. She relished the thought of Hans bent over the dough tray, kneading and kneading, the bread crumbling away at the touch of the butter knife.

The children regained their health, the storm blew itself out, and Hans left the house to change a few of the box stalls in the barn.

When spring arrived that year, hearts everywhere celebrated. Housewives sang joyously, and men walking behind their plows watched rolls of fertile soil turn over and whistled praises.

Swallows wheeled in the sunshine. The air was heavy with the scent of honeysuckle vines and wild strawberry blossoms. The grass grew thick, the sheep and cows gorged themselves on the tender new growth, becoming fat and contented. The cows' udders bulged with new milk, and Hester made butter. She packed the excess away, and Hans took it to the trading post to sell, coming home with coins weighing down his pockets. He emptied them furtively into the redware cup by the fireplace.

Hester also collected buttermilk, which she set in the springhouse to keep cold. Now and then, when more had accumulated than she could use, they sold it, too.

When the hens occasionally laid more than usual, and the family could spare some eggs, Hans sold them by the dozen at an exorbitant price.

The gray mare produced a fine colt—a bay foal—which had its mother's fine, long legs. This fine animal lifted Hans's spirits to a higher level than they had ever been since his beloved Kate's death.

Hester laughed aloud at the antics of the new calves and chased them about the pasture. She gathered great armloads of wild iris and honeysuckle and fitted them into earthenware bowls, filling the log house with a scent that was unmatched by anything Hans had ever smelled.

It evoked a sadness in him, an unnamed longing for someone to call his own. He would need a wife in the future, a mother for his children, a helpmeet to share his life. The thought terrified him and made him feel very small and ashamed of who he was. Only a man, with nine children, no, ten, counting Hester. Who would be willing to give him her hand?

Chapter 14

Ever since the local school had resumed in March, Theodore Crane was dreadfully behind with the year's lessons. His stomach soured from his nervous tics, and his eyebrows jumped unceasingly as he passed about the classroom like a caged lion.

When a line of children stood side by side in the front of the room to read from their small, hardcovered readers, he tipped forward and backward so fast, Noah's eyes widened to Isaac, and he jerked a thumb in the schoolmaster's direction. Isaac bent his head behind his slate, desperately striving to keep a straight face.

Theodore called a school meeting for the parents and asked for any available volunteers as tutors to help the little ones with their work, a plan that seemed excellent to him at the time. When Lissie Hershberger volunteered, raising an ample, well-rounded arm and stating her eagerness to help, he floundered like a catfish caught on a hook. What a woman.

Anyone, simply anyone else, would be fine, but not Lissie. He turned his head very slowly at the meeting and acknowledged her raised hand with one shaggy, gray eyebrow climbing halfway up his forehead, the other one refusing to move.

"Yes. I believe you are Elizabeth Hershberger. Is that correct?"

"Yes. You can call me Lissie. I would be willing to help three days a week in the afternoons." Her voice was low and rich; it carried well across the room.

Theodore pulled on his Adam's apple with his thumb and forefinger, adjusted his stiff, white collar, and cleared his throat in a rattling fashion before blinking two or three times.

"Ah, yes. Elizabeth. I believe I can . . ."

Here he broke off with a terrible coughing spasm, lifted his right leg, fished around in his pocket for a clean handkerchief, and proceeded to finish coughing into it.

"I do beg your pardon."

The occupants of the room were unsure exactly whose pardon he was begging, so ripples of acknowledgment spilled across the many faces.

Lissie, however, believed he was speaking solely to her and replied loudly, "You are so pardoned."

Theodore felt as if he had been led to his own execution, with his fate changed by Lissie Hershberger, but he coughed a while longer to erase all that.

"Yes, yes, Elizabeth, I accept your kind offer. I thank you very much."

He felt like a traitor, untrue to his own heart, but he could not bear to hurt the lady. She was a hard worker and sincere, and he was also quite sure she had a good head on her shoulders.

But my, she was so large. It seemed as if those yards and yards of fabric gathered across her bounteous hips would scrape the smaller children right out of their seats. She was like a great ship plowing steadily through the sea, her sails all unfurled. It was a bit frightening.

The evening closed with a discussion about the older boys' behavior. They were almost never on time in the morning, or they loitered unnecessarily at the end of the school day. Comments came from one of the boys' parents and then another and another. Finally, they voted unanimously to discipline their children to try to make his workload easier. They agreed there were only six more weeks of school and much to be done in that short period of time.

And so it was that Lissie drove her well-fed, old horse down the road through the lush green forest to school. The shoulders of her cape came well down the sides of her arms, and the cape was pinned closely and modestly around her neck. Her cap was white as snow and pulled well forward over her thick ears. She parted her graying hair severely in the middle, and then greased it back in a small roll along each side of her forehead. Below the sleek sheen of her graying hair, her blue eyes sparkled in anticipation.

Here was a challenge, something new. Hadn't she changed enough diapers and swept enough dirty houses? Hadn't she slaved over stinking farmknee breeches soaking in lukewarm wash water when the soap no longer formed decent bubbles, with her arms too tired to stir or pound the dirt out properly?

She'd tended to ailing mothers and screaming babies, comforted the dying and smacked the newborns' backsides. She'd cared for her own husband and children besides, and then lived through the shock of his death and the deaths of two of her children.

She thought it was time for a change, so she took great care with her appearance. She turned this way to catch the light on her forehead, then another way to see that her covering was just so.

Yet, she still owned some snap, so she did. She deemed herself quite agreeable, perhaps even charming.

Theodore opened the door at her knock, stepped aside—very far aside—and ushered her into the schoolroom. She sailed through with the light, quick step of a much younger person, smiled at him, and said, "Good afternoon, Theodore."

"Good afternoon, Elizabeth."

He showed her the classes she would have and introduced her to the first-, second-, and third-graders who smiled guilelessly, genuinely happy to have Lissie Hershberger for their teacher. Everyone knew Lissie. She'd been to all their homes many times.

Theodore watched from his vantage point in the back of the room as Lissie launched into her first assignment, explaining multiplication to the third graders, German alphabet to the second, addition with three numbers to the first. She was thorough, well spoken, and patient. She smiled often, encouraged the slackers, never intimidated by the strongest.

However, when the last pupil ran yelling out the door, she lingered, exactly what he was afraid of. He wanted nothing to do with this outsized Amish widow. It was only his impeccable English manners that kept him from telling her so.

She spoke only of the children—who was capable, who was lagging behind. It seemed she knew each household intimately, knew what the problem was if a child seemed insecure.

He was beginning to fidget, thinking of his chores at home in the small brown house by the trading post not quite six miles away. He was hungry. He had stuffed only a portion of cold corn pone in his haversack that morning.

Lissie heaved herself to her feet, the yards of fabric swishing—why did he always think of a ship?—smiled up at him, and said she'd made ginger cookies. "I brought you some in a bag."

She sailed through the door and across the schoolyard to her wagon, bent to retrieve the cookies from beneath the seat and sailed back, her wide face radiating happiness. "Ginger cookies."

He opened the cloth sack immediately and came out with the largest, thickest ginger cookie he'd ever seen. It was like a small, round cake, dusted liberally with sugar and ginger. The first bite was ambrosia, chewy, soft, and fragrant with spices. He closed his eyes and chewed appreciatively, his eyebrows jiggling with the movement of his jaw.

Lissie watched him, waiting eagerly.

"The best," he said simply.

"Thank you," she answered, turned lightly on her heel, went to her wagon, untied the old horse, and was gone.

He should have offered to help, but he was too busy stuffing ginger cookies into his mouth. Besides, he was glad she had left.

Lissie rode home in the late afternoon sunlight and thought that Theodore Crane was just a bit *schnuck* (cute), the way his eyes came alive when he spoke.

But he was English, perhaps a Catholic or a Protestant, so that meant he was quite worldly, and likely she'd not be able to think of him as a potential husband with the difference in religion.

Her golden years stretched before her, bereft of a close relationship with a husband, something she had cherished, nurtured, and appreciated. She liked to set a good table, cook wonderful meals, try different recipes, loving to see a man eat.

Ach well, he was very English. He couldn't even say Lissie. It came out "Elizabeth."

As different as day and night.

Noah was the first to notice. He told Hester that Lissie Hershberger dressed awful particular to teach school. Hester said teachers were expected to dress in Sunday clothes, and Noah said it wasn't just her clothes, it was the way she seemed to watch the schoolmaster with a bright face or something like that.

Hester shrugged her shoulders, and went back to the butter churn, lifting the dasher, plunging it up and down, the muscles in her young, brown hands tireless. Now that Lissie had taken the job of tutoring, Hester was on her own. Hans was a big help with the garden and the planting, and he put the boys to work as well, helping carry wood and water, hoe the garden, and perform any chore that saved Hester's endless hard work.

She had little time to spare. Forbidden to ride her horse, she had no other activity to think about, so she became a young mother years before her time.

All that mattered to Hester was being able to feed everyone and keep the laundry done and the house decently clean.

The sewing, however, was another matter. She could sew strips of cloth by hand with tiny stitches, but she had no idea how to go about sewing a dress or shirt or pair of knee breeches.

All the boys' knee breeches were much too short, and she had applied patches to them over and over. Sewing the patches on with firm, necessary stitches, Hester had whipped the needle in and out, her mouth set in a determined line.

They all needed clothes to wear. Without Kate, where should she begin? Noah's and Isaac's knee breeches were creeping up their legs, but no one thought anything of it. Lots of boys wore their breeches short, before they were handed down to the next younger brother. But Hester knew something needed to be done before school started in the fall.

She approached Hans, finally, when the spring warmth had turned to summer's heat, when the corn was already knee-high and the hay was ready to be cut. It was late, after the children were all in bed. Hans noticed Hester's reluctance to retire for the night, so he sat watching her. She folded a small coverlet and put it across the back of the rocking chair, then picked up a few playthings and placed them in the basket by the fireplace. She stooped to pick up a washcloth someone had left on the bench, folded it across the wooden rack by the dry sink, her back turned, straight and still, for too long.

She was not wearing a cap again, and here she was, fifteen years of age. Hans knew the matter needed to be addressed.

"Hester." The voice was not unkind. But it was authoritative, jolting.

"Yes." Hester's voice squeaked, and she stammered a bit.

"Why aren't you wearing a cap?"

"I don't like them."

"But you were taught to wear a cap in the manner of our people."

"Yes."

"Then not liking it is no reason, when the *ordnung* of the church requires it."

"Yes."

"You must give yourself up as Christ did, dying for our sins. Do you think that was easy for him, our Lord and Savior?"

"No."

"Then wearing a cap is a small thing, is that not so?"

"Yes."

"Then you must begin to wear it."

"I have only one, my Sunday one."

"Who knows how to go about getting fabric? Or making it?"

Hester shrugged, her eyes lowered.

"I'll speak to my mother," Hans offered. "You might also want to consider more sewing. All the boys need knee breeches and shirts. The girls need dresses."

Suddenly Hans's face became very soft, his eyes warm and moist. "Ah, yes, Hester. That was the joy of my life when you were small—buying the fabric to make little dresses. Colors of wild roses, the blue of cornflowers. You were like a colorful little fairy."

Hester lifted her eyes, surprised to find the emotion that memory brought to his face.

Hans met her gaze.

Hester looked away, uncomfortable, now.

As quickly, Hans said gruffly, "So, you'll promise me you'll wear a cap?"

"If I have one."

The truth was, she hated to wear a cap while she worked. They were big, and the strings tied below her chin were itchy and warm in summer. Besides, what was the point? If she said that to Hans, he would never get over her flagrant display of rebellion, so she dusted the corner of the table with the tip of her apron, a movement so graceful it reminded Hans of a dancer he had watched as a young man in Switzerland.

"Go to bed."

"Yes. You will see to it, about the fabric?"

Hans only nodded, his eyes hooded. He turned from her as something black and frightful, like a shadow of fear, rolled across his features.

"*Denke*" (Thank you).

She slipped through the door to her bedroom, closing it softly behind her.

Far into the night, Hans sat. He was tired, his legs aching from the long day of loading hay after cutting it with a scythe. His thoughts were tumultuous as he tried to decipher his own rush of feeling for Hester. It was the little girl he loved. It was not appropriate to feel any fond emotion for her at this age. Somehow he needed to tread carefully and be the father she so desperately needed.

Sleep eluded him. The wolves' spine-chilling song added to his loneliness. An unnamed fear of the future tormented him as he thought of Hester. She was a young woman now. Who would be a fitting husband for her? His mind traveled, resting on each young man of the community. Jacob. David. Abner. Joe. All of them were either too short, too immature, too lazy, or had no character. *Ach,* it would be a few years yet.

He wanted to buy her yards and yards of beautiful hued fabric, but that was no longer a luxury he could allow himself. She needed to be restrained and come to understand the way of the cross. It was best for her soul.

He got down his heavy German Bible and immersed himself in the words he found between the leather-bound covers. Slowly he relaxed. He prayed for strength, the will to do what was right. As he prayed, he began to realize that Hester's beauty was a thing he cherished, even held with pride. And pride was wrong.

"Forgive me, Father, for I have sinned." Again, he sank deep into spiritual ashes, imagining gray sackcloth covering his head completely. He emerged some hours later, knowing the joy of his life would remain with him, the young Indian maiden named Hester.

It was only a matter of ridding himself of the pride he carried.

Rebecca came, stern and overbearing. She swooped through the log house like a hawk, her sharp, beady eyes missing nothing. Everything was out of place. She meant well. She just came to teach Hester how to be a better housekeeper.

She sewed a white cap for Sunday. She placed the used Sunday one on Hester's head, tying the wide strings beneath her chin.

Hester stood, her soft brown chin lifted, her eyes flat and black, veiled by lowered lashes. A hatred so intense built up in her chest until she felt as if she was on fire. Abruptly, she turned on her heel and left the house, walked swiftly to the spring, and climbed the ridge behind it. She moved in strong, hurried strides, on and on, over rocks and through brambles, until her breath came in short gasps. Her heart pounded with her swift ascent. Clambering up the side of an outcropping of limestone, she crawled out to its edge and flopped onto her stomach, folding her arms beneath her chin.

She had no tears, only a knot that was so hard she felt as if she had swallowed a large, mysterious object. Hatred for Rebecca swam in her veins. She wanted to chase her out of the house like a vermin-infested dog, drive her across the yard and down the road until she disappeared, then send the stodgy old horse and wagon after her.

It felt good to acknowledge and finally understand the emotion that rocked her. Hatred was wrong; it was evil. She knew it inhabited her mind and heart. All her life, she'd sat in church services and heard the Amish ministers speak of heaven and say that the only way to go there was through Jesus Christ. The way you went to hell, they said, was not to believe in him as your own personal savior.

So where was Jesus? What did you do if you accepted the fact that you were such an awful sinner but you still wanted to drive your grandmother down the road? Besides that, you hated your cap.

Slowly, Hester lifted her head. The summer's heat radiated from the rock she lay on. It shimmered and waved above the multicolored green of the treetops, which waved and rolled away as far as she could see, blending into the distant purplish-blue haze that was Hawk Mountain. There was no break in the sea of green. The sky was the azure blue of summertime with fluffy, fat clouds lazily floating along.

She became aware of birdsongs and butterflies. Suddenly, she sat up, untied the scratchy strings, tore off her cap, and placed it carefully on the rock. She lifted her hands to the back of her head and pulled out the hairpins. She ran her fingers through her heavy black hair and shook her head to loosen it.

Leaping to her feet, she lifted her arms, spread them slowly, then flung them out, on her tiptoes now, her bare feet lifting her body as high as it could go. She threw her face to the sky, her eyes closed, as she absorbed the movement of the trees below her, the rustling of the branches around the heat of the sun, the rolling of the white clouds.

Here I am, God. It's just me. You created me, you made me who I am. I know I sin. I know it's wrong, but alone, I cannot do everything I should.

A puff of wind caught her black hair and lifted it, sending it rippling behind her.

I am flesh and bone. An Indian. My skin is a different color. I am different. Why am I here?

Slowly, she lowered her arms and dropped her head with the grace of a ballet dancer.

Overhead, a shadow crossed her. She lifted her head and caught sight of a bald eagle as it soared directly above her, so low she could see the strength of its intense yellow eyes, the strong curve of its noble white head, the great lift and swell of its massive wings.

Cold chills washed over her as tears squeezed from between her thick black lashes. She felt alive. She felt the spirit of the eagle, inseparable from God. God was the eagle, and the eagle was God. He was so big, her mind could not accept it. He was so strong, she could not fathom it. Everything was possible, everything was wonderful. She had nothing to fear.

She stood on the limestone rock, the sun blazing down from the summer sky as the great bird soared, circled, dipped, and lifted on swells of air, her heart following its movement.

Strength flowed from its wings. Redemption immersed her yearning heart. She understood that God had created her, knew her nature, knew every cell in her body. She was his. He alone could guide her, save her, by sending his Son to die for her.

If someone had asked her to put her heart's song into words, she could not have done it. Words were untrustworthy. God was not. Humbled, satisfied, her spirit rejuvenated, she turned. The wind caught her hair and blew it across her face as she lowered her eyes to find the offending cap.

Quite suddenly, the corners of her mouth lifted, and she sat on her haunches to retrieve the hairpins. The eagle's head was white, too. God had made him in that fashion. She would wear the cap. In her heart, it signified the strength of the eagle. She would live the life he required of her, a small price to pay.

Gathering her thick black hair, she twisted it into the usual bun, placed the cap on her head, and tied the strings loosely. Then she knelt, lifted her face to the sky, and said, very soft and low:

"*Denke, Gute Mann*" (Thank you, good Father).

I am a child of his, and he will give me courage and strength for each new day.

She would certainly need it.

Chapter 15

When Hester returned to the log house, the air had become stifling in the hollow surrounding it.

The bake oven radiated heat, so Rebecca must be baking bread, she thought. She was surprised to find the family gathered around the table for the noontime meal. Had she been gone so long?

Hans pushed back his chair, rose hurriedly to his feet, then stood, uncertain, stifling the strong feeling that rose in his chest as he faced Hester, who had returned unharmed.

Rebecca's sharp words rang out. "Where were you? Disobedient child."

Hans's tortured eyes went to his mother's sharp features, and he folded into his chair, trembling before the familiar sound of his mother's temper.

"I went for a climb up the mountain."

"Why? With all you have to do here?"

"I don't know."

"You don't know." The words were a mockery, a bald-faced slur that hung in the room like a stench.

Hans sat up, opened his mouth, his eyes going to Hester's face. He wanted to protect her. He wanted to keep her from the grinding, twisting wrath of his mother.

Hester sat down when no more words were forthcoming. Noah poked Isaac's thigh with his forefinger, and he slid down the bench to make room for her. She sat close to Hans, whose unveiled eyes revealed everything Rebecca needed to see.

Rebecca's breath hissed between her lips as she lifted the spoonful of bean *schnitzel* to her mouth. Well. So this was how it was.

Hans praised the bean *schnitzel,* saying he had never eaten a better seasoned dish than this one. The mixture of cut green beans, bacon and onion cooked in butter was a combination he had always loved. All she said was, "You have onions in your beard."

Hans's face flamed.

Rebecca reveled in his discomfort. A talk would be in order.

They all bent their heads to the fried salt pork, the cooked turnips and the *knabrus,* the dish of buttered cabbage with onions, and no further words were spoken. The children were not allowed to speak at the table. They were expected to eat everything placed before them and to remain completely silent. There was no asking, no questioning about the amount of food each one was given. They accepted the food, receiving it as nourishment, and that was it.

When Rebecca served the warm *Lebkuchen,* the silence was broken by Hans's gleeful laugh. "Did you make the sauce, too?" he chortled.

"Yes, I did." Rebecca placed large squares of the moist, warm cake on the scraped-off plates, then poured the sweet brown sauce over it. There were walnuts and dried apples in the cake—a very special and infrequent treat. Every spoonful was eaten with gratitude, plates scraped noisily, and spoons licked clean.

Afterward, they bent their heads in prayer for the second time to thank God for what they had just received. Then they sat around the table, drinking cold mint tea sweetened with honey.

Rebecca told Hans he needed a bigger house. He needed to buy a new stove, the kind she had heard about. She knew he had money, so why not use it to the children's benefit?

Hans smiled, his round cheeks glistening with sweat, his stomach overly full, and stroked his beard. "If I build a house, it will be built with stone."

"Ooh." Rebecca was impressed. A son who built a house of cut limestone was, indeed, prestigious. Someone of high status.

Hans smiled at his mother with benevolence in his large, dark eyes. Yes, he had money put by. The farm was growing, the pile of coins accumulating.

Before Rebecca took her leave, she cornered Hans in the barn. Wasting no time, she told him it was high time he sought a wife. She told him the children were running wild, that Hester was incompetent, the house was dirty, the clothes unwashed, the sewing undone. He needed to find someone.

"I don't want a wife."

"No, you want Hester."

Hans recoiled from his mother's words. He could not help the heat that rolled across his full cheeks or the accompanying confusion.

"No, no, no."

Rebecca waited, haughty, enjoying her son's floundering.

"No, Mam. No. Not in that way. She is my daughter."

"Piffle. She's not your daughter, and you know it."

"But I have no feelings for her in that way."

"Then get a wife."

"Who?"

"Annie Troyer."

Hans's eyes bulged with disbelief. "Mother!"

"Don't 'mother' me. If you're going to compare every available woman with Hester, you'll never get anywhere."

"Mother!"

Later, swinging the scythe through the tall, waving grasses, the sweat rolling from his wide forehead and down the sides of his cheeks, he thought about his mother's words. Yes, she was right. But, oh, the thought of someone replacing Kate was unthinkable. *Mol net die Annie* (Certainly not Annie). Honeybees buzzed through the grasses, crickets chirped and hopped, crows wheeled and cried their unnerving squawks, but his mind was far away.

No, it was not true. Hester did not leave the house dirty or the clothes unwashed. None of it was true. Perhaps not to Rebecca's standards, which were ridiculous. She was one of those Swiss women who scrubbed her doorstep every morning, living in a house so clean you could eat off the floor.

Hester did well. Not like Kate, but good enough. He wondered idly why Hester had taken to wearing the cap. She had put it on for his mother's sake today, perhaps.

His ears burned as if she had cuffed him the way she always had when he was a boy. He cringed within himself. That was not true, either, that outright lie about his feelings for Hester. His mother had always had a sharp tongue, unguarded, as loose as a flopping fish. Of course it wasn't true. He loved Hester only as a daughter, that was all.

He prayed for guidance, for strength in the coming days, as he rested on his scythe there in the middle of the hayfield in the blazing sun.

A few weeks later, Hans made up his mind. He polished the leather harness until it shone, instructed Noah to wash the spring wagon, and curried Dot and Daisy until their coats shone. They were going to the trading post, then to Berksville.

Hester's heart beat rapidly, her eyes snapped and sparkled as she washed dishes and laid out the children's clothes. She picked the cleanest, least-patched knee breeches for Solomon, John, and Daniel.

For herself, she chose a dress of bittersweet, a rust-colored hue. She loosened the small drawstring in the back of her cap, then tightened and retied it. There. That was better. The cap did not have to hide so much of her straight, black hair. She liked the way Mary Fisher's cap fit much better than the one strict Rebecca sewed for her.

They did the chores, ate a quick breakfast of porridge with bread and milk and got everyone dressed and combed before seven o'clock. The sun was a red orb of resplendence, already giving off heat for the day. Hans wore his long-sleeved linen shirt, vest and knee breeches, and a wide-brimmed straw hat, placed squarely on his head.

The horses sensed a long drive and trotted gaily, their heads lifting as they followed the dusty, sun-dappled road between the trees, down steep inclines, and up more hills and turns. After an hour of steady traveling, Hans stopped the team beneath a tree, threw the reins across the dash, and let the horses rest awhile. The children scrambled off the high spring wagon, stretched their legs, and raced in circles, chattering like a flock of colorful birds.

Hans smiled. He looked at Hester beside him holding Emma. What was so different about her today? Beneath the shade of the oak trees, she was radiant with beauty, an inner light making her brown skin glow, her large dark eyes like liquid fire. He looked away.

"Come, children," he called, his voice choking.

When the road led down to the river, Hester caught her lower lip between her teeth and her upper one. Padriac. Would he be there? She could smell the river, the wet bottomlands, where the dusty, crumbling earth turned to soft black mud that squished beneath toes and smeared easily across skirts and breeches.

A row of thick bushes almost hid the raft, but Hester spied it long before they reached the crossing. An old, grizzled man unfolded from his seat on a wide stump, a blade of grass dangling from his teeth. His hat was a questionable shade of brown, made of felt, the brim waving and flopping around his face. His stained, collarless shirt was open at the neck, his knee breeches held up by a sturdy rope with frayed edges.

He removed the blade of grass, spit a stream of green juice, and rumbled, "Howdy."

"Hello, there."

"Goin' across?"

"Yes, we are. If you'll take us."

"Sure thing." Going to the rope that circled a sturdy post, he unwound it slowly, then coiled it and laid it on the raft. Picking up another rope, he hauled the large, flat raft to the bank, secured it, and went to Dot's bridle.

"Horses skittish?"

"I doubt it."

Hans lifted the reins and clucked to them as the old man tugged at the bit. The horses stepped gingerly, bending their heads as they walked across the planks and up onto the raft.

Hans got down out of the wagon and went to stand next to the horses' heads as the old man poled them away from the bank. The children's eyes widened with apprehension, but they remained seated, obedient.

"These all yours?" the man asked, looking directly at Hester.

"Yes," Hans said, gazing across the water.

"Where's your wife?"

"In heaven."

Up went the old man's eyebrows. "Can't beat that."

"No."

"When'd she die?"

"It'll soon be a year."

Hester looked straight ahead, clutched Emma on her lap, and remained silent. She knew the wizened old man wanted to ask more, but he chomped on the blade of grass, watched Hans, busied himself forming his own opinions, and kept his questions to himself.

When Padriac returned the following day, he told him about the Amish man and his wagon load of kids, his wife dead. "Either them Amish allowed young wives, or that oldest daughter wasn't his," he mused. "Them Amish is odd," he finished.

Padriac watched the old man's face intently, but he only nodded his head and asked if they had come back in the evening. Frustrated, he kicked the raft, balled his fists, and stalked off, leaving the old man looking after him with questioning eyes, shrugging his shoulders and shaking his head before sitting back down on his overturned, wooden crate. He pulled his felt hat down over his eyes and leaned back against a tree. Young chaps nowadays!

The trading post was a long, flat building made of logs. Two windows with a door in the middle looked like eyes and a nose, Hester thought. The hitching rail in the front was strung with horses of every size and description, some carrying saddles, others without. Men lounged against the front wall, eyeing them curiously. Hester sat very straight, looking neither left nor right as Hans guided the team up to the side of a hitching rail. He tied them with the neck rope, then told the children they were allowed off, but to stay with him.

Inside, the light was so dim, Hester had to blink her eyes to be able to see anything. After a minute or so, she could see the long, high counter along the side, the form of a man behind it, and a knot of Indians talking in low, guttural tones.

The smell that assaulted all of them as they stepped inside came from the great pile of furs in a corner of the room, tied in bundles with heavy string, a great stinking heap of them. Noah and Isaac held their noses, rolled their eyes, and made gagging sounds, until Lissie plucked at Hans's sleeve and whispered to him about the boys' bad behavior.

Hester had never seen so many objects in one place. Her large, dark eyes roamed every wall, taking in the bolts of fabric, rope, plowshares, lanterns, hooks, utensils, tools, rakes, pitchforks, dishes, books, long rifles, and evil-looking pistols.

There were barrels of molasses and herring and pickles. Drums of vinegar, barrels of sugar and flour and salt. Tentatively, Hester reached up to touch her cap and adjusted it slightly.

One Indian who caught sight of Hester stopped and stared. Speaking rapidly to the others in his group, they all turned and stared, their black eyes keen, their bodies held very still.

They were tall with straight black hair tied with lengths of rawhide. They wore linen shirts, leggings made of deerskin and brown, beaded moccasins on their feet. Heavy ropes and necklaces made of bear claws, bear teeth and shells hung from around their necks. Each had many bracelets of Dutch beads strung around both wrists.

Hester lowered her head. Her stomach flopped when one of them approached the family. He spoke to Hans, who spread his hands and shrugged.

"Come." The Indian led him to the counter and began a series of rapid-fire questions, which the owner of the trading post translated to Hans in German.

Yes, Hester was an Indian. A foundling. She was fifteen, maybe older. They had never been sure of her birth date. Yes, she was Amish.

After this had all been translated back to the Indians, they nodded eagerly and became quite excitable. They came to stand close to Hester, examining her with their eyes, reaching out to touch her, but stopping before they actually made contact.

Hans fought to remain calm, the looming fear of losing her seeming like a sudden reality.

The Indians were quiet, well-spoken, and strong. Their bodies were honed to perfection by long hunts, their travels through the forest, their way of moving constantly.

Hans thought they were likely of the same tribe as Hester as he observed their stature, the contour of their faces, the way they walked.

When he felt it was polite, he pointed Hester toward the fabric, in spite of the Indians' interest in her. They chose bolts of linen to make knee breeches and shirts, shortgowns and dresses for the little ones.

Hester could not help but look longingly at some purple fabric, too, the shade of violets nestled between their waxy green leaves in early spring. Her eyes begged Hans. At first he shook his head no. But when she bent her head gracefully, the thick lashes sweeping her cheeks, and when a painful blush crept across the swell of her face, he caved in, sinking like a man caught in quicksand.

He bought a plowshare, a length of rope, and a new axe blade. He bought hard candy for the little ones. Lissie pouted prettily until he bought a beautiful square of fabric for her.

They sat beneath the shade of a great locust tree behind the trading post. Hester spread a cloth on the ground, and they ate bread and some dried deer meat.

It was very good. They were all hungry, so everything tasted especially fine out in the open air, away from the pile of furs, thinking of the new colorful fabric they had just bought. The dried venison was salty and tough. They chewed it for a long time, finally washing it down with spring water, which Hester had put in a wooden pail with a tight-fitting lid, then wrapped in heavy coverlets to keep it cool.

It was a wonderful day.

Hans asked Hester how she felt about the Indians who were so like her. She kept her face averted and said she didn't know. She couldn't sort out her feelings yet. It was too soon. The Indians had not repulsed her; neither had they attracted her.

She knew her skin was the exact same shade of brown, her hair straight and sleek and thick. God had created her an Indian. And he loved her. He loved her enough to have her be discovered by Kate, a childless mother whose arms had ached to hold an infant of her own. But then he'd taken Kate away. She'd figure it out later. Today was too perfect.

They traveled on to Berksville, where a group of houses huddled in tired rows lining a dusty street, like maids trying to appear as wealthy women.

Hester knew now why they were called false fronts. A lot of Amish people had false fronts—perhaps English people, too—appearing to be a lot more than they really were. Behind the fronts were the brownish, gray-weathered lumber buildings that looked exactly alike, but people couldn't see that. Only God did.

In Berksville, Hans bought a great copper kettle that cost a lot of money, he said. He also said it was a necessary item, one that would pay for itself at butchering time, and in the fall, when they cooked apple and pear butter.

The children saw a livery stable, a hotel, and a drunken man who was weaving in and out of other pedestrians' paths, singing a ribald song at the top of his lungs, hiccupping in between his off-key words.

Hans's face became set and severe, thinking how he'd brought his innocent children directly into the maw of the world. What if Noah and Isaac wanted to try that? Well, he certainly couldn't say he had always abstained. But that was in the days of his youth, when the Amish leaned toward tolerating youth who sowed a few wild oats before they were ready to settle down.

They met an English couple walking arm in arm, chatting happily, their faces turned toward one another, and Hans experienced such a pang of pain, he thought he would fall down in the dusty street. How he missed those moments with Kate! Hunched over on the front seat, he became weary of life with such an uncertain future before him. Yes, he needed a wife, a helpmeet, a fine Christian companion. The thought settled into his brain, bringing a kind of hopelessness he hadn't thought possible.

He glanced over at Hester, who sat like stone, her perfect profile etched into his heart, impossible to remove and as lethal as smallpox.

He heard the children's noise in the background. Lissie was seated in the copper kettle, wagging her head in time to the song they were punching out in various keys. He smiled to himself.

The sun was not yet setting when they crossed the river again. Hester watched for the flaming head of Padriac, but only the old man rose from the stump he was seated on, shuffled over, and poled them across.

It was not yet dark when tired Dot and Daisy pulled the spring wagon up to the barnyard. They stood with their heads drooping, eagerly awaiting the removal of the heavy leather harness and a long, cool drink of water from the trough, a fine pile of oats and corn, and a forkful of hay thrown across the stable door.

Chapter 16

Almost to the day, a year after Kate's death, the deacon, Amos Eash, announced the upcoming nuptials of Hans Zug and Annie Troyer.

The well-trained congregation remained in their seats, faces solemn, showing no emotion. The number of the last song was given out, and the slow rhythm of German singing followed. No one cracked a smile.

The children had been told the evening before. Noah's face closed like a book. Just folded up, unreadable. Isaac searched Noah's face to see what his own reaction should be. Finding no clue, he shrugged his shoulders and figured Noah would let him know sometime.

Lissie jumped up and down and clapped her hands in excitement. Then upon finding out who the bride was, she wrinkled her nose and said, "Ew. Why her?"

The three boys, "the stair steps," as they were often called—Solomon, Daniel, and John—said it was all right and that it would be nice to have a mother again.

The three little ones jumped up, eagerly imitating Lissie. But they were confused by her nose-wrinkling and went outside to play.

Hester said nothing. She watched Hans's face, and thought he had done well, asking Anna Troyer. She was young, never married, slim as a rail, and probably prettier than Kate had ever been. She had brown hair, the color of most white people's, and a round, comely face, if not beautiful. Yes, Hans had done well.

Like a stone rolling off her young shoulders, the burden of keeping house, the washing, the baking, just everything slid off as she thought of having a mother in the house.

The wedding could not be soon enough for Hester. The Amish neighbors gathered around and planned a "sewing" for Hans's family.

One day after another marched by in quick succession, unraveling life as Hester knew it.

After a year on her own, she was the one in charge. She decided when to do the washing, when to light the bake oven, when to put in the bread and cakes. The wood was chopped and carried in under her supervision, the bedding washed in her time.

Now and then Rebecca swooped into the house, a great beaked crow of disapproval, shouting at the children, simpering with pleasure at Hans's appearance, and sending Hester to do the meanest tasks she could think of. The farm had to come up to Annie Troyer's standards, and she was fastidious, Rebecca said. She came from Germany, where the people worked hard, lived clean, and never shirked a duty. The children would have to live up to her standards now.

The day arrived when Hans brought Annie to meet the children, only a few hours after Rebecca prodded her horse down the road, the house cleaned to her satisfaction.

He unhitched Dot with Annie's help, who seemed flushed, radiant, and eager to help. Together, under Hester's watchful eye, they entered the house, Hans stepping aside, a hand on Annie's back, to introduce her to the children.

She was thin as a rail like a young sapling. Her skirts hung straight and full, touching the heels of her shoes, her cape pinned close under her chin, falling across her shoulders, revealing not the slightest hint of a womanly figure. Her eyes were large and set far apart, her whole face quite comely except for the uneven row of teeth that revealed themselves when she smiled.

Hester watched warily as she shook hands with Noah, then Isaac, saying softly, hardly above a whisper, "How do you do?" The boys nodded awkwardly, the late afternoon sun's rays illuminating their tortured eyes as they searched Annie's face for signs of approval.

When Annie reached Hester, she put out her hand yet again, grasped Hester's in a firm grip, and said, "Hester." Hester's eyes met Annie's with a flat, expressionless appraisal. She held her lips straight and taut. Annie was struck by her beautiful face, crowned by a sheen of black hair, while noting that her cap was too far back on her head. Hester's eyes were like the eyes of a cat, mere slits, awaiting its prey, Annie thought. Her knees went weak.

Hans saw. Ah. Hester didn't like Annie. A fierce possession welled up in him, and he was strangely comforted. His heart was a tangled mass of knots, a disorderly jumble of feelings he was struggling to unravel. The display of animosity in front of him only heightened the tension by far.

His heart pounding, he smiled untruthfully while showing Annie the remainder of the rooms. He sat with her at the clean plank table and laid out his plans for a new stone house. When the children gathered around shyly, Annie lifted little Emma onto her lap, and they resembled a family.

The wedding was held at Dan Troyer's, and a fine one it was, everyone said.

The great house was emptied of its furniture. The summer kitchen filled up with women, who, although dressed in their Sunday finery, cooked and stewed and baked as the wedding guests were seated in the main house on hard, wooden benches. The gathered community listened to the traditional sermon as the minister spoke of creation, of Ruth and Samson and Tobias of the Apocrypha.

Hans was large and dark-skinned, his full cheeks flushed with color, his eyes bright with renewed vigor. His Annie sat beside him, meek, quiet, her eyes lowered, dressed in a navy blue dress and black cape and apron, pinned snugly about her neck. Her white head covering hid most of her brown hair.

It was a solemn occasion. The children were in everyone's thoughts and were being closely observed. Poor motherless little ones. The women sized them up, clucked their tongues, said the little boys didn't look happy. *Ach*, Annie would be good to them, poor little boys.

That Hester. Good luck with her, they said, shaking their heads. Annie would have her hands full with that one. Well, they never should have raised her. She was, after all, an Indian. Mark my words, she'll bring sorrow on the family. So the talk drifted in half-whispers behind palms held sideways, as people are wont to do on occasions such as this.

Hans ate turnips with dark streams of browned butter running from a pool on top of them. He ate large spoonsful of *roasht,* the traditional chicken filling, with rich brown gravy, and shredded cabbage mixed with vinegar and sugar.

There were cakes and pies, cookies, stewed apples, and apple butter bread.

Annie smiled, her eyes sparkling as she looked at the tools people had brought as gifts. She gazed at her new husband and felt a lucky girl.

Hester sat with her friends but remained strangely silent most of the day, except when she answered questions or lifted the corners of her mouth in a half-hearted attempt at gaiety. This was not what she wanted. She wanted Kate, her mother. Her loyalty, her love, was with Kate. Why had they gone that day? If they never would have picked raspberries and disturbed the mother bear, Kate would still be here.

The wedding songs rose and fell as the guests sang lustily. The children ran outside to play, eating all the cookies and doughnuts they wanted with not a care in the world.

Hester thought of the old Indian woman and wondered if she was still alive. Suddenly, she had an overwhelming urge to see her and to visit the magical place. She knew without question that she must go. She needed her in a way she could not understand.

"Hester?"

She looked up.

"Come. The girls are getting ready to go to the table."

Hester shook her head.

Annie's sister, Barbara, questioned her with lifted eyebrows.

"I'm not sixteen."

"Oh, but you may go to the table with a boy."

"Going to the table" meant standing in a group with other white-faced, nervous girls, waiting for a single young man to reach for her hand, then lead her to the table and join in with the hymn-singing. She wouldn't be able to participate, being an Indian. No boy would choose her to accompany him to the table.

She shook her head.

"Come on."

"No."

"Please?"

Hester lowered her head. "No one will want me."

Barbara was shocked.

"Oh, but that's not true."

"It isn't?"

"Why, no."

Hester wanted to believe her. Her friends prodded until she gave in, standing miserably behind the rest of the colorfully clad young women who giggled and made small talk, trying to appear nonchalant when, in truth, they were bordering on hysterics.

Who would ask for their company? Would anyone? Would it be the one they preferred, or one they could barely tolerate?

Hester's heart pounded as she stood in the room upstairs. The young men would come trooping up the stairs, their hearts pounding as well, jostling, joking, combing their hair, bending to check their appearance in small mirrors, held discreetly.

Hester almost elbowed her way out of the room. She wanted to flee, to run and run and run out of sight, away from this ghastly wedding, this disturbing, unnerving day, when her father took this questionable, skinny girl to be his wife, her mother.

The first young man appeared. Gigantic, wide-shouldered, his head scraping the low ceiling, his hair as black as midnight on a rainy night, his eyes as brown as a shelled walnut.

One glance, and Hester's eyes fell.

His eyes surveyed the room from left to right and back again. He stepped forward. Softly, he made his way through the over-eager young girls, parting them, his eyes telling them to step back.

Hester could not look up. Her eyes were held by the hem of the dress in front of her. When the skirt moved aside, she saw a white sleeved arm, a large brown hand extended, the fingers long, tapered, the nails clean and cut evenly.

She hesitated, unsure. She waited for another girl's hand to take the one that was offered. When none appeared, she looked up, afraid of making a mistake. The brown eyes looking down at her were the gentlest thing she had ever seen.

Slowly, trembling, she placed her hand in his. She was led away, the girls parting for them, faces showing the extent of their congratulations or misery. He took his time, walking slowly, holding up his hand so she could easily descend the narrow staircase.

Heads turned at the first couple's approach. There were broad smiles of approval, eyes following their every move. This was a wedding, and matchmaking and romance swirled in the very essence of the room.

Other couples followed, but Hester was guided to the bench by the wall, facing the wedding guests.

Gracefully, she slid into her place on the bench beside him. Her shoulder touched his solid one. Quickly, she leaned away, lowering her eyes, folding her hands in her lap. She felt as if her breathing brought no oxygen to her body, as if her heart would lose its power to keep going. There was no way she could speak to him.

He propped his elbows on the table. His shoulder came solidly against hers, and he kept it there. "Hello," he said, very softly.

Hester only nodded. She had no power to speak.

"Can you say, 'Hi'?" he asked, so gentle, so easy.

She nodded again.

"All right. That means 'Hi.' Do you speak Dutch?"

Again, the nod of her head.

"I'm William."

When the singing began again, it was easier to look at him. She felt as if the guests were watching their hymnbooks and not her, so she lifted her head, turned it slightly to the left, and opened her eyes. Her lips parted in a soft smile. Gladness rose in her dark eyes, and she said, simply "Hester."

He could not answer. He had not thought this feeling possible. The welling of unexpected emotion that rose in his chest brought tears to his eyes. All his life he had prayed. When he reached his twenty-sixth birthday, he stopped asking God for a woman he could love. He fought bitterness, sure that God had forgotten him.

Thinking she had been too bold, Hester bent her head, misery suffusing her face.

"Esther?" he asked, finally.

"No, I am Hester."

"Hester."

"Hans Zug is my father."

"The groom?"

"Yes."

"Forgive me, but are you his daughter?"

"No."

"I didn't think so."

"I am a full-blooded Indian." She turned her head, and he drank in her beauty—the glow of her caramel-colored skin, the perfection of her nose, her mouth. Her eyes were sad, too old. She couldn't be more than eighteen. Perhaps he had no chance.

"Why are you Amish?"

"They found me as an infant. Kate did."

"Kate?"

"My mother. The one that died."

"Oh."

The sweet treats that were offered, the cider that was served in redware cups, turned to sawdust and vinegar for Hester. She could not eat or drink, for she had been held captive by kinder eyes than she had ever thought possible. She wanted to hold his eyes with her own, drain all the caring from them, and hold it in her heart forever.

She wanted to keep that gentleness so that she was rooted to something, no longer floating between the fractured family she belonged to and the distant calling of the old woman's heritage.

"How old are you?" he asked, when he was able to speak.

"I am fifteen."

The disappointment was so heavy, it left him speechless, yet again. Too old. Too old. You're twenty-six. The words in his head mocked and shamed him. He could not rise above it.

"*Ach,* you're a slip of a girl. I'm twenty-six."

From the weight of his letdown, his spirits soared to unnamed heights when she shrugged her perfect shoulders.

"What does that mean?" he dared.

Anything she said would be too bold, so she remained silent. While she knew she was risking straying out of her rightful place, she desperately wanted to reassure him that twenty-six was perfectly acceptable. Sometimes she felt older than that. So she looked at him. She looked into his dark brown eyes, realized the perfection of the contours of his face, the rightness of it, and let her eyes tell him what she could not say.

How could they leave this hallowed place that was only a hard church bench?

Quickly, he told her he was from Lancaster County. A group of Amish had migrated there from Chester County. His name was William King. His father was a brother to Annie. He was the youngest of ten children, four of them dead from smallpox. He had just bought one hundred acres of land.

She listened, nodded, then whispered, "I am nobody."

"Don't say that."

"I am. I don't know where I belong."

You belong with me, his heart cried out. How to let her know? In answer, he reached over, gently pulled her left hand away from her right, and held it in his own.

No one else would have to know, just them.

Unbelievably, he felt her fingers slip into his own like a trusting child. If he had no more from her for the rest of his life, this was enough. The moment would be etched into his mind forever, a gift of God to the end of his days.

Seeye, der bräutigam kommet
Gehet ihm entgegen.

The words of the German wedding song rolled through the house, its joy rising to the rafters, the house filled with goodwill and forbearance. For the lonely widower had found a wife, the children had a mother, and that oldest daughter would have her workload taken from her.

God was in his heaven, and all was good in the fledgling Berks County Amish settlement.

William looked down at Hester, trying to absorb the blue-black of her hair, the perfect part in the middle, the white, white cap, like an angel. He memorized the way her black lashes fell heavily on her glowing brown cheeks, the high cheekbones tinged with the whisper of a blush. Her lips were more than he could ever hope of touching, but he could remember them.

He shuddered, thinking of his Aunt Annie and her family, the ragged tear that was so desperately hidden, the pride, the blatant lies.

He couldn't stay quiet. Bending his head, he leaned his shoulder solidly against her.

"Hester."

"Yes."

"Promise me if things don't go well, you'll let me know."

"What are you saying?" Frightened, she lifted large dark eyes to his.

He drew in his breath. "If Annie proves to be less than, well, how can I say this without disappointing you? I'll just say, if Annie is hard to get along with, if she hurts you, will you let me know?"

"I can't. I don't know your address."

"I'll give it to you before the day is over."

"I think Annie will be kind. She seems nice. I just want a mother and not a stepmother."

William nodded. "Do your best."

How could they explain the agonizing loss at leaving a hard wooden bench, their time together? Years stretched before them, she too young, he too old. How many young men would want her first? And him so far away. He almost wished he'd never settled for the one hundred acres. But he had, and he would remain true. He could not let an Indian girl's beauty derail him like this.

The remainder of the day was nightmarish. He only wanted to be with her. He couldn't find her. He thought she'd gone home. Beside himself with fear, he rose a head above the crowd, his eyes searching anxiously, but she was nowhere to be seen. He left the wedding heartsick.

He stayed at his uncle's house for the night. He was tempted to ask for a horse and ride out to Hans Zug's house, but he thought better of it and decided to let his fate rest in God's hands.

Alarmed at the feeling of losing her, of never seeing her, he felt the memory of her like torture now, an agonized longing that threatened to send him into despair. What color was her dress? He didn't know.

All he knew was that he understood, at long last, what it meant to be in love. That secret no one could fully express made young men do silly things, made them forget the ordinary daily world and dwell on utterly useless things.

Ah, but it was priceless to be able to savor this once in his life. He could wait, placing his trust in the One above.

A cold fear gripped his heart as his Uncle Dan yelled at his wife, then followed his words with a quick fling of a shovel in her general direction, leaving her scuttling for the house and muttering to herself. When William came to talk to Dan, he gave a quick start. A smile spread across his lean face, his blue eyes crinkled in pleasure, and he said jovially, *"Da Villie!"* his favorite nickname.

William kept his manners, held them in front of himself like a shield, but a foreboding gripped his spirit. He wanted to ride to Hans Zug's, grab Hester, and ride away with her, a knight in armor.

Chapter 17

Hester awoke on the first morning after the wedding and remembered William, her new mother, and the fact that neither of them seemed to mind that she was an Indian.

She stretched, luxuriating in this new and astounding discovery. She had never imagined being accepted in this way. Every word they spoke, their every touch, were like drops of pure gold, covering her whole being with grace and love.

She rolled over, buried her face in the pillow, and allowed the happiness to overtake her. She would never again have to wonder where she belonged. It was here with her family and her sweet new mother, whom she would learn to love in time. When she was old enough, she would marry William King, her newfound beau.

She got up, dressed, and went to the dry sink to wash her face.

"Hester!" The sharp word caused her to jump instantly.

She stopped, water dripping from her face. She lowered her hands slowly to the edges of the dry sink and gripped it tightly.

"Hester!"

"Yes?"

"Do not! I repeat—do not ever let me catch you washing your face in the dry sink again!"

"I'm sorry," she whispered, shocked into a low voice.

"Just so you know."

Unsure what to do, Hester turned to the right slowly, afraid the sight of her dripping face would only inflame Annie further. She sidestepped like a crab out of her eyesight, then rubbed her face dry with her apron.

Unsure of exactly what was expected of her, she turned, meaning to ask Annie what she should do to help.

A stack of plates came crashing down in front of her. "Wipe these."

Hester looked at the clean plates, the shelf they had rested on, and then Annie's face.

"What? Weren't they washed?"

"Of course. But an open shelf? Think of the dust."

Nodding, as if it was perfectly understandable, Hester began wiping, placing the dishes on a stack. Then she went to the pantry to retrieve the tablecloth that they always used two or three times before washing it.

Instantly, Annie was by her side, fingering the tablecloth, then whisking it out of her hands. "No. It's dirty. Always use a clean one."

Hester obeyed, quietly placing the plates on the clean tablecloth. Then she stood uncertainly at the corner of the table, one hand placed over the other.

"Don't you milk?"

"I do in the spring. Four cows are dry now, so Noah and Isaac milk."

"That's a girl's job. You should be at the barn."

"I can go if you want me to."

"Yes. Go."

Uncertainly, Hester entered the barn, meeting Noah and Isaac, who were letting the cows out to pasture. When they asked what she had come for, she said that Annie thought she should be milking, not them.

Hans walked in on their little huddle, his face set grimly, boding no good for any of them.

"What?" That was his way of greeting.

"Annie told Hester she should be the one milking, not us boys."

Hans eyed Hester, shrugged his shoulders, and said it was all right with him. "If Annie wants to make breakfast by herself, that's all right with me."

The first meal together was a lesson in Annie's way of life. Everything was perfect. The eggs were cooked just right; the *ponhaus* (scrapple), cut not too thick and not too thin, was fried crisp. The tea was hot and sweetened with honey, the milk cold, the water chilled as well.

Annie was an expert housekeeper, but she avoided Hans's intense eyes. Her conversation to him was civil although a bit stiff, containing none of Kate's closeness. Hester reasoned that a marriage was not created in one day.

But the minute Hans was out the door, Annie turned on Hester, berating her for not setting the water on to boil so she could properly wash the dishes. Had Hans not taught her the ways of a household?

Hester thought Annie had already heated the water. She figured if she told her that, she'd not accept it as a valid answer, so she simply bowed her head, set about filling the water pot, and swung it over the flames of the log fire.

By the time the children were off to school again, they were glad to go. Annie was trying to be a good mother, but she was a new one, one they were not yet comfortable with. School was their refuge, a place familiar, old, and dependable, like Theodore Crane, the schoolmaster, and his helper, Lissie Hershberger.

They loved school, every one of them. They loved the order of their days, the hard work, the lessons they learned. Lissie enjoyed the lower-graders immensely, especially the little Zug children. Poor motherless babies. That Annie Troyer was like a scarecrow, she thought. Good for nothing except scaring away birds. Whatever ailed that Hans she'd never know, but she kept her thoughts to herself, knowing gossip did no one any good.

She watched Lissie closely. Her face was like an open book, revealing everything that was on her mind. She asked her questions when she thought Solomon or John or Daniel looked white-faced and peaked. And she confided in Theodore, who had become quite accustomed to her solid, comfortable presence. He concluded that she wasn't after him at all. She simply enjoyed cooking and baking, which was a profound relief.

Today she offered him a pie, saying she would enjoy a slice with him, bringing out two pewter plates, two forks, and two cups. Had he ever eaten her pumpkin pies? No, he shook his head, no, never.

She cut him a high, wide slice, then served it shivering and custardy on his plate. He cut into the very tip with the side of his fork, brought it to his mouth, and chewed with his eyes closed as he savored every creamy, spicy bit of it.

She leaned forward, her eyes expectantly on his face, then clapped her hands high in the air, a child's yelp of glee following. "Yessirree! Yessir!"

Theodore was not known to burst into spontaneous laughter, being a solemn man and not given to any emotion, but at the sight of Lissie's unabashed delight, he burst into an unusual croak of loud laughter.

He ate the entire slice of pumpkin pie, then another. He became quite talkative, bolstered by the energizing pie, and told Lissie where he lived and why he lived alone. He'd had a sweetheart once, but she had died before they made it to the altar, and his vow to remain single was still as sincere as the day he made it.

"*Ach,* yes, yes," Lissie answered. "But you know, Theodore, you don't know what you're missing, living alone like that. You have no one to eat with, no one to laugh with, no one to wash your clothes."

"Yes. Yes, I do."

"Who?"

"Some old Indian woman, who comes to the trading post."

"Piffle."

"What does that mean?"

"Just piffle, I guess."

He almost laughed again but caught himself and remained decorous.

"Well, I guess if you enjoy living by yourself, that's none of my business. I guess you've been on your own long enough to know what you want. And look at that

Hans Zug and his children. You'd never know it, but mark my words, those children have a hard taskmaster now. I'm afraid Hans was swayed by that Rebecca and his own loneliness."

Theodore nodded wisely. "Indeed. Indeed."

Outside, the leaves began rustling dryly as black clouds piled up to the north. The door swung back, groaning on its hinges as it was swept outward. Theodore got up to close it and latched it firmly, leaving them together in the confines of the classroom.

The room darkened as the sun slid behind the bank of clouds, and Lissie heaved herself to her feet, gathered up the plates and the remainder of the pie, and put it all in her cloth bag.

Stopping, she held her head to the side, considered, and yanked the pie back out of the bag. "Yes, I will have another piece." Expertly, she slid her fingers beneath the wedge of pie, brought it to her mouth, and ate half of it in one hearty chomp. She chewed reflectively, then asked if he liked fried cabbage.

Yes, he certainly did.

Well, why didn't he drop by on Sunday, and she'd make him fried cabbage.

"I go to church on Sunday."

"So do I. After church."

Theodore thought of his dusty old Sundays, when his bones ached as he got out of bed, padded around his cluttery, cobwebbed little rooms, made his eggs, and ate them with salt and pepper. He listened to the minister, helped sing a few songs, and went back to his disorderly home to eat boiled cornmeal mush.

Dinner with Lissie seemed like a bright possibility, but he eyed her warily and said he slept a lot on Sunday afternoon, which did not deter her in the least. She informed him quickly that he could eat at her table and then take a long afternoon nap.

Theodore considered this, but in the end, he declined. What great juicy fodder for gossip would that be? Lissie getting company on a Sunday afternoon and the schoolmaster asleep in her bed! Well, he would be every bit as bad off as that poor fellow who was caught by the old maid when he was stealing her valuables, and she cried out, "At last I have a man."

So Lissie drove home beneath the gathering storm clouds, but she did not despair. She was making progress. She couldn't wait till the time came when she could call him Ted. Or Teddy. She chuckled and then slapped the old horse with the heavy leather reins, whose only response was the flicking of his left ear.

The storm lashed Berks County with unprecedented fury, driving a cold, slanted rain from the north, battering every structure with high winds that bent the trees of the forest, laying flat the ones that were not deeply rooted.

Lissie barely made it home before the rain sluiced against the log barn. It was cold and wet against her face as she hurried to the house, her flat hat slapping her face. She was glad to enter her cozy kitchen, the fire burning low on the hearth, the white linen tablecloth a welcoming beacon.

She lit a betty lamp to ease the darkness away from the corners, then put the pot on the flames for a cup of spearmint tea. She thought she still had enough bacon to fry up with some dried string beans, brown bread, and apple butter.

Theodore arrived home well ahead of the storm, the fire out and mice munching the crumbs on his table. He whacked at them with his broom, then went out through the wind to cut kindling, shivering as the icy rain blasted straight through his trouser legs.

He bet someone like Lissie could make the winter nights quite comfortable, then was overtaken by an awful attack of coughing, so that he choked and had to go to the pump for a drink of water.

The Zug house was warm in the middle where the leaping flames from the fireplace gave out a steady glow, but the corners were drafty. Hester reached for a small shawl to wrap around her shoulders, then sank into a rocking chair. She pulled Emma onto her lap and cuddled her beneath the warm folds, bending to kiss the top of her fair head.

She was weary, and a few minutes with Emma were a good reason to sit. She watched Annie from the corners of her eyes, turning her head slightly so Annie wouldn't know. The late afternoon sun cast a square of yellow light on the oak floor. The light from the fire illuminated the remainder of the house in a warm glow, reminding Hester that a house was a home, as long as there was a group of people in it.

She was trying hard. She scrubbed floors, wiped walls, washed bedding and blankets. She took on the hardest tasks, trying to win her stepmother's affections. Her shoulders were wide and capable, her arms rounded and muscular. The seams of her dresses strained beneath the power of her arms as she hoed the corn, cut it with a sharp scythe, and carried it to the barn for bedding.

As the winds became colder, rustling the last of the clinging, brown oak leaves, she was in the fields. With her ungloved hands, she ripped the ripened ears of corn from the stalks and threw them on the wooden wagon, her nose red from the cold, a warm scarf around her head.

Lissie was helping her. Noah and Isaac had gone to help Hans with the foundation of the new stone house. The corn rustled in the wind, a dry brittle sound that spoke of the coming winter. The mound of golden ears was reaching above the wooden walls of the wagon. Hester's stomach growled.

She lifted her face, searching for the sun, but the gray clouds had reduced it to a shaded, white light. It would rain. The clouds in the evening sky had resembled fish bones, a sure sign of rain, Kate had always told her.

Thunk. Thunk. The ears of corn flung into the wagon made a satisfying sound. This was sustenance for the horses, as well as the family. They would roast the ears of corn in the bake oven, then shell the corn into the wooden dishpan. The next step was to grind the kernels into a fine, golden meal, set it to cooking with water and salt so that it bubbled slowly in the black cast iron pot hanging above the fire, then pour it into pans. The cornmeal mush would set, so that it could be sliced and placed carefully in sizzling lard, where it was fried to a rectangular piece of crisp goodness.

Or Annie would dish the bubbling corn pudding from the pot, lace it with molasses, and pour rich, creamy milk over it. Sometimes she made cornbread. It was all very good.

Thinking of it made Hester swallow, her eyes searching the clouds yet again. Surely the dinner bell would soon ring. Unaware of any changes, Hester continued stripping ears of corn from their husks, flinging the cobs onto the wagon, a mindless repetition, until she called to the horses. "Dot! Daisy! Giddup!" Dutifully, the horses leaned into their collars, tugging the wagon through the emptied cornstalks, until Hester said, "Whoa."

It was only then that she noticed Lissie's absence. She stooped, her eyes searching the cornstalks. "Lissie!"

"Hm."

"Where are you?"

"Here." Lissie lay on her stomach, her face in her cupped hands, her feet kicking the air above her.

"What are you doing?'

"I'm lying on my stomach."

"Why?"

"Why do people lie down? Because they are tired."

Hester laughed quietly. "Come, Lissie. It's almost dinnertime."

"I'm starved. I'm falling-down tired. I can't pull one more ear of corn."

Hester knew she meant it. Lissie was young to be husking corn all day, but Hans had said he felt the hurry in his bones. Winter was going to catch them this year if they didn't stay steadily at the husking of the corn.

There was no doubt about it, with Annie as his wife, Hans's stride matched hers, side by side. He began laying the foundation for the new stone house after digging the cellar with shovels. Neighbors lent a hand, with Noah and Isaac helping after school.

Annie was the taskmaster, the one wielding the scepter, barking orders, shoving the family into a regimen of good management. Where Kate had been relaxed, her work done well and in an orderly fashion, content with her log house and small farm, Annie's goal in life was getting ahead, attaining status and wealth. Of course, she never spoke of it, but Hester knew by the narrowing of her eyes and the lift of her chin when they drove into Amos Hershberger's farmyard, that she aimed to have a house like Mary's, and soon. So Hans took his place beside his thin, energetic wife and met her requirements.

It was only at times, at unguarded moments, when he sat pensively staring into the fire at night, that Hester saw the longing, the remembering, and she wondered. Did he really want this stone house?

Some things, you never could know, but as the days grew colder and Hans redoubled his efforts, laying one stone upon another steadily, week after week, his cheeks became gaunt and lost their rosiness. His shoulders stooped with tiredness, and his eyes glittered with a strange light. Hester shivered. Where would it end?

In due time, the house was built with frolics, those days when men swarmed into the farmyard with wagons and carts, their able bodies a boost to Hans as they bent to the task of cutting and laying the good, solid limestone.

Before those days, Annie and Hester worked from dawn till past sundown, preparing food for the hungry men. They made *Leberklosschen,* the dumplings made of chopped liver and onions, boiled in a good, rich, beef broth and served with pungent mounds of sauerkraut from the crocks in the cold cellar.

Annie made the most wonderful chicken they had ever tasted, serving the dish on a big redware plate with creamy chicken gravy poured over it. There were great dishes of *Schpeck und Bona*, beans cooked with ham, a salty, savory dish served with cruets of vinegar for those who liked the beans strongly flavored. Filling out the tables were stacks of homemade bread and apple butter.

Annie loved to cook, using her mother's recipes whenever she could.

Hans proudly hosted these wonderful meals for the men who came to the frolic. He urged the men to fill and refill their plates, and he ate two platefuls himself. But never once did anyone see him lift his face to find his wife or speak to her as she darted from oven to table and back again, holding her head just so, a bit to the side, away from him.

Isaac observed this, beginning to understand his son's empty eyes. A great sadness lay like a heavy stone on his chest and his breathing, so intense was his pity. And when he observed Hans's eyes on Hester's face, a look that struck Isaac with the force of a sledgehammer, he knew the power of his prayers were more necessary now than they had ever been before. He knew the way of life with a woman like Annie. Rebecca was so much the same. He knew the sacrifices his son would need to make.

Yes, a man gave his life for his family. It was in the Word of God. For years, Isaac had struggled with this monumental sacrifice, this giving up of a close relationship, a shared intimacy, the relaxed and loving way of a wife.

He had much, Hans had. A mother for his children, a willing and able worker, a manager, a zealous woman, but one who left him with an empty heart, a longing. And there was Hester. Isaac shook in his shoes.

CHAPTER 18

DURING THE SUMMER MONTH OF AUGUST, THEY moved into the new house. It was a house that exceeded even Annie's expectations. The floors were wide, golden oak, set with wooden pins, smoothed, sanded, and oiled to a fine, glistening sheen. Winding steps led to the second floor with two bedrooms, each one containing a glass-paned window.

Large pieces of furniture held all of Annie's blue and white dishes, which she had brought from Germany.

A fireplace was located in the center of the house, with a wide hearth for cooking.

Noah and Isaac cut wood for cooking and for heating the rest of the house from the fireplace, the back wall of which jutted into a large room for gathering opposite the kitchen.

Annie kept the floor of the big room swept clean. And when visitors came, she often put down some hand-sewn rugs she had made. The chairs were always dusted, just in case someone would drop by. She hung some of her favorite coverlets over the backs of the chairs to add warmth to the room. She liked doing needlework and wasn't shy about displaying her skills to others.

It was a fine house, with closets built under the stairways and little pantries built in nooks off the kitchen. One of the pantries contained a small window that Annie always left open in winter, which was a wondrous idea. That kept food from spoiling for a week at a time, but no one needed to go outside to bring it in. Water from the spring stayed cold in the large, covered bucket inside this pantry, as well as many foods.

Annie was always pushing for more. She thought a black stove would allow her to do more efficient cooking. And she had heard talk of a pump in the house, which would bring in water at the lift of a handle. Hans knew how expensive these conveniences were, but he kept thinking about the possible depletion of his saved coins, plus the burden of owing a debt to his father. How he hated to ask his own father for money. He eventually had to admit defeat and allowed himself to ask for help to keep his new wife content.

He trembled under his mother's wrath. "Neither a borrower nor a lender be," she said, the words like icy pellets ingrained into his conscience.

"Yes, Mam. But I did not have quite enough money to finish."

"Hans, it's all right for you to have this big house, but not with our money." To have a son who was well-to-do was one thing, but to give up her own pot of coins was quite another.

"He'll pay it back," Isaac offered.

Rebecca chose not to answer. She leaned against the doorframe, crossed her arms, lifted her chin, and asked, "How's it going, son? With Annie?"

"Good. Everything's fine."

Rebecca's eyebrows shot up, disbelief lifting her upper lip. She snickered. "Well, good."

That was all she said, but Hans felt as if his mother had seen straight into his soul, leaving him struggling to put up the shield of happiness he had been accustomed to holding. "She's a good cook."

Isaac nodded.

Rebecca said, "That's about it."

Hans left his parents' house with higher resolve. He would work harder, hide his feelings with more ease, and become the son his mother expected.

When the new house was finished, Annie turned on Hester. She rarely performed any given task properly. The washing was not done to her specifications. When she cleaned, she left dust in the corners. When she washed windows, they were streaked. Her sewing had to be ripped apart and done over.

Hester could not cook, she was told over and over, until she believed it was true. She avoided the kitchen as much as possible and took on more and more of the boys' chores.

For reasons beyond Hester's understanding, Lissie seemed to be able to fulfill Annie's expectations, spending hours in the kitchen producing cakes and biscuits, bread and cookies, with Annie's assistance. It was only Hester who rankled her moods.

Hester climbed the mountain to her rock, as she thought of it now, the great ledge of pure limestone that jutted out over the hillside allowing her a view of the hills surrounding her home, her community of Amish people, the only way of life she had ever known.

She was almost seventeen now, so she was allowed to go with the youth. But so far, she'd chosen not to socialize with them. There wasn't anything she wanted there except to be with her girlfriends, whose inane giggling set her teeth on edge.

Her eyes took in the sky, the heat shimmering above the restless, green trees. She watched a few brown birds wheeling in the sky, those daring swifts that flew so gracefully.

She drew up her knees and laid her head on them, closing her eyes wearily. She felt beaten today. Finished. Surely there was more to life than this endless round of disapproval. She woke up to it and went to bed with it, a knowledge of all her shortcomings. She was never quite enough in Annie's eyes.

The next day, Annie asked Hester to cook a huge kettle of apples, so none went to waste. She had built a good-sized fire, burning hot, so the apples would finish cooking before it was time to start supper. She was struggling to lift the heavy kettle onto the hook set over the fire, but she bumped it when she swung the loaded pot up and over the bank of flames. Determined not to ask for help, Hester pulled the kettle back again with a broad arc of her arm, balancing herself carefully so as not to have the sparks that were racing across the hearth catch her skirt.

But as her elbow flew back to its highest point, Hester felt a burst of heat at her feet. Her skirt had swept the edge of the hearth, and flames ran quickly across the width of her hem.

Determined to achieve the perfection Annie required, Hester landed the pot of apples onto the hook over the crown of flames. Perspiration formed on her forehead and beaded on her upper lip, but she didn't slacken her pace once.

She bent to smother the flames on the bottom of her skirt before they could race up the threads, consuming her weekday clothing. But as she stooped to stamp on the smoldering cloth, a stinging slap connected firmly with the side of her face, then another. "You're just a strong-willed, insolent Indian," Annie hissed, her wide eyes alive with the anger she felt, never acknowledging the danger Hester had been in.

Hester escaped in the only way she knew how, straight up the mountain to her rock, the only place of solace she knew.

Today, she did not see the eagle, as she often did. Where was her God? Did he hear when she prayed? It seemed as if God had hidden his face from her, the way he had allowed Annie into her life.

It was the endless, mind-numbing disapproval she felt continually. She tried and tried, doing her best each day, but she guessed Indians must be like that. What other explanation could be valid? Indians were incapable, untrustworthy, slackers who shirked their duty, unable to perform the way white people did. At least that's what Annie wanted her to believe. But did she? Her thoughts jumbled and twisted painfully. Stuck in self-hatred, she examined each of her flaws and cringed before them.

Yes, she was unworthy, but there was nothing she could do to help that.

Gott im Himmel (God in heaven), she prayed. I know we are not supposed to ask for signs, but today, when I am not sure if you are there, please show you care about me. I need something or someone to show me how to be a better person.

The sky remained blue and bright and empty. The leaves whirled and danced, the thin, brown branches waved in the summer breeze. A curious green lizard scuttled out on the edge of the shelf of rock and watched her with wide red eyes, its sharp, forked tongue darting in and out so rapidly, Hester could see only a blur. Bees hummed past on their way to a certain type of nectar from a flowering bush.

Hester lifted her head, her eyes searching the great blue sky so empty today, devoid of one puffy white cloud. She sighed, straightened her legs, and propped her shoulders by extending her arms behind her.

A clear, melodious whistle entered her consciousness. Not a bird, certainly. She held her body motionless, a part of the limestone. The whistle was clear, a melody, a song, although she didn't know the tune or the words. Who would be here? Noah or Isaac? It was a beautiful tune. It sent chills down her back. Had God heard her? Was this an angel? In the German Bible she had learned to read, a visitation from an angel was always frightening. Should she be afraid?

Slowly, the whistling faded away into the distance, leaving Hester frustrated, longing to know.

Sighing, she prostrated herself on the rock, hid her face in her hands, and thought of William King. What a name! Worse than the red-haired youth named Paddy. The King of England, this one.

Yes, it had been nice, and oh, he was handsome. A fine man. But if she harbored thoughts of him, it would only lead to heartbreak. She could never have him. She wouldn't be white enough, with skills to do housekeeping properly.

A butterfly hovered over her, then danced through the sky with its fluttering, erratic pattern of flight. Perhaps she was like this butterfly, made to be the way she was. Hadn't God created her? John Lantz, the bishop, had explained it very well. God had taken a rib from the man he created and formed a woman. That was a wonderful idea.

Hans was not like Annie. He was a good person. Perhaps all men were better than women. She knew that thought was incorrect. Kate had been the best person Hester had ever known. And Lissie Hershberger. She smiled. Local gossip swirled around the portly woman and her tall, skinny co-worker, Theodore Crane.

She strained to hear the whistling, unafraid, curious, but there was no sound except the leaves rustling, distant bird song, the faraway cawing of crows.

Hester sighed. She did not want to go back. If she stayed here on this rock, would she suffer much if she didn't eat or drink for days and days? Now that was only being foolish.

One thought became very clear to her. She would find the Indian woman who gave her the herbs to heal Kate's wounds. She sat very still as the thought saturated her being. Yes, she would go. Somehow she would find her way, perhaps only to the river, but perhaps Padriac Lee would go with her.

She felt a clear direction, a newfound purpose. The old woman would help her in much the same way she had healed Kate's wounds. Lifting her hands, she felt thankful for the direction. It was a simple thought, but a belief so strong it was like an object she could hold.

She drew a sharp breath when a doe stepped out of the trees, followed by a fawn, its white spots already disappearing. The doe's ears flicked forward, her large, dark eyes examined Hester quietly, then she lowered her head and lifted her feet delicately, disappearing into the surrounding trees, the fawn at her heels.

Again, Hester lifted her hands, then flung her arms to the sky. Freely, her spirit worshiped the Creator. She praised him; she thanked him for sending the deer and her fawn. She would go to the Indian woman.

Revived, she didn't dread her return to the house like an unwanted chore. Everything was possible. She could survive, even prosper, under Annie's disapproval.

Later, when she retrieved the twice-washed bed linens from the line, she lingered by the emptied washline, the courage she had felt earlier in the day slipping away from her. Footfalls behind her made her stand erect, at attention, waiting for the harangue that was sure to follow.

"Hester." It was Hans, the soft word a boon to her flagging spirit.

"Yes?" Turning, she faced Hans with tired eyes.

"I need horseshoeing supplies at the trading post. Annie says it's a waste of time in the busy month of August to go after them. Would you please go with Noah?"

"Tonight?"

"Tomorrow."

He watched the expression across Hester's face. Suspicion, fear at first, then acceptance, and what else? "Hester, are you doing all right?" he asked suddenly.

"What do you mean?"

"Is Annie too hard on you?"

She wanted to tell him. She longed to let him know how unkind Annie was but knew it would only make her life worse. Hester shook her head. She would not look at Hans.

"Why don't you go with the youth?"

"What do you mean?"

"You don't try to attend the hymn sings. Why not?"

She shrugged her shoulders.

"The only way . . ." Hans's voice trailed off. "Hester, the only way out of here is to get married."

Anger sliced into Hester like a knife, catching her unprepared, unable to control herself. "Oh, marrying would be a fine kettle of fish. Who would have me? Not an Amish person. Every last one is self-righteous and pious beyond belief. The day Kate picked me up, she should have dropped me in the spring and let me drown like an unwanted cat."

"Hester!" Hans was shocked.

"Don't 'Hester' me!"

"You have no right to talk this way."

"Yes, I do. She hates me."

"No, no, you have it wrong. She's just like that. Annie means well, Hester. She's teaching you the ways of a housewife."

Stepping closer, Hans was overcome by his strong feeling for the Indian foundling, the sweet baby he had helped Kate to raise, appreciative of her grace and beauty. "It's all right, Hester. She treats me the same way. You must forgive her if she seems harsh. She really does mean well."

His hands went to her shoulders. She bent her head, letting go of her anger.

"Promise me, Hester."

She nodded.

He stepped back, feeling more alive than he had in months.

From the front living room window, Annie moved to the kitchen, just in time to see Hans place his hands on Hester's shoulders. Her eyes turned to pools of jealousy; her lips tightened into a fierce line of determination. Hester would have to go.

Energetically, she began cleaning the new stovetop, her anger giving her all the speed and force she needed. She served warm wild plums and dumplings for supper, along with a pitcher of cold, creamy milk. She praised Hester's fried rabbit until her face burned with embarrassment, not knowing how to tolerate the wrong, the treachery in Annie's voice.

Annie approved of Hans's plan to let Noah and Hester take Dot and the wagon to the trading post, making it unbelievably easy for Hester to get away. She guessed that if God cared, he made things possible, and that was the truth.

Hester's face was flushed with excitement as she pinned the black apron around her red dress. She took great care in combing her thick, black hair. Tying her white cap strings beneath her chin, she hurried out of her bedroom, down the stairs, and across the living room before Annie's voice caught her unexpectedly.

"Hester, here are two quarter pieces to buy yourself something."

Hester stopped but would not look back.

"Your father said you can use them for a dress."

"I don't need a new dress."

"He said you're supposed to."

"I'll get one for Lissie."

"He said it's for you."

Turning, Hester faced Annie, summoning the courage to look into her eyes. Reading nothing, she reached out her right hand, and Annie placed the two coins into it. Hester folded her fingers around them, then reached into her pocket to leave them there.

"Aren't you going to thank me?"

"I thought they were from Hans . . . Dat."

"They are."

"Then I need to thank him."

"We are married, Hester. To thank me is to thank him. Although, I'm sure I won't place my hands on your shoulders the way he does."

"Thank you." Her face burned yet again, humiliated by Annie's evil surmising. Hester stumbled through the door, wiping at her swimming eyes with the backs of her hands, hardly able to breathe for the gigantic lump in her throat.

There was no getting away from her. Well, she was on her way, so Annie's jealousy would be of no consequence. She would tell Noah where she wanted to go and hoped that Padriac would be at his post, taking people across the river.

So far, God had been with her. Or had he? Could she bring herself to question her reason for being on earth? Should she return to her people, the Lenape? Could she adopt another way of life after living the white way for so long?

The mockingbird's song from the hemlock tree reflected the scornful voices within her, telling her she could never be white nor Indian. She should have drowned as a small, helpless infant.

CHAPTER 19

SHE TOLD NOAH.

Noah nodded his head, listened to her, then his lower lip trembled, and he begged her not to leave them, telling her she was the only one he could depend on anymore. "Dat and Annie are married, but she can't stand him, and he goes around pretending to be happy. It makes me sick."

Hester nodded.

"Don't leave, please don't." Noah's large green-blue eyes pleaded with her, but all she could do was nod her head. One little slip of her iron control, and all would be lost.

She genuinely loved Noah. In spite of having lost their mother, he had done a great job of dealing with all of it, including Annie's ambitious cruelty.

"You have Dat."

"You mean what's left of Dat."

A small smile lifted the corners of Hester's mouth. "You mean, a pair of shoes and his straw hat and nothing in between."

Noah's loud roar of laughter frightened Daisy, who leaped, jerking the wagon up and forward, flinging their heads back against the seat.

As the wagon bounded across the rutted road, veering left and right, Noah fought for control, still chuckling to himself.

When they arrived at the river, Padriac's bright head of hair was visible on the water as he poled the raft across with a lone rider on it. He caught sight of their wagon and waved his hat.

"He knows us?"

"Yes." Hester said the simple word, but her heart was pounding.

Noah climbed off the wagon, his youthful face watching Padriac intently. He gave a low whistle. "Look at the way he poles that raft across. I bet he could wrestle anyone down."

Hester smiled. Her knees felt soft and weak, as if she had been running for a long time.

Leaving the rider on the opposite shore, Padriac poled back in a short time, his face showing his eagerness. "It's you! Hello, there!" he called, long before he reached the shore.

Noah was puzzled, looking from Hester to the youth with the flaming hair.

Padriac went straight to Hester, took her hand, and bowed over it.

"My Amish Indian princess," he said, so soft and low only Hester heard him.

She looked into his blue eyes, so open and honest, so completely without guile, it was like a refreshing drink of water on a very warm day. "I have a favor to ask of you."

"Gladly. Anything, anything."

She told him.

Plans were made. They would ride together while Noah went to the trading post. He would return, waiting here till they returned. If anyone came along, they would have to wait to cross, or if Noah was here, he could navigate the raft and its freight. His eyes shone with anticipation, thinking of poling that raft across the river.

It was so easy being with Padriac. He was confident, at ease with the world around him, carefree and lighthearted. He responded to questions in a way that left a smile on Hester's face.

The way was longer and more complicated than Hester remembered, but his horse was surefooted, taking the streams, ravines, and hills easily, picking his way along. Padriac kept up a steady flow of words, while trying to keep his arms from going around her slim waist. As he watched Hester's white cap bobbing up and down just by his chin, he wondered what she would look like with that thing off her head.

Again, it was the birds' cries, their warbles and whistles and liquid trills that gave Hester an otherworldly sense, as if she had stepped into the *Paradeis* (Paradise) that John Lantz spoke of in his sermons. The pine trees were as mighty as she remembered, the waterfalls even more so. The flowers were startlingly unreal, their splendor completely unmatched. Why had no white man ever stumbled on this place? she asked Padriac.

"Oh, they did. A bunch of people know this place is here. Only they're scared of the old woman and her powers. Some say she's the devil; others say she's a witch. Everybody's just glad to let her be."

"Where are the goats?"

"She must have penned 'em up to milk them." Padriac stopped his horse, slid off, and reached up to help her down, then tied his horse to a sapling, returning to her with a smile-chiseled face.

"Ready?"

She nodded.

"I'll leave you alone with her as long as you need to be, okay?"

Again, she nodded, letting her eyes thank him.

Except for the birds and the sound of the falling water, everything was eerily hushed as they made their way down the narrow pathway. They came upon the hut covered in bark. Padriac called out once, then again. Hester was aware of her pounding heart and a rushing in her ears.

"She must have left."

There was not a sign of the clean, white goats. The door of the hut was closed. Padriac tried the latch, pulling on the knotted rawhide, then pushed the door in on its creaking, rusted hinges.

The smell was overpowering at first, but after a minute or more, she was aware of the odor, an earthiness, a scent infused with herbs, dried and preserved in whiskey.

It was so dark, they both waited by the door until their eyes adjusted to the stingy light. Slowly, objects came into focus. She was not here, but her house was filled with the essence of her. A bed on the floor with skins to lie on and to cover her comfortably when the nights were cool. A betty lamp, a fireplace of sorts, an assortment of boxes and crates containing bottles and skins.

Arrowheads, turquoise jewelry, spears, a tomahawk, pipes, dried plants hanging from every available inch of wall space, the floor littered with dried, broken leaves.

Hester's eyes fell on a leather-bound book. A section of brown skin lay across it with Hester's name scrawled in large shaky letters. Hester gasped.

Padriac hurried to her side, bending his head to see. Slowly, Hester reached out to remove the skin. She meant to toss it aside, then decided better of it, folded it tenderly, and placed it in the wide pocket of her dress. A feeling of awe enveloped her as she opened the cover of the book.

"I can't see."

Padriac led her outside and pulled her down on the grass beside him. They bent over the ancient volume.

"It's in English."

"Some of it isn't."

"To my companion, Hester."

"Companion?"

"She probably meant 'friend.'"

"I have gone deep into the forest to die. My time is here. The Great Spirit is calling me. I told you I would leave these ancient herbal remedies, which tell how to cure sicknesses of every kind.

"You will come again to question me. My time is not long, and you have not come. You are misplaced, a sheep among goats, a bird among bats of the night. But you cannot return. You are raised in the way of the white man, and you will never be a true Indian.

"I am very tired, and cannot go to the post to have the schoolmaster help me. The remedies are written as best I know how. To find further instruction, go to the schoolmaster.

"Your God is mine, and my Great Spirit is yours. We are bound to the Great Earth. It is our duty to protect it, care for it. The Earth gives us its food and its animals of the forest. The way of the Lenape will soon be lost as time marches past swiftly, day by day. To prosper, you must trust your own instincts. In our veins runs the pure blood of the Lenape. Courage and strength are your virtues.

"Stay with your people. They have been kind. Do not let the evil slay you. Let the Great Spirit lead you. When the night is dark, the path is hidden. Wait. Wait on the eagle who rises up in due time.

"I will leave now. My heart is very slow. Do not look for me. My body will return to the earth, from which it was made. Someday, we will meet again."

Hester was not aware that she was crying. She didn't know the wetness that fell on the brittle pages was from her own eyes.

She consumed the words the way a starving person ravenously gulps food that is finally available.

She lifted the leather-bound book to her breast and bowed her head over it, as pent-up emotions propelled the tears in an endless, satisfying stream. She was not aware of Padriac's arm around her, of the comforting touch of his hand on her shoulder. She knew only of the wonderful gift she held in her hand.

She dragged the back of her hand across her dripping nose, sniffing, then leaned against Padriac as a fresh wave of all the sadness and pain in her life swept over her. She felt guilty for her revulsion at the odor of the Lenape, her own tribe, coupled with the great chasm between them, accompanied by the betrayal of her mother's dying, and now Annie's hatred, if that's what it was.

The words of this Indian woman were a rope thrown to a struggling person.

John Lantz would not approve of this, but he had not been born an Indian, adopted by the Amish. He would say the Bible is the only true road map. This thought made her sit up, look at Padriac with streaming eyes, and say, "Do you have a handkerchief?"

"Not a clean one."

"Doesn't matter."

Grateful, she took the crumpled piece of cloth, frayed at the edges, and blew heartily. "Thank you."

"How come you're crying so hard?" Again, his eyes were blue and clear and guileless, the question in them kind and honest.

"You wouldn't understand."

"I bet I would, in a way. It can't be easy, born an Indian an' bein' Amish with them strict, bearded, old men hovering over every move you make."

"It's not like that."

"Huh."

"What does that mean?"

"Nothing."

Hester took a deep breath, then held the book out to Padriac. "Just go ahead, read what you can of it."

He was finished long before Hester thought it possible. Reading was still very hard for her, and she took a long time to decipher any words.

She looked deeply into his eyes, taking from him everything he had felt while reading it.

"This must be absolutely profound for you."

"What does 'profound' mean? I'm Dutch, you know."

Patiently, he said, "It must be amazing, meaningful."

She nodded.

They sat in this way, a comfortable silence between them, only the birds' voices in the distance. A sense of belonging, coupled with reverence for the Indian woman's death—the intriguing way she had departed, giving herself to the earth from which she was made—left them in awe.

What faith and simplicity, Hester thought.

"Are you going to the schoolmaster?" Padriac asked.

"Yes. Oh, yes. I know him."

"Is he Amish?"

"No."

"What's his name?"

"Theodore Crane."

"That skinny nervous guy? Bounces his eyebrows?"

"That's him."

"Can I come with you?"

Hester looked at him. "Why?"

"How else am I gonna see you again?"

"If you're thinking about . . . you know, courting, you better not. Amish girls are only allowed to date Amish boys."

Padriac thought on this blunt statement. "I could be Amish."

"Probably not."

"What's the difference?"

Hester shrugged.

"Not much."

"More than you think."

"Yeah, well, I'm Irish. Red hair, blue eyes, a temper. We're all Catholic."

They rode back in silence, Padriac regretting his own Catholic life, the Irish way, vowing to give it up. He wasn't steadfast at all. He never confessed his sins to the priests, figured it wasn't their business. No, he was not devout about anything—not Amish, Catholic, or the Indian's Great Spirit. He just wanted Hester Zug. He wanted to be with her every hour of every day, make her life happy, and protect her from every stepmother and father that treated her wrong.

Could love transcend every culture? He didn't know. He knew those Amish men were some sour-looking individuals. He bet if some of them laughed, their faces would break like glass. The women didn't look much different, except for their white caps or bonnets or whatever you called them. They didn't dance or play musical instruments, so things would be pretty flat. But he'd make it.

Again, Padriac felt a devastating sense of loss when they reached the river. Noah was sitting patiently on the stump. Daisy was unhitched and chomping on great mouthfuls of lush, green grass. Padriac helped Hester down, looked longingly into her deep brown eyes, drinking in the loveliness of her face, and stepped very close to her. "Please say it won't be almost two years till I see you again."

"I can't tell."

Noah sauntered over and began firing questions. His mouth formed a perfect O of astonishment at the book, vowing that between him and Isaac, they could decipher the ancient remedies, couldn't they?

Hester said they could try, laughing her rippling laugh as she helped him hitch up Daisy and left, a cloud of dust obscuring them at the edge of the forest.

Padriac paced the bank of the river, mumbled nonsense, and vowed to appear at Theodore Crane's door, even if the man's eyebrows drove him nuts.

For reasons of her own, the leather-bound book inflamed Annie's hatred. She found it beside Hester's bed, picked it up, and confronted her immediately, her face white and pinched, her breath coming in small gasps of agitation.

"You may as well go back to your people. You are nothing to us."

The words were rocks raining on Hester's head. Her hands went up to defend herself from the pain.

"You think Noah and Isaac and Lissie love you. They don't care a lick what happens to you." Annie stood, her thin fists held to her gaunt hips, leaning forward at the waist, her face only a few feet from Hester's.

"You think Hans cares for you, too. You think your pretty face will have everyone bowing to you. Well, you are about to be surprised."

Hester began to tremble. Like a leaf in a storm, she was shaken by Annie's words. Unable to form any words of her own, she cowered beneath the onslaught of displeasure. But she did not cry. She stood, her arms at her sides, her fingers playing with the folds of her apron, her head bent so that Annie could only guess at the expression on her stepdaughter's face.

"Another thing you need to understand. You won't be able to find a husband here among the Amish. Who would want to have the impure blood of an Indian in their *freundshaft*? So don't go around harboring ideas about this handsome boy that had you at the table at my—our—wedding. He didn't pick you to go to the table. You don't know that boys make bets. They earn money taking the unwanted girls to the table."

Breathing hard by the force of her words, Annie fell silent, glowering.

Still, Hester would not raise her head.

"Look at me!" Annie shrieked, her voice a hoarse whisper.

Hester obeyed. Her eyes were half-closed, expressionless, her mouth a straight, perfect line, her caramel-colored skin flawless, shining with an inner light.

"Look at me!" Annie whispered.

"I am looking at you," Hester said, soft and low.

"Open your eyes when you do, you rebellious Indian."

Hester opened her eyes.

"You see this book? It's full of witchcraft. It's evil and must be burned." She shoved the precious, leather-bound book into Hester's face, forcing her to turn her head away.

"Now I'm going to burn it." Gleefully, Annie held it just out of Hester's reach.

Hester knew if she protested or cried out, it would serve to goad Annie's fury to new levels, so she stayed still.

"Do you want to put it in the fire, or shall I?"

Still Hester remained as still as a stone, immovable.

The front door opened, and Hans entered the house, followed by Noah and Isaac.

Quickly, Annie lowered the book and lifted her lips into a caricature of a smile. Her eyes widened, her eyebrows lifted, and she stepped back, laughing a low, mocking laugh.

"My, Hester, this book is full of drivel, isn't it?" Annie looked at Hans, her face contorted with the effort to swallow her anger.

Hans stopped, taking in the scene in one glance. "Give her the book."

"No."

"Give Hester the book."

"No, Hans. It's full of witchcraft. If this book stays under our roof, evil will befall us."

"Annie, stop. You have no reason to say such things. It is a book containing old herbal remedies and medicines. It is worth a lot to Hester, who needs to learn some of these things."

"It will not be in my house." Annie said evenly.

"Give it to Hester."

Annie would not. She crossed the room slowly and placed it on top of the warm kitchen stove. "I mean to burn it."

She said the words to no one, her back turned to them all, her thin shoulders held squarely.

Hester moved so quietly Annie did not hear her. With speed borne of desperation, she grabbed the book off the stovetop, clutched it to her breast, and stood aside, her eyes alive with hope as she searched Hans's face.

Whirling, Annie snatched the book from Hester's clutching hands.

"No!" The involuntary cry was wrenched from Hester as she gave up the book.

Hans stepped forward, took his wife by her thin shoulders, wrestled the book from her grasp, and handed it to Hester. "Take it away," he barked, his eyes like black fire.

Hester ran through the door, down the slope, and into the green forest, silently holding the precious book to her chest, her only link to hope.

Chapter 20

From that day, Hester's fate was sealed.

She was an unwelcome addition to a family that was changing under Annie's tutelage. As subtle as an approaching change in the season, so was the web Annie wove among all the members of the family.

When did Noah and Isaac begin to keep their distance from Hester? She couldn't be sure. She just knew they no longer talked openly and unashamedly around her, the way siblings do with each other. It seemed to Hester they harbored a suspicion of her behind a wall of mistrust she did not understand.

Lissie remained the same for some time, but her ego was so swelled by Annie's praise that she soon formed an air of superiority over Hester that she may or may not have been aware of. Her cookies were soft and moist, her bread light as a feather. Annie taught her how to make pumpkin pies. Hans's eyes shone at his daughter as he praised her baking, knowing he could enter Annie's graces by doing so.

Hester began losing weight. Her dresses hung loosely on her thin frame, her facial contours became more pronounced. If anything, she was more beautiful than ever.

Hester hid the book away under a stone below the limestone overhang of rock. She wrapped it carefully, put it in the wooden box, and never looked at the words again. They were imprinted on her heart.

To live without love is one thing, but to live with suspicion and displeasure is quite another, she soon found out. Even Hans seemed to stay away from her, avoiding her at all costs, afraid of Annie's wrath.

One Sunday in late autumn, Lissie Hershberger placed herself squarely in Hans's path when church services had just come to a close. He was surprised to see her large bulk obstructing his way and stopped, his eyes wide.

"Lissie."

"Hans."

They shook hands, in the way of the Amish. They spoke of the weather, the crops.

Lissie wasted no time. "Hans, what is going on at your house? Hester is not well."

Her eyes bored into his, quick, alert, and knowing.

"What do you mean?"

"You know what I mean."

Almost, Hans broke down and told this capable woman all his troubles. Almost, he told her of the division that tore Hester from him, the fear of Annie driving Hester away. Almost, he confessed that the only reason he soothed Annie by agreeing with her disapproval of Hester was to make it possible to continue living as her husband.

"Oh, it's all right, Lissie," is what he said.

"It's not all right, Hans, and you know it. What will become of Hester if someone doesn't intervene? She's looking thin and sad, and I know Annie is mistreating her."

"Lissie, everything is fine. You stay out of it. Hester is happy. She really is. She just had a summer spell."

There was nothing to do but step back and let Hans continue on his way.

When Theodore Crane began attending the Amish church services, he was met by looks of disbelief, suspicion, and then acceptance when they saw he was making an honest effort to learn the German language.

He was respected by the community as the industrious schoolmaster who kept unflagging order in the classroom, taught the three Rs thoroughly, and went to eat Sunday supper with Lissie Hershberger. That was all they knew.

They didn't know everything about Lissie, either—the merry whistling that accompanied her swiftly moving hands as she kneaded the biscuit dough on the floured dough tray. Her lighthearted singing late on Sunday afternoons as she cut up the carrots, thickened the chicken broth, and dipped out cream to drizzle over the berries.

Neither did they know the anticipation Theodore felt as he drove his rickety black cart with the gold stripes painted on the wheels. He had never known a warmer, more caring person than Lissie Hershberger. She never failed to administer a kind word to a failing student, hand a hungry child her own lunch, or give a word of praise to a discouraged one.

She was large and soft and filled with goodness. She infused sunshine into his world until he no longer felt old and rickety and dried up, even when his bones hurt with the cold and his cough heaved from his chest when he rose from his chair to add a few sticks of wood to the cranky, low-burning fire in his fireplace.

Every Sunday, she made roast pork and sauerkraut, or a chicken or some beef if she had them. She often fixed stuffing, stirring in broken chestnuts if they were in season. Sometimes she made duck *und* kraut, which was one of his favorites. She made so many different pies, he didn't know if he liked one any better than all the others. Raspberry, strawberry, pumpkin, custard, apple, they were all delicious. He would tuck his napkin into his shirt collar, lean forward slightly, and eat two or three wide wedges of pie, never failing to praise her with flowery words.

And yet Theodore spoke neither of love or marriage. That was all right with Lissie. She chuckled to herself as she mixed up a cake with brown sugar crumbled over top. She thought the dear man couldn't live without her, he just didn't know it yet. Give him time.

It would be wonderful to cook his breakfast and wash his clothes, to sit with him in the morning and discuss their day, to refill his cup with steaming coffee and bend to kiss the top of his head. She would sew his shirts and wash them. He could learn enough of the German that he could understand the sermons in church. He already knew each family, having taught their children. He knew the Amish ways, so it was only a matter of time.

It was on a blustery evening, as the pumpkins lay rotting on the dry, brown vines and the yellowing corn stalks rustled in the gale, when Theodore thought he heard a sound in the wind. He put down his fork and looked at Lissie, who stopped chewing, held very still, and thought perhaps this was the moment when he would finally propose. But what he did was hold up one finger and tilt his head to one side so he could hear better. Lissie's blue eyes watched his face intently, then cut into the pie she was eating once more.

"Sh. There it is again."

Lissie heard nothing. She resumed eating her pie.

"I hear a sound of whistling in the wind."

"*Ach* piffle, Theodore. Who could tell? It's so windy that everything flaps and whistles, howls and roars on a night such as this."

Theodore shook his head, lowered his eyebrows, then raised them again, before bending to his pie. He drank two cups of hot milk, putting off going out to his cold cart, cranky horse, and weak lantern light. The thought of entering his cold, disheveled-looking house gave him a decided case of the blues. How would it be to rock without interruption in Lissie's chair by the fire on a night like this? He could stay here and would not have to go out and hitch up the ill-tempered beast or light the smelly lantern hanging on the cart's side. He just did not want to do that.

Sometimes he wondered if there would be any room left over on her fluffy, goose down mattress, if he ever decided to ask for her hand in marriage. She was a large woman. More and more, he found thinner women quite unappealing compared to Lissie. Take that Annie Hans had married. My goodness, she was like peanut brittle.

Oh, he just wasn't sure. For years, he didn't think about women, didn't even notice them. Then Lissie pushed herself into his life, cooking all this food, and he felt himself slipping, losing his handhold on his vow to remain alone all his life.

Abruptly, he said, "Lissie, you know I don't hold with shunning."

In answer, Lissie laughed, her stomach shaking up and down. "What makes you say that?"

"Well, this ban and shunning is not something I would hold to."

"Why would you have to? You're not a member of the Amish church."

"But if I were."

"Why would you want to be?"

Feeling the noose tighten about his neck, he said gruffly, "Oh, nothing."

When he left, Lissie whirled about the kitchen, singing and whistling, scouring pots and pans, her cheeks pink and shining, her eyes snapping. He was surely thinking about something, that Theodore was. Coming up with that statement out of the clear blue sky. Yessir, he was thinking of joining the Amish church. There was not one other reason on earth to make him pop up with that statement.

She thumbed through the greasy, dog-eared, old book that contained her recipes, planning next Sunday night's supper. Dried plums. She'd never served them to him. Or would dried apples be better? He'd never eaten them either.

She set the old recipe book aside, placed her hands across her rounded stomach, and thought of Hans, his evasive manner, and Hester, that poor, unwanted soul. What kept her in that house?

Hester wrapped her black shawl expertly around her thin shoulders, shivered, drew her knees up to her chin, and laid her head on them, as she sat perched on the limestone rock that jutted out over the side of the steep mountain. Beside her lay the opened book, bound in leather, the one the Indian woman had left her. It was her heritage, the link to something true and real, an object that gave her direction. Over and over, she read the words of wisdom, memorized them, spoke them to herself.

Here on her rock, she felt as one with the earth and its Creator, exactly the way Uhma had written. She could identify with ease the things Uhma portrayed on these pages.

She had never had a chance to visit the schoolmaster. Never had a chance, or was she too ashamed?

She had a constant companion now. Everywhere she went, she imagined herself carrying a handicap, like a growth on her back or one leg too short to walk properly. She was an Indian. Ingrained in her mind, for everyone to see as plain as day, the color of her skin marked her as strange, inferior, less.

The small changes had grown steadily, fueled by Annie's distaste for the Indian. Savages, she called them.

Hester kept the book hidden away, opening it only in rare moments when she could get away without being seen or needed.

The rock had become a place of worship, an altar, a place she came to be comforted, to feel as one with her Creator.

She so wanted to find the secrets of the book and understand the way of the Lenape, which she carried as an unexplored longing in her heart. The old woman had written instructions for her, it was true. She had told Hester to stay among the white people because they were kind. That was not true. They were no longer kind, so that would give her the right to leave.

Hester had a birthright. She had the right to search for her beginnings. A place where every skin was the same color as hers. "My people," she said aloud to herself. The thought brought a thrill, an intense desire to be among them, to live with them in peace and harmony so she could experience a true and pure sense of belonging.

She remembered the distasteful smell permeating the interior of the trading post on the day she had finally encountered the men from the Lenape tribe. Could she learn to live in this primitive manner, now that she had lived all her life in the German culture of cleanliness and hard work?

And there was Jesus, her Savior, who redeemed her from sin. There was her promise to the Amish church to be baptized and live by their rules, to help build the church, to be honest and good and obedient. Like Kate. Like John Lantz, the bishop. And like Hans and Noah and Isaac used to be before Annie came into the family.

Why did Annie dislike her so? For the thousandth time, the question tormented her. Annie's dislike was deeper than the color of Hester's skin.

She did not want to leave her family. Not now. Winter was coming. She wouldn't survive. If she stayed, she would have food and shelter.

Well, she would try harder. She would work more, do everything better. Perhaps her family would change again.

Hester went home and threw herself into every task required of her, again.

She spent days husking corn, forking manure, hauling hay with Noah and Isaac.

When the snows came, the woodhouse was jammed with expertly cut wood, probably half of it done by Hester. She directed all the frustration and loneliness in her life at the cut log pieces, the blade of the axe biting skillfully, severing the pieces easily. Hans praised Noah and Isaac, telling them they were tremendously capable of sawing and splitting wood.

Hester left it at that, lowered her eyes, and swallowed her pride. Annie's mocking eyes laughed at her.

Every Sunday when they had no church services, Hans gathered his children around his chair, and they took turns reading from the great German *Schrift* (Scriptures). Noah and Isaac were fluent, rattling off one difficult sentence after another, but Hester stumbled over the words, mispronounced them, or sat silent, feeling the sneers behind her heavy eyelids. Hans was always patient. Once, when she dared lift her eyes, she found his dark ones on her, brooding, mysterious, containing an expression she did not understand.

Reading and writing had always eluded her, but since she was older, she was getting better at words. That was why Annie told her to go to the schoolmaster for awhile.

"What a dimwit! If you'd sit with Theodore Crane for awhile, he could knock some sense into your head," she said one Sunday after a particularly grueling session of German reading. Suddenly the atmosphere in the house was stifling. Hester got up, wrapped herself in her shawl, and headed out the door.

No matter that she slipped and slid, Hester pulled herself up the side of the mountain by any young tree that offered itself. She was gasping and heaving by the time she reached the rock. Falling on her knees, she dug frantically, her breath coming in quick puffs of steam, searching for the box.

Her mittens were soaked, her fingers icy, her arms aching with effort when her heart leaped. It was there! Pulling out the wooden box, she grabbed eagerly at the volume inside wrapped in cloth. She held it to her body and calmed her breathing.

A clear whistle edged into her senses. The tune was as melodic as the first time she'd heard it. She froze. The sound was undulating, a series of warbles, chirps, and whistles, a liquid, tumbling sound like the waterfalls near where the Indian woman's hut had been.

Slowly, Hester turned her eyes, searching the surrounding forest. The trees were bare and black against the mounds of drifted snow beneath them. The sky was whitish-gray, almost identical to the snow, with a weak winter sun shining faintly as if it was veiled. There was no wind, no sound. A few chickadees scattered a dusting of snow from berry bushes, twittering and chirping to themselves.

Her eye caught a movement beneath the trees. A small brown form, leaning a bit forward as if stalking his prey, moved through the trees. He was too far away to calculate his age or his size. When the whistling began again, she could see that the figure was clearly its source. Hester watched, holding as still as possible until the form moved farther along on the side of the mountain. It was only then that she allowed herself a deep breath, turned, and made her way carefully down the side of the slope.

Neither Noah nor Isaac would accompany her. They said she'd be safe on her own. She asked Hans if she could ride. With all the snow, it would be better. He said no, so she threw the harness on Dot, hitched her to the wagon, threw a few furs across the seat, and left without looking back.

The lump that wanted to rise in her throat was an unhandy thing and served no purpose but to bring on the hated self-pity. She swallowed, resolved to forget there was a time when Noah and Isaac would have helped her hitch up, accompanying her eagerly anywhere she wanted to go.

Lifting the reins, she slapped them down on Dot's rump, relishing the fast trot that ensued, reveling in the dangerous swaying of the wagon as it slid back and forth. Fiercely, she hoped Hans had seen. In the past, she would have pushed such thoughts back, but now there was a difference.

Out of the sneering, the life-draining disapproval that she eventually experienced from each family member, came the small steady flame of Hester's independence. If the wagon rolled over, crushed its shafts, and broke a wheel, there was no one to worry. She felt a freedom somehow. Perhaps a lonely kind of freedom, but she was breaking away from the chains of self-loathing.

The icy air hit her face like a slap, yet she lifted it to the elements, savoring the cold and the pure white world around her. A red bird flew away, its dipping flight pattern carrying it aloft, followed by his dull red-brown mate. Dot clopped along, throwing snow from beneath her hooves, her head held high as she pulled the wagon through the snow.

She passed Amos Hershberger's, the smoke from the chimney wafting in gray plumes into the metallic sky. Looking up, Hester noticed the sky was turning darker. She brought the reins down on Dot's back, who answered with a flick of her ear and an accelerated pace.

When she pulled up to the schoolmaster's house, she was alarmed to see dark windows with no smoke coming from the chimney. Perplexed, she sat in the wagon, unsure.

The light was fading fast, the graying clouds bringing along clumps of snow that had not yet fallen but would come swirling in from the north before the night was over. Uncertainly, she stepped from the wagon. Her black shawl was in stark contrast to the snow. The steaming horse enveloped her in a gray cloud, the white of the sky behind her.

Theodore Crane stretched and yawned, pulled himself up out of his chair, scratched his ribs, peered through the glass at the darkening world outside, and yelped. Surely that was not a ghost.

He peered again, blinking his eyes as Hester moved through the fading light, the steam, and the snow. She pulled the horse and wagon to the hitching rack and threw a blanket across the horse's back. It was only then that he recognized the dark face beneath the large flat hat. The Indian girl. Relieved, knowing it was not a ghost, he opened the door before she had time to knock.

Hester was as relieved as he was. Her quick smile showed the appreciation she felt, and she was promptly drawn into the cold, cluttered house, with Theodore's affable words of welcome. He fiddled around with the fire until it roared up the chimney, filling the small room with radiant heat and light.

She took off her shawl and hat and held her cold fingers to the raging fire, while watching two mice nibble on a bread crust beneath the table. She smiled hopefully at the schoolmaster.

He voiced his enthusiasm when she produced the Indian woman's book and nodded his head in understanding. He said that all the English she had written she had learned from him, and, yes, he would love to try to decipher everything else she had written in the book.

Chapter 21

In the morning, when Hans discovered Hester's absence, he raved and yelled, his worry causing him to become alarmingly out of control. He told Noah and Isaac they should have listened to him and accompanied her, and when Isaac stood up to his father and said they were not told to do that, he received a stinging slap on his shoulder.

Annie was terrified. She had never seen her husband so irate. She didn't know what to make of it and set about frying bacon and stirring up biscuits, as if the sight and scent of her breakfast would mollify this awful yelling.

Hans would not eat. He told Annie to feed the children, he couldn't eat, not with Hester gone. He yanked on his boots and fur coat, smashed his felt hat down on his uncombed hair, and lumbered through the door, still accusing Noah for not accompanying her. Were they aware that she might be lying at the bottom of a ravine, dead and frozen?

For one searing instant, Annie felt cold dread, guilt piling in on her as she remembered all the times she wished Hester ill.

Lissie cried, and Annie felt worse. What had they done? Oh, surely God's judgment would be swift! She trembled in her shoes but kept her fears hidden from the children by firmly reprimanding them to sit up and eat, Hans had gone to fetch her back. One terrified thought after another crowded itself into her mind, and she wondered if she would be accounted for a murderer in God's sight. The Bible plainly said that to hate someone is as bad. Annie wasn't sure if it included humans of another color or not.

Hans searched every ravine, his eyes combing the surrounding trees as terrible thoughts of Hester's demise ran rampant through his fevered brain. The snow was coming down in earnest, hard, stinging little pellets of misery that raked across his face beneath the wide brim of his hat.

He found himself talking out loud to Kate, telling her he was sorry. Memories of the two of them, the perfect child between them, became a fine torture, the denial of his love for Hester an exquisite pain.

A shower of snow enveloped his head as it fell from a weighty pine branch. It knocked his hat into the deep snow, leaving him wailing and floundering, searching desperately for the necessary headgear.

By the time he arrived at the schoolmaster's house, his teeth were chattering, his hands were stiff with cold, and his toes felt like ten chunks of ice. He flung himself off his horse, pounded on the door, rattled the lock, peered in the windows, then paced the small porch, his hands behind his back, his face thrust aggressively in front of him, muttering questions and answers to himself.

He looked off across the falling snow and tried to come up with a plan. Had she arrived here at all? He looked wistfully in the direction of the trading post, wondering if the proprietor had seen her go.

But where was the schoolmaster? Oh, at school. No, this was Saturday. He should be at home.

Finally, he lay down his pride, shouldered his resolve, and pushed through the deepening snow to the front porch of the trading post. A handful of slovenly looking men stepped aside, allowing him to enter. He nodded shortly without meeting their eyes and walked quickly up to the counter where a youth with red hair looked down on him, a good-humored grin on his freckled face.

"What can I getcha?" he asked, without any greeting.

"Have you seen my daughter?"

"What's she look like?"

"She's Indian."

"Yeah. I bet. Move on. Next? What can I getcha?"

When Hans realized he was not going to be helped, he walked back and forth between a bale of furs and some fencing tools, muttering, trying desperately to come up with some way of locating Hester. He tried talking to a stolid Indian wrapped in blankets but was glad to get away from his penetrating, black eyes.

He walked back to the schoolmaster's house and rattled the doorknob before sinking onto the snow-covered bench. Where could she have gone? Was the schoolmaster with her?

He retraced his route, a tortuous journey of fear and indecision, hoping to find her, afraid to look down rockslides and ravines.

He reentered his house around noontime and was met with questioning eyes. He shrugged his shoulders, then tore off his hat, peeled off his wet coat, hanging it across the back of a chair, and sat, starved and dejected, blaming Noah and Isaac, then Annie. Even Lissie had a turn, blamed for her baking skills.

Hans wept openly. His hands shook as he lifted the cup of scalding tea laced with whiskey to his quivering mouth. He refused any food. Annie stayed out of his way, finally understanding why she disliked him so much.

He hitched a fresh horse to the cutter, the small sleigh that whispered through the snow, and made his way to his parents' house, pleading with them for help.

Isaac told him to sit down, think rationally, calm himself. Had he prayed? Was he seeking the face of the Lord to help him? For without faith, nothing was possible.

Out of his son's mouth, then, came the tale of misery—Annie's hatred of Hester, his fear of Annie, the entire family's mistreatment of Hester—leaving Isaac without a trace of surprise.

Rebecca nodded, her mouth prim with the knowledge of having seen this all along—where had Isaac been?—but she said nothing until Hans's voice wobbled into silence, accentuated by the shaking of his shaggy head, left to right.

Finally, Isaac spoke. "Well, Hans, perhaps this is meant to be. It is better for your household with Hester gone. You know that, and I think you know why."

"Why would you say such a thing?'

"Hans, face it. You feel for Hester what you should be feeling for Annie."

Hans's denial was so emphatic, his outrage so complete, that Isaac apologized in the end, saying perhaps it was incorrect to put it that way.

Rebecca turned her back to hide her feelings, then asked if he had checked the widow Lissie Hershberger's house. Rumor had it that Theodore Crane spent Sunday evening with her.

"Why would Hester be there?"

"It's worth a try."

"No. Fat Lissie doesn't have to know."

"Perhaps she has returned to her people, the Lenape."

Up came Hans's red face, shock and disbelief written all over it. One single word was forced from his mouth, in a wail of denial. "No!"

Rebecca stepped up to Hans then and spoke her piece.

In the end, he drove his horse through the snow to Lissie Hershberger's house and found the wagon in front of her small barn, Dot munching oats in the box stall beside Lissie's horse. He fell on his knees there in the hay-strewn barn and thanked *der Herr* over and over for guiding him to Hester. Relief pulsed through his veins; redemption shone from his dark eyes. He adjusted his hat, blew his nose, took a deep breath to steady himself, and walked sedately up to the porch of the little log house.

Lissie answered the door.

"Good afternoon, Lissie. I came to get Hester." He hoped his tone of voice was normal, his countenance calm and friendly.

Lissie pulled herself up, glowering from her blue eyes. "She's not here."

"The wagon is."

"Well, she's not."

"You're hiding her from me."

"I sure am."

"Lissie, I beg you, let me see her."

Lissie considered, then stepped aside, motioning him in with one hand.

Hester was seated at the small linen-covered kitchen table with Theodore Crane, steaming bowls of thick soup in front of them. Hester rose, holding onto the back of the chair, her eyes so large and dark in her thin face, they were like dark, turbulent pools.

With a glad cry, Hans moved swiftly across the room, gathered her against him, and held her there. He bent over her, crooning as he would to a small child, murmuring words of endearment, jumbled with soft apologies.

Uncomfortable, Hester tried to extricate herself from his embrace, her face a mirror of Lissie's own.

Theodore choked on his soup. His eyebrows began raising and lowering themselves of their own accord, but he remained seated, unable to watch.

Hans let Hester go, but his eyes remained on her face as if he could not bear to let her out of his sight. Finally, he realized how he had lost control of his emotions in Theodore's and Lissie's full view, lamely telling them how precious the small babe had been, this foundling who had made his and Kate's home complete.

Lissie nodded, her mouth a slash in her round face. "If you like her as much as you say you do, why would all of you mistreat her, then? What explanation do you have?"

"Mistreat?"

The question quivered in the air, a bubble of hope, Hans's desperate wish that Hester had not spoken of her life as she knew it since Annie had become his wife.

"You know what I mean. Hester went to Theodore's house for tutoring in the German language and stayed with him, unable to bring herself to go home, that's how bad it is. So you're not getting her. She's staying right here with me, and this time, I mean it."

"Oh no, Lissie. You're mistaken. Hester comes home with me."

"She stays here."

"She's my daughter."

"Tell that to the ministers when they come to call on you."

"*Ach* now," Hans's tone became a whining, nasal plea. "Let's work this out like two Christians should."

"How?" Lissie demanded.

"Hester, you want to come home, right? To Lissie and all the others, your own bed, all the good food Annie prepares for you. Please return with me now, and this will all blow over. No one needs to know that any of this occurred." His voice rose an octave, his eyebrows elevated, his tone becoming eloquent in his earnest desire for Hester's return.

They all stayed silent, looking to Hester for an answer. She stood behind her chair, tragic in her beauty, her eyes sad and much older than her years. Quietly, she began to speak.

"I'm not sure what I need to do. I can't go back with you as long as Annie is your wife. I'm not sure if I want to return to my—to my people, the Lenape tribe of Indians who live in the Pennsylvania forests and mountains. I have the book from the Indian woman. She says to stay among my people. They are kind.

"And you aren't anymore. Annie is cruel. I'm not sure who I really am. I partly belong to two peoples, to two ways of life.

"When Kate was my mother, I never wavered. I became Amish; I was Amish. It was a good way to live life on this earth. Annie takes all that away, making me wonder why I am here. Maybe my life as an Indian would be better. I would be accepted."

"You are accepted by me, by the Amish community," Hans broke out, spreading his hands wide for emphasis.

Without wavering, Hester asked coolly, "Am I?"

Hans floundered, said he'd talk to Annie, but Hester shook her head.

"Annie will not change."

Hans knew the truth of her words. He knew, too, that he was caught. He could not turn his back on Annie, but he would suffer unspeakably without Hester.

"I suggest that Hester stays here, away from Annie, until she chooses which direction she will go," Lissie said, testing the situation.

"But she has chosen. She is one of us. She professes to be part of the church."

Around and around the dizzying conversation swirled like clouds of wearying gnats that only served to heighten tempers. Hester saw this and knew it would be unwise to stay with Lissie. For the sake of peace, for Hans, she would return. He had given her a home when she was a helpless baby. Now she would return.

She told Hans she would go back, then proceeded to dress in her outdoor clothes and never said another word. She walked woodenly through the drifting snow, lifted the reins onto Dot's back, and moved off, a dark, lone figure wearing a large, flat hat that hid her face completely.

Hans followed in the cutter, resolve in the way he smashed his hat onto his head, memorizing the speech he would give to his family.

The speech was never delivered.

Annie's face was radiating her disapproval, her body taut with it. Her arms moved like jerking sticks as she loudly derided Hester's behavior.

Fear of his angry wife crowded out Hans's words of bravery. He kept his eyes hidden from Hester as she hung up her shawl and hat, and he tried not to see the puzzled expression on Isaac's and Noah's faces. He was a man caught in the middle between two women, indecisive and afraid.

No one spoke.

Hans cleared his throat.

Annie thumped serving dishes of creamy cornmeal mush on the table top and poured water in redware cups so fast, it splashed on the tablecloth. Her mouth quivered. Her hands shook with repressed fury.

Hester took her place, choked down a small amount of the mush, and drank a sip of water while the rest of the family bowed their heads and ate hungrily. Hans kept his face averted, talking only to the small children. He never looked straight at Hester or Annie, the unresolved issues hanging between them like an invisible partition.

The snow piled around the stone house, mounded on the roof like heavy frosting, loading the pine trees with its weight. Upstairs, one lone window shone with a dim yellow light, barely visible through the white semidarkness of the night.

Hester sat on her side of the bed, Lissie a lump beneath the covers. She was bent over the open book, one forefinger placed beneath the English word Theodore Crane had written below each word scrawled in Uhma's handwriting.

Carefully, her tongue catching between her teeth, she read slowly in whispers, storing the words deliberately in the deepest recesses of her memory.

"For Fever. Take one pound of the bark of the yellow birch tree, half-pound sweet flag, half pound of tag elder bark, two ounces thorough wort, two ounces tansy dry. Boil down with water to a liquor. One dose every two hours till shakes come on."

She stopped, staring wistfully at the black, cold rectangle of the window, wondering. Would Kate have survived had she been given these ancient remedies?

"For Weakness."

"To Strengthen the Leg and Feet."

"For Coughing Blood."

"For the Lungs."

"For the Pleurisy."

"Burdock leaves, white root, unkum root, pennyroyal tea, bud of lobelia, skunk cabbage, Indian turnip, chamomile flowers, seed of the silverweed."

Hester knew all of these.

She wrinkled her nose at the prescribed "ox dung, mixed with yarrow, half part Jacob's ladder."

Sighing, she held the book to her breast, bent over it, and thanked her Father in Heaven for Theodore Crane's assistance. She smiled, remembering the way his blue eyes danced with merriment, reciting the old Indian ways of healing.

"Mouse dung mixed with the lard of a boar"?

"Coltsfoot snake root"?

What was "gravel"? "A glass of the juice of onion tops" to cure the "gravel"?

Theodore said he believed that "gravel" meant kidney or gallstones. Hester nodded, wrote it down carefully, asking how to spell kidney.

They laughed together at the remedy for dull sight. "The skunk's musk bag steeped in boiling water." The laugh they shared was so genuine, Hester felt as if she had made a lifelong friend.

Theodore was so polite that night as he scurried around, seeing to her needs. He spread a clean, white sheet on his bed and turned the pillow over. He insisted that he would be fine rolled up in a coverlet by the fire.

She'd slept in her dress, for there were no partitions for privacy. He assured her he would leave the house when she crawled into bed, but she wanted to sleep in her dress. He lay awake, blinking into the red embers of the fire, thinking how strange this was to have a woman, no, a girl, in his bed, something that had never occurred before.

For Hester, there was only a sadness, a fondness.

He could not fathom what would become of her. He had no doubt in his mind that she could survive on her own if it came right down to it. He knew she was treated only slightly better than a slave, and that happened because of the base nature of the woman Hans had the poor fortune to marry. Well, he'd take her to Lissie. She'd know what to do.

Hester's life continued much as before. She counted the days by Xs inscribed in the old book of Indian remedies. She took the hissing, scolding voice of her stepmother like a bitter potion, swallowing it, hiding her pain.

She put on the same serene face for church every two weeks, dressed in brilliant dresses covered by a white cape and apron. Her face was as undecipherable as everything else about her. Refusing to go with the youth, she had no friends. The few girls who coaxed her to go to the hymn singings and Saturday evening hoedowns dwindled down to one, and finally she gave up.

Hester roamed the woods on those days when other girls were preening, dressing themselves in their finery, making plans and giggling, their main interest the boys who would pick them up in their wagons. She found the plants and roots she searched for, held them, cradling them in the palms of her hands. She sniffed them all appreciatively, storing each scent in her memory.

When the snow melted, leaving old, wet undergrowth exposed but patches of snow still lay beneath the pine trees on the north slopes, she searched the woods with new desperation. She dug feverishly at the roots she believed would be needed, and soon. Her keen eyes had observed the involuntary quivers in Annie's hands. Often the plates she carried to the table rattled without reason.

Sometimes, when Annie sat at her spinning wheel, she would suddenly throw the thread of flax, but her foot would cease its pumping, bringing the whirring sound of the wheel to a stop. She would shift her hands between her knees, bend forward, and rock over them, her lips twisted in frustration.

Hester believed she had palsy of the hands. She would need a concoction of sage mixed with mustard root, stirred into boiling water. She should soak her hands in this mixture as often as possible to get relief.

Would she be able to redeem herself in Annie's eyes, Hester wondered, by the cures from her ancestors? She thought of it, dreamed of healing Annie's hands. Perhaps Annie would be able to forgive the color of her skin, the alien brown hue that forever marked her.

Hester stored the herbs in the box, separating them with scraps of stolen skins. She read the old volume scrupulously now. Very seldom did she sleep before the clock struck midnight.

She found the flax plant and tore it excitedly from the earth. Mixed with ewe's milk, it was a powerful source for healing swollen, painful joints. She thought of Hans sitting before the fire, rubbing his right knee, his brows lowered, a grimace on his face at times when Annie was out of the house. Once he'd looked up, saw Hester's eyes on him, and kept her gaze for only a few seconds before removing his hand from his knee. He got up, went to the wooden peg holding his straw hat, slammed it on his head with unnecessary force, grabbed the door handle, and let himself out, not looking back.

Hester folded the tablecloth she was holding. Years ago, she would have approached him with the remedy and gladly administered the poultice. Hans would have gratefully accepted it, but now, with the poison swirling among them in the form of Annie's displeasure, she did not know how it could be possible anymore.

Chapter 22

When the snow turned to patchy slush, rivulets of muddy, brown water wet the dead, wilted plants by the roadside. The sun became a bit warmer each day, drawing tender green and yellow shoots from the cold, wet earth.

Hans was sharpening his plowshares and oiling the heavy leather harnesses in preparation for the long, hard days of stumbling behind the plow. Noah could work with the harrow, preparing the soil for the corn and the tobacco. Hans wanted to clear at least five more acres this summer. More, if possible. Hester would be able to harrow. He'd put Noah instead to work felling trees.

He shook his head as he thought of Noah. That homely baby, that clumsy boy who ate at the table with fewer manners than a dog. What, indeed, had happened to his son? He was powerfully built, a great hulk of a boy, with shoulders that strained against the seams of every shirt he owned. Narrow in the hips, with powerful legs and feet that filled shoes a size bigger than Hans's own shoes, he was clearly in awe of his son. Now that he was grown beyond the awkward stage of boyhood, Hans wanted to have a close relationship with Noah, but he felt shamefully inept.

Hans shivered, thinking of his oldest son's clear, light eyes mocking him, the slight upturn of the left side of his well-shaped mouth, so like Kate's. Why did he always feel as if Noah was disgusted with him?

Isaac was not like that. He was still awkward, shy, and not as powerful as Noah, with a merry spirit, quick to laugh, easy to control and advise. A shadow crossed the doorway, darkening the plowshare he was holding. He looked up. It was Noah.

"Too wet to plow?" The voice was low, rough, gravelly, a sound that sent shivers up Hans's spine.

"*Ya.*"

"What does today look like?"

"Well, I'd like to clear at least five more acres this year. If you think it might be dry enough, you could start."

Noah nodded and walked off. Hans heard him sharpening the axe. How did one go about starting a friendly conversation? He wanted to. He wanted to ask him how many trees he could fell in a day, for there was no doubt about it. Noah could fell a tree twice as fast as Hans, cutting into the wood with unfailing accuracy, the tree crashing within a foot of where he wanted it to go.

Hans was irked, jealous at first, then grudgingly proud. He wanted to convey some sense of this to Noah, but always, his tongue remained tied. Ah, he had never expressed much interest or love to his sons from the time they were born. Hans knew he rarely acknowledged their presence. It had been Hester. All Hester. As it was still. A flush crept up past his linen work shirt and hid behind his thick black beard, which was already turning white along the side.

It was only the Bible's teachings, his obedience to the church, to God, to John Lantz and Simon Yoder, and to the memory of Kate that guided him. He remained distant from his sons and now subservient, obeying Annie's will.

In his own mind, Hester belonged to their family and to the Amish, no matter that the blood of the Lenape flowed in her veins. He knew many good Indians. But since Annie harbored a firm and unrelenting distaste for every native man, he kept his opinion to himself.

He could accept his life and appreciate Annie's housekeeping skills, her management of the household, the mothering of his children. He had to give himself up to her treatment of Hester. As long as Hester remained with them and he could see her, that was all that mattered. It was enough.

He knew Annie deserved much of the credit for his prosperity. The great stone house was finished and contained many things other Amish women envied. It stood sentinel, surrounded by clearings, the trees felled by the sweat of his and Noah's brows. The barn had been elongated and held a fine herd of six cows, twice what other landowners possessed.

Annie had shown him what hard work and perseverance could accomplish, no doubt. With Kate, there had been a contentment, a peace in gathering around the hearth, going on picnics in the summertime, attending every frolic or get-together in the neighborhood. No matter that the barn was piled high with manure, or the calf had not yet been weaned, or the rabbits were getting into the beans in the garden.

He remembered his Kate, large and soft, laughing as she collared the errant creatures and hauled them out of the garden, only to have them return the following day. Yes, his life had changed.

But now he was someone. He was a highly respected member of the Amish community, a man others went to for advice and looked up to. His ways were esteemed. That was another reason he kept the true nature of his household well hidden.

He could grind his teeth, thinking of Annie's swollen ego, her big mouth, the speed with which she voiced her young, inexperienced opinion. He often wanted to smack her, doubling his fists beneath the wooden family table, swallowing his anger for his pride's sake.

All the while, he watched Hester bloom into the full beauty of her womanhood, sweetened by her rare sense of innocence.

It was when the wind carried the scent of violets and honeysuckle, and the hollows on the south side of the ridges grew thick with spring morels, those delectable mushrooms that camouflaged themselves among wet winter leaves, that Theodore Crane, the stern and capable schoolmaster, opened his heart to thoughts of love. He was riding in his cart, a nice bunch of morels in a redware bowl at his feet, on his way to Lissie's house. He had dropped the "Hershberger" name from his mind a long time ago, thinking of her only as "Lissie."

His thoughts of her surpassed fondness now. He wanted to be with her each hour of every day. He was not quite sure how to go about the next step, but he believed she would be willing, perhaps even eager. His eyebrows went up as a smile creased the lines around his eyes. Yes, Lissie would make him a fine companion.

She met him at the door, her usual welcoming smile especially wide. She threw up both hands at the sight of the large, succulent morels as she chortled with pleasure. "My dear man! Where have you found them?" she asked, her round face pink and creased.

"Oh, I have my places. I try to keep it a secret."

"Well, they will certainly go well with the greens I'm cooking."

The squirrel, fried in the pan and finished in the oven, fell off the bones, seasoned with plenty of salt and pepper. The greens swam in a thick, brownish white sauce topped with bits of dried beef. The accompaniment of the stewed morels was superb.

They bowed their heads over the ample table, Theodore's mouth moving with his whispered silent prayer, Lissie's eyes closed tightly, her hands folded neatly under the table as she thanked God for the food they were about to enjoy. She added a footnote to her prayer, requesting that God please let today be the day. For how many springs had gone by, and Theodore's thoughts still had not turned lightly to thoughts of love, the way young men's often did.

She ate with great relish, enjoyed the morels with satisfaction, and brought out the cake and applesauce, saving the plum pie for last. She reveled in Theodore's praise as she always did.

She had her spoon in the cup of coffee and was stirring it when the conversation flagged, and the comfortable silence between them settled softly through the small house. It had been a wonderful meal, truly one to be remembered. Theodore cleared his throat. She looked up.

His eyebrows stayed perfectly level, and he said very soft and low, "I don't want to go home tonight."

At first, she thought he'd meant the cranky, obstinate horse or the lack of good lantern light, so she just shrugged her shoulders and asked why not.

"I've come to dread the ride home."

Still, Lissie missed what he was trying to convey. "You need to get a better horse."

Sadly, he shook his head. "No, I don't believe that has anything to do with it."

"Maybe a new seat."

"No, no," Theodore said, shaking his head sadly.

Lissie was genuinely puzzled.

"No, what afflicts me is far more complicated than acquiring a new horse or wagon seat. I am caught in a serious malady that often attacks much younger men."

Afraid suddenly, Lissie gasped. "Theodore, whatever is wrong? Surely it isn't consumption or pleurisy?"

"Oh, no, no. Much worse than that."

In answer, Lissie flung her apron over her face, unwilling to allow him to see the tears forming quickly in her tender blue eyes.

She froze when she felt his hands grasp her soft ones, and when she lowered her apron, could hardly believe the sight of Theodore bending toward her, his thin face earnest, a new light radiating from his eyes.

"Lissie, my malady is love. I believe I love you. Will you be so kind as to consent to be my wife?"

Lissie didn't wait, not even for the space of a heartbeat. "Yes." The word was out, as breathless and as eager as she felt.

"Thank you, Lissie. I will try and be a good companion."

Lissie leaned forward and placed a hand on each side of Theodore's face. Her eyes shone into his with a warm light. "*Ach* now, my man. You will be more than a companion to me. You will be my husband." And with that, she gathered him into her lonely arms and kissed him soundly.

He blinked, his eyebrows danced madly, and they got to their feet, where he promptly embraced his beloved Lissie. Moving his feet, he took her slowly around the kitchen in time to the music in his head. She rested her round head on his small shoulder. His long, thin arms went about her bountiful waist, and the little house was suffused in a soft yellow glow of love.

At last, Lissie's lonely heart was filled.

That Sunday in church, John Lantz spoke eloquently of marriage, the raising of children.

Theodore and Lissie kept their heads bowed, then walked out as soon as the last prayer was read from the German prayer book. Before the congregation realized the fact that both of them had gone out, the deacon, Manasses Yoder, announced in stentorian tones that he wished to let the congregation know that two souls had agreed to become man and wife, Theodore Crane and Lissie Hershberger.

The closing song was a rousing rendition of God's love, fueled by the anticipation of the wedding day to be held in the community. As soon as the last strains of the old hymn had died away, the sedate service turned into mayhem. What a fuss! The women shrieked and giggled, threw their hands in the air, and said the fact that Theodore had joined the church should have given this away.

"*Dumbkepp* (Dumbheads), that's what we are!" laughed Mary Troyer.

"Oh, I thought about it. Those two were together longer than we knew."

"Every Sunday night, no?"

"No, just for supper."

"Oh, well, she took the route through his stomach."

This brought howls of laughter.

Hester sat alone, her face impassive, at the long table holding the Sunday lunch that accompanied Amish services. She spread a slice of bread with the home-churned butter, then speared some dried apples with her knife, the only utensil provided, and chewed quietly.

Around her, girls chattered, planning the afternoon's get-together. Babies cried. Children ran, calling to one another, stopped suddenly by mothers' firm grasps of their arms.

Hester took a sip of her water. She turned when she felt a touch on her shoulder. It was Ruth, her friend. "Would you like to go with me this afternoon? Davey will take us to Bertha's house if you want to go?"

Quickly, Hester shook her head.

"Hester, please come. You can't always remain alone."

"I'll talk to you after I'm finished eating."

She told Ruth there was no point in joining the youth's activities, being Indian and of different blood.

Ruth assured her that made no difference, but Hester held steadfastly to the conviction Annie had successfully branded into her consciousness.

She was different and still unsure which way her life would go. For now, she was content to have a roof over her head and be a servant to Hans and Annie, daily storing in her memory vast quantities of information about the Indian way of healing with plants and herbs.

Sometimes she thought of Padriac, the ease with which they communicated, or the hand of William King, which she had held discreetly beneath the wedding table. And always, she dismissed both of them. She could never taint a *freundshaft* with her Indian blood. It would not be fair to future generations.

To have a husband, she would need to return to the Lenape. The whistling youth had perhaps been sent by God. He would grow up to be her companion, aiding her return to the people of her birth. Today she had no doubt. The whistling had moved her deeply, bringing a sense of her own longing for something she did not understand.

In spite of her many unanswered questions, she did have the leather-bound book of Indian wisdom. It would remain with her wherever she ended up.

She had convinced herself that it was right to leave the Amish people. This thought had been brought about by Annie's hatred, but now, as she bowed to Annie's will, she wondered if everyone in the tribe of Lenape was kind. Wouldn't there be unkind ones among them? Certainly. They were part of the human race. She began to wonder if leaving one group of people for another might not give her the answer she hoped for.

She was surrounded by mountains, great hills, and valleys, an endless schoolroom containing a vast store of knowledge.

She knew which birds migrated south and when. She knew where the mother fox hid her kit. She had found all the plants and trees and roots mentioned in the book, easily identifying them. She watched the bald eagles build their nests and knew where the spotted fawns were hidden. She could tell by the swallow's flight when a storm was approaching. The beavers' houses told her how harsh the winter would be, as did the thickness of the acorns scattered on the floor of the forest. The jay's screaming heralded the approach of another animal or human being.

She was an expert marksman with the handmade slingshot she'd fashioned while still in school. She supplied the household with rabbits and squirrels and an occasional pheasant. Many deer had fallen when one of Hester's arrows lodged in precisely the right spot, bringing them down with a minimum of suffering.

She always thanked God for giving her meat for her family, then dragged the deer to the side of the barn, where Hans or Noah or Isaac would *fa-sark* it. It was an unspoken secret, for nothing inflamed Annie's seething temper like the thought of Hester's hunting or Hans admiring her skills. Annie never knew who killed the wild animals.

Theodore and Lissie's wedding was held at Hans Zug's because his and Annie's stone house was the largest in the community. Annie and Hester had scrubbed and washed, painted and toiled, until the place was perfectly groomed and shining. Already, the additional five acres had been half cleared, with the stumps burned.

Because it was springtime, many families offered a chicken for making *roasht.* There were plenty of turnips, and even some celery and cabbage. They added fresh greens with hot bacon dressing. The women made *schnitz* dried apple pies instead of the traditional pumpkin that was made during the fall of the year when most Amish weddings were held.

The wedding guests were duly impressed by Hans Zug's fine farm, his wealth, his hardworking children. Strapping sons, they said. What a fine child, that Lissie!

Tongues clucked over the Indian girl. What a pity. The prettiest girl many of them had ever seen, but her eyes contained a pool of unnamed sadness in their black depths. What would ever become of her?

Theodore and Lissie, however, eclipsed every guest's happiness, their joy shining visibly through their otherwise reserved demeanor, which was fitting and proper for a sober Amish wedding. They stood side by side, their hands placed in the bishop's as he pronounced them man and wife.

Sadie Fisher told Mamie Troyer that Lissie was twice as wide as her husband, but Mamie frowned at Sadie's remark, ruining the festivities for Sadie entirely.

Well, Mamie thought Sadie was making fun of Lissie, and everyone knew Sadie prided herself by maintaining her trim figure, which wasn't right in the sight of God, or at least, in Mamie's.

They ate vast quantities of *hinkle dunkus*, that good, rich, salty gravy that was ladled generously over the *roasht*.

Lissie leaned over and told Theodore that her own bacon dressing was better, although she wanted to remain appreciative. Theodore smiled at his radiant bride, agreed wholeheartedly, and thought himself the most fortunate man on earth. To think of having a good hot breakfast, with the scalding coffee she drank every morning, was a luxury he could not begin to imagine. The long cold nights spent shivering in his bed would be a thing of the past, as well as eating burned toast and poorly cooked eggs with the mice, that pestilence that dogged every day of his life.

The warm touch of his beloved Lissie had already taken up a place of wonder in his heart. The pure enjoyment of being in her company, the way she touched his arm, his shoulder, his cheek, the way she cooked his supper, he wondered why he'd waited so long.

Lissie's smile faded and then melted away when she caught sight of Hester standing off by herself, dressed in the traditional blue wedding dress, a black apron around her slender waist. She was indeed, by far, the most beautiful person in the room. The most tragic as well.

Lissie pursed her lips, laid a hand on Theodore's leg, leaned into his shoulder and jutted her chin in Hester's direction. "Look."

Theodore followed Lissie's gaze. His eyes found Hester. "What?" he asked, unsure of what she meant.

"She's so alone. Couldn't we find a young man for her on this, our wedding day? Wouldn't it be perfect?"

Theodore nodded. "But they do not pair the young people at a small wedding like ours, do they?" he whispered.

"No, you're right."

They watched as the young men filed in, observing carefully the way they behaved as they sat across the table from Hester. They all watched her discreetly, as she kept her eyes lowered to the German hymnbook placed on the table in front of her. Her lips moved along with the singing, but not once did she look up or as much as lift her face an inch.

At the next table sat her brother Noah, a blond giant of a boy, his face darkened by the early spring sun. His shoulders pushed at the white fabric of his shirt; his black vest fit seamlessly. His hair was cut shorter than the suitable *ordnung* for young men.

Some said Noah was "turning wild." Some said he'd spoken of joining the lumber men, those crews of rough men without scruples who felled trees as fast as they could, hacking away at the forest with nothing in mind but making as much money as they could.

Noah had the most unusual eyes. They were not quite blue or green. Hans had dark brown eyes. His mother Kate's eyes had been an astounding shade of blue.

Lissie watched, her eyes narrowed. Not once did Noah acknowledge his sister's presence. He spoke to the young men beside him, smiling and laughing, but Hester may as well have been invisible for all he cared.

Yes, Hester may as well disappear for all that family cared about her, and it was all Annie's doing. All of it. For the rest of her life, Lissie would remember her perfect wedding day, filled with love and anticipation, containing only one gray cloud named Hester.

Poor, darling Indian foundling. Surely God had a purpose.

CHAPTER 23

ANNIE'S HANDS WORSENED CONSIDERABLY. SHE could no longer lift the heavy crockery without using both hands. She hid this fact from Hester's eyes repeatedly, covering one hand with her apron whenever Hester was in the kitchen.

One summer day when the heat and humidity had lifted, mercifully cooling the damp earth, Annie was in a better state of mind. She allowed Hester the luxury of ironing instead of hoeing corn, which she had done every other day of the week from sunup to sundown. Calluses formed on her hands where the dreaded blisters had been, which eased the pain and made the hoeing bearable, in spite of the fiery sun beating down on her head.

All girls strove to keep a pearly white complexion, devoutly wearing a straw hat to work in the garden. Annie required that Hester wear a hat as well, although she reminded her many times there was no use trying to keep her white since she never was and never would be. But it was the *ordnung* of the church, and no child of hers would be seen in her garden without a hat.

The minute Hester entered the back field, she untied the hated straw hat and flung it to the ground. All day, till she heard the dinner bell, she hoed, listening to the bird calls around her, identifying each one, as her hoe rose and fell and sweat trickled off her forehead and down her back.

Today, she cleaned up after the noon meal, washing all the dried food off the plates and forks while moving as quickly as she could. Annie watched with narrowed eyes as she quietly dried the many dishes and put them all back in their places.

Turning, Annie lifted a heavy crockery pitcher, gasped, then screamed shrilly, as the pitcher crashed to the oak floor, a wide pool of milk spreading across its gleaming surface. Instantly, it was all Hester's fault, but she had expected that and didn't reply. Bending, she lifted the broken pieces, went to the pantry for a rag, and began to clean up the milk. Annie turned away, her tirade finished, satisfied that Hester had taken the blame.

Little Emma voiced her opinion with Barbara's support, whereupon they were both paddled firmly and told to sit on the bench until they were sorry for their *grosfeelich* (proud and cocky) ways.

When Annie became agitated, her hands were always worse, causing her to clench them together, her fingers interwoven, her shoulders held erect.

Suddenly, Hester stood, having cleaned up all the milk and holding the bucket of soapy water she had used. "Annie, I believe I know a solution that would help your hands," she said firmly.

Annie snorted. "Out of that devilish book, I suppose."

Hester did not answer but simply took the bucket to the back porch and flung the water over the steps. Immediately, a bevy of geese came waddling, their necks outstretched, lifting their wings in warning.

"Can I mix a few herbs and steep them in boiling water?"

"No. You'll kill me with that witchcraft."

"It's not to drink. It's to soak your hands in twice a day."

Annie scowled, and the vertical furrows on her forehead deepened as her narrow face took on a look of undisguised suspicion. She pursed her lips, smacked them with an unappetizing sound, turned away, and said, "No."

"Please."

"What kind of herbs?"

"Sage and mustard seed."

"We don't grow either of them."

"I know where the wild plants are."

Suspicion was replaced with hope, but then pride cast its shadow across her face, and she turned away. "No. And don't mention it again."

Hester returned to her ironing until the basket was empty, with the ironed garments hanging from the back of a chair. She folded the rows of white shirts and then put them in the wardrobe for Sunday's use. She sewed missing buttons on knee breeches and searched all the everyday work breeches for holes and patched them.

Annie ran a terribly efficient house, every hour of every day producing something worthwhile. She had no use for any person who shirked a distasteful duty, all heavy people who ate more than was necessary, and anyone who spent a penny without considering the true necessity of the purchase. Hester knew she was too frugal to visit the doctor in Berksville, so she decided to bide her time, to let the matter drop for now.

Hans found Annie watching Hester with a wary eye. There was a difference in the way she looked at her, with a hesitation of sorts. For one hopeful moment, Hans wondered if Annie was indeed changing her opinion of Hester before he discarded the thought as foolish. He knew his wife's ways all too well. She did not budge once she formed an opinion.

What did the scriptures say? Ah, but it was unthinkable. As he watched Annie hide the shaking of her hands with her apron more than once, he brought a fresh resolve to be more patient, more understanding of her tense moments with Hester.

Annie sent Hester to bring Noah and Isaac for the evening meal. Unsure about the borders of their property, she asked Hans where they might be.

"You'll know. You'll hear their axes."

Annie asked loudly how she could traipse all over God's creation and not know where the property line was.

"I know where the east and west borders are. I'm just not sure of the north."

"You'll find them."

It seemed odd to Hester that anyone would be sent to fetch the older boys. Didn't they always come in when dusk ushered them home? No one seemed particularly worried about their absence or their return. She decided to use extreme caution and keep her eyes and ears open. Annie had proved to be as untrustworthy as a wolf or a cornered rat, although neither of those descriptions suited her really. Hester knew she was more cunning than either one.

Walking through the cornfield, she entered the woods, staying on a straight course to the north. The land sloped uphill gently, then abruptly changed to a steep incline at the top. Undecided, Hester stayed still, evaluating the terrain. Yes, she'd been here many times. She'd always imagined the property line would be the top of the incline, along the crest of the hilltop.

She heard the ringing sound of an axe meeting solidly with wood. Clunk. Clunk. Clunk. A steady rhythm, faster than Hester thought possible, and then a cracking, ripping sound, a moment's breath, a fearsome sound of branches breaking and cracking. A giant oak disappeared from view, coming to rest in a newly created clearing.

Noah stood hatless, his blond hair stuck to his head by the perspiration that soaked his body. One hand was coiled loosely around the heavy, wooden handle of the axe; the other rested low on his hip as he watched the tree's descent. His feet apart, his strong legs made him appear a ruthless giant, taking control of every tree's demise, destroying the pristine forest as if he were God himself.

Hester felt an inexplicable sadness, a tender pity for the great tree that stood so proud, its green leaves shading the forest floor, providing homes for woodland creatures. How could Noah spend his days whacking through the forest, cutting the beautiful trees without a thought in his head? Hester visualized the bald mountains and ridges littered with dead growth, the good, rich soil washed off the hillsides by torrential rains, the creatures of the trees having no home.

The old woman had informed her about the way of the Lenape. To fell a tree was unthinkable. Wrong. The Creator had placed trees on the earth for shelter and protection, and they should not be disturbed. They were sacred.

Suddenly, a rage so violent it was physical lent wings to her feet. Silently, she moved, swiftly hurrying down the incline, sliding, grabbing small trees, making only a minimum of sound. Noah looked up at her approach, his face masked. When he saw the agitation on her face, he stepped back, watching her uneasily.

On she came, her chest heaving, her fists balled tightly by her flowing green skirts, her black eyes flat with displeasure. She strode up to Noah, raised both hands, and thumped her fists against his wide, solid chest.

He stepped back, catching her hands, but so powerful was her dislike of him, she wrenched them free, delivering another blow to his upper arm. "Hey! What is wrong?"

In answer, she flung her head back, her black eyes snapping her anger. "I guess you're happy to spend your days ruining the sacred forest!" She spat her words.

Isaac stopped, watching his sister intently.

"Oh, come on, Hester," Noah said, grinning.

In answer, she reached up and smacked his face, hard. "Don't you make fun of me! You mark my words. The time will come when you'll regret this. All of you will."

"Stop acting like an Indian. We are only obeying our father's wishes. We need the land."

Hester raised herself to her full height, her black eyes conveying her contempt. "Believe me, the time will come when the white people will need the land more than they do now."

There was nothing to say to this, so Noah looked off across the woods where the tree lay in his path.

"Annie says supper is ready."

Instantly, Noah loosened his grip on the axe, letting it fall to the ground. Then Isaac led the way up the slope, their heavy boots crashing through the undergrowth. Hester followed soundlessly, a few steps behind her brothers.

At the evening meal, Hans watched his two oldest sons with new respect, seeing the way they stayed silent, shoveled the hot food into their mouths, thanked Annie, and left the table immediately after the second prayer was said in silence.

Hester ate very little. She kept her head lowered except when she helped Barbara with her meat or spread butter on a biscuit for Emma. Hans sensed agitation and wondered what had occurred, if anything.

A new thought snaked its way into Hans's mind. Had the boys behaved unseemly toward Hester? A great and palpable fear entered his heart. He had no clue how he could ever approach these grown boys with his fear, his suspicion. It was unthinkable.

He could not talk to them of his feelings on any subject, so how could he approach them about Hester? He would need to be her guard. Every waking moment of every day, he would need to look out for her.

The thought placed a crushing responsibility on him, so he shared it with his wife, who watched her husband's face go from red to white and back again as he spoke of his concern about the boys growing into men, perhaps thinking of Hester in ways other than merely being their sister.

Annie listened gamely, choosing to keep her face averted, unable to meet her husband's too-bright eyes. Yes, she agreed, it was a reasonable concern, but she was certain the boys would not think of her as anything other than an Indian and want nothing to do with her.

"Unlike you, Hans," she added.

For Annie was shrewd and watchful, her skill at deciphering looks and attitudes honed by her years of surviving a family that had hardly been better than a battlefield of wills.

Hester would have to go. How to go about that was a challenge she had not figured out, at least until now. No matter how she was treated, Hester became more of a servant. Annie would need to figure out another way.

These thoughts were all hidden as she watched the display of emotion on her husband's face. Her husband. Hans. The Hans who did not love her.

Well, the rejection, the denial, could operate both ways. With her lips compressed into a thin line, her eyes doe-like, her head nodding in agreement, her will given to her husband, Annie plotted a plan that would not fail.

The trees continued to fall. Black smoke poured from the stumps that were removed. The boys had lit them on fire, and they were so thick and heavy that they burned endlessly.

They hauled firewood into the lean-to, and Hester took her turn with the axe. She walked behind the cultivator, following the harrow; she planted corn and helped with the tobacco through the cool spring days.

The sun turned warm. Soon they had spring onions to place on the table, along with freshly churned butter, which the family spread on thick slices of wheat bread. Annie served great wooden bowls of greens flavored with a hot dressing made of eggs, vinegar, and bacon, seasoned with chives. They ate sugar peas, small and green and limp, flavored only with salt, a dash of black pepper, and a touch of butter. The greens grew tall and thick. Annie cut them in bunches, gathered them into her apron, and then cooked them in a cream sauce with nutmeg. The table was laden with the gifts of the earth, Annie said demurely, often noting the plentiful rains, the goodness of God.

Even the women at church noticed the change in Annie and wondered at it. Some said Hans was good for her, and so she could act kindly toward Hester, noting that she was not even his own child. He was certainly good to his own children, something you could plainly see by the way they sat so quietly beside him in church.

And so the family prospered, growing substantially in prestige, their status among the Amish steadily improving. For Hans had really made something of himself with that Annie by his side. Look at the way those children behave themselves in church, they said. Hans just had such a nice way about him.

Hester came to believe that times were, indeed, changing. Annie displayed a new tolerance of her knowledge of plants and their ability to heal. Annie even allowed her more time to pursue her interests, so Hester often found herself on the rock, her favorite place of meditation. She never heard or saw the whistling youth again, although she kept her eyes and ears alert, curious.

Annie asked Hester and Lissie to see if the trout had spawned yet. She was hungry for a mess of fish. They would eat them fresh and salt the rest in barrels for winter meals. Hester's heart leaped unexpectedly as she thought of the creek's emptying into the river, close to where Padriac shuttled traffic across on his raft. Would she be able to speak to him again?

Hans decided to take the day off to accompany the girls and help them with the net. When he asked Solomon, Daniel, and John to ride along, his request was met with whoops of joy as they clambered onto the back of the spring wagon with Lissie. Hester sat on the front seat with Hans, wreathed in smiles. The color of his face brightened, and his eyes sparkled.

Annie stood on the porch, waved a thin, shaking hand, then turned, her hand on little Emma's head, letting herself in the door slowly. Once safely away from anyone's prying eyes, she clasped her hands behind her back and paced, her mouth working.

Before they knew it, fall would be here, and with it, winter close behind. Hester could not leave in winter because she would freeze or fall prey to wild animals, and Annie could not live with the guilt of having her blood on her hands. Yet this plan was going entirely too slow. By all appearances, Hans loved his wife, and his mindless infatuation with Hester was completely disappearing. But Annie was running out of patience. She wanted Hester gone.

She swept the kitchen, her agitation causing her to draw the broom stiffly across the well-worn floor, her thoughts in turmoil.

When Padriac spied the spring wagon with Hester seated beside Hans, he didn't try to veil the all-encompassing joy that shone from his blue eyes. "It's you!" he shouted, making a mad dash for the spring wagon, holding up his hand to help her down, holding the small, well-formed fingers in his own entirely too long.

Hans felt anger rise within but told himself it was his fatherly instinct wanting to protect his eldest daughter.

Padriac showed them where the trout were heavy with roe, some of them sleepy. He caught the huge, fat trout with his bare hands, his enthusiasm rolling with his easy laugh, a sound so genuine it was infectious.

Hans had not heard Hester laugh so often or so freely since she was a young child. Lissie giggled and floundered about, soaking her skirt and the front of her dress as she came up, gasping, with yet another trout.

The afternoon was filled with the smell of fish, the blazing sun, the skittish dragonflies hovering over the tall grass on the bank of the creek. The low-hanging branches trailed their leaves in the water, as Padriac and the girls dragged the net through the still, green pools.

When Padriac had to leave to ferry a team of horses across the river, Hans watched Hester as he walked to the small building, an expression he had never seen etched on her lovely face. Well, he would have to nip this in the bud. This fellow was not Amish, and Hester knew it.

Cold fear of her disobedience wrapped its stifling tentacles around his heart. His breath came quickly.

What would such a romance do to his pride? How would it appear to the Amish community if one of his children went off with an *Englisher*? Such an occurrence would only flaunt his failure at raising the Indian foundling in God's way so her soul would be saved and she would go on to lead a true Christian life by choosing the way of the cross.

Hans called a swift halt to the afternoon's activities, his face pinched and white, his eyes darting furtively from Padriac's open, joyous demeanor to the blush on Hester's perfect cheeks.

Quickly, he threw the flopping, dirt-encrusted fish into the wooden barrels, tied them securely to the sides of the wagon with strong hemp rope, called his children, and told them it was time to go home. The children wailed their disapproval but climbed onto the back of the spring wagon obediently, where they sat smelling like fish, wet, bedraggled, and tired.

Hans hitched Dot in anxious jerks, snapping the traces hurriedly to the singletree, his eyes going repeatedly to Padriac and Hester as they stood aside. He couldn't hear what Padriac was saying. He just saw that Hester's eyes never left his face. When Padriac reached with his hand to clasp hers, Hans became inflamed like a man possessed.

"Hester!" He shouted the word once, harshly.

Hester responded as if she'd been shoved. Without another word, without a backward glance, she ran to the spring wagon, leaped lightly to the seat, and spread her wet skirts carefully around her feet.

Before Padriac realized what was going on, Hans held the whip aloft, brought it down on Dot's back, and startled her into a wild plunge up the slope and away from the river, the wooden barrels swaying and creaking against the heaving sides of the fast-moving spring wagon.

The children clung to the sides and to each other as they bounced and swayed from side to side, leaving wet spots when they moved from one location to the next. Lissie became angry and yelled at her father in her brash manner. Hans told her to close her big mouth. Hester hung on, braced her feet against the dash, pulled her cap strings forward, and thought surely Hans didn't have to be in such a hurry to start the milking.

When they clattered into the barnyard, Dot was soaked with sweat, the lather white against her black harness, her sides heaving, the pink nostrils dilated, her eyes rolling behind the blinders on her bridle. Noah straightened from the water trough, ran his fingers through his soaking wet hair, and watched with narrowed eyes.

Isaac opened his mouth on one side and said with certainty, "Dat has seen a *schpence.*"

Noah only shook his head, his mouth grim, his eyes slits against the brilliance of the late afternoon sun.

Chapter 24

From that day on, Hester became uneasy with Hans's behavior. He dogged her footsteps. Some days it seemed she was never out of his sight. He popped up in the house when she least expected him. He hired Noah and Isaac out, putting a much larger workload on Lissie and Hester. Even Annie took her turn in the fields, forking hay and chopping thistles.

When Hester realized the new kind of prison that had closed its talons around her, she resigned herself to whatever God, the one who controlled her life, would allow. She had long ago reasoned to herself that he was the only one she could trust. Her people called him the Creator, the Great Spirit, and he was the same to her.

She had found an uneasy truce, as well, between the Amish and the Lenape. In her heart, she no longer tried to divide them. They were all God's handiwork, the same as the tall pine and the lofty oak, made according to his purpose. In the Indian tribe, there was good and evil. In the Amish community, there was the same. Human nature contained tempers that flared, jealousy that reared its poisonous head, covetous folks, and dishonest ones.

There was kindness, so much goodness, pity, and compassion, plus a spirit of helpfulness, all things that kept her within the culture in which she was raised. Deep in her heart, she believed that to be among the Amish was a privilege. It was a blessing to be shown that you needed Jesus Christ and the power to overcome the nature one was born with.

Of course, people were imperfect. Even Annie had good qualities—her discipline, the way she managed her family's duties, her financial outlook.

Hester tried without success to gauge Hans's odd behavior, then decided to give in and stop thinking he was unreasonable. He was concerned about her welfare, that was all.

It was in the evening, when the katydids and locusts were already in full symphony, their whirring, chirping chorus the music of the forest in Hester's ears, when Hans approached her.

Dusk was only a few minutes away, the light was slowly leaving the front porch where Hester sat shelling pole beans. She popped the pods with her thumb and caught the heavy beans in the palm of her hand before dropping them into the wooden bucket beside her chair.

He stood above her, his breathing hard, his hands held loosely by his sides. Hester could smell the soil on his shoes and see bits of earth clinging to the rough fabric of his trouser leg. He smelled of straw and warm grass, of honest perspiration after a day's work in the field.

"Hester."

She remained seated, the urgent note in his voice keeping her face lowered.

"Hester."

The word was not a question or a command; it was more a sound of desperation. Why was Hans so frantic on an evening such as this?

"Yes, Dat."

She hardly ever called him that, so why now?

For reasons beyond her understanding, "Dat" seemed necessary suddenly, the proper word, the needed fence around her.

"Look at me."

She obeyed.

"You know I have loved you as a father should from the day my beloved Kate found you by the spring. I have given you a home, fed you, raised you in the fear of the Lord in the Amish way."

Hester dropped her gaze away from the wrong in his. In one jolt of awakening, she understood. She sat still, as if she were part of the stone wall behind her, except for the white of her cap, listening to the words he said, his breath catching on phrases, his eyes boring into the top of her head.

"Promise me, Hester. Promise me you will not begin a courtship with this Irish heathen. For you are preserved among the Amish. God would not want you to consort with the Irish."

On and on, his voice rose and fell, the words true and Christian, fatherly and caring, the motive behind them another thing entirely. Hester was no longer an innocent child. The knowledge of Hans's caring and Annie's hatred—all of it—suffused her mind and heart like a white-hot iron, branding her with its pain. Hans knew, as did Annie, that he loved her in the way a man loves a woman, in the way God designed that two people fall in love, and that, as time went on, it would become harder and harder for Hans to deny this. This Annie knew, as well.

A great pity welled in Hester's heart for the thin, hurting Annie with the palsied hands. Ah, how Annie must hate her! She loved Hans, Annie did. But his love eluded her, and she saw the reason why.

Before Hester now lay the great unknown, a vast new world without the safety of the Amish fold. There was only one remedy for this situation, and that was for her to disappear. Hans must never know what had become of her. Unlike Joseph in the Old Testament story, she would leave behind no evidence. All this flashed through her mind as Hans talked on. Bits and pieces of what he said pierced her consciousness, but nothing mattered, nothing was of any consequence.

"You were more precious to me than my own sons," Hans spoke heavily. His hand came down on her shoulder, the touch like that of a viper.

Leaping to her feet, Hester scattered the bean pods. She kicked the wooden bucket to one side as she stood erect, facing Hans squarely. Her voice was low, well-modulated, but terrible in its depth. "Don't you touch me ever again, Hans Zug. Your words are righteous, but your foul breath contains the wrong that battles in your chest. You will never have the right, from this day forward, to tell me how to live my life. You are living in hidden adultery, and you know it."

She was crying now, with the weight of his wrongdoing, the uncovering of his intentions. His betrayal was a blow so crushing, Hester dealt with it in the only way she knew how. With her foot, she kicked his shin again and again. She pummeled his forearms with her fists, then fled around the corner of the house as he watched her go, helpless as she unveiled his innermost secret.

She slammed through the back door, found Annie at the hearth, grabbed her forearm, and spun her around. "You will never have to look on my face again after this night. I wish you and Hans a long and blessed life together with his children gathered around your table."

Annie's mouth opened, then closed. When it opened again, a mere squawk emerged. She stopped and licked her dry lips with an anxious tongue.

Hester had already gone to the stairs, her feet pounding up the steps. Annie stood stiffly, her breathing so rapid she felt lightheaded, listening to the sounds overhead. She heard Hester take the wooden box out from under her bed, then slide her feet across the floor. She opened and shut the wardrobe.

Hans came into the kitchen. His face searched Annie's. "Where's Hester?"

Silently, Annie pointed to the ceiling.

"What is she doing?"

Annie shrugged, her face chalk-white, her eyes dilated with the stark fear that was wreaking havoc in her conscience. What if Hester died? Quickly, she moved to Hans and grasped his shirtsleeve with nervous fingers.

"Hans, the winter is coming. She won't survive."

"What are you talking about?"

"Hester is leaving."

"No!" The cry exploded out of him. He was completely unable to stop himself from that burst of fear. He leaped up the stairs, two at a time, and tore open the door to Hester's room, begging her to stay.

She didn't know how it happened; she just knew her fury and disgust propelled her across the floor. The great banging and thumping that ensued was Hans's heavy body falling backward down the stairs, the breath leaving his body in drawn-out "oofs" and "ahs" of pain before he lay sprawled out on the kitchen floor at Annie's feet, doubled up in hurt and humiliation.

Hester grabbed the sack she had filled with her earthly possessions, with the only coat she owned stuffed on top, and lunged down the stairs after him. Without a word of goodbye, she let herself out of the house and into the deepening dusk to the sound of the katydids and crickets.

"Hester! Wait! Where you going?" Little Emma came flying across the yard, her strong young legs propelling her.

A groan escaped Hester's lips. She dropped the sack she'd slung across her shoulder and bent to reach for Emma, the true little companion she loved. Lifting her, she held the small body close to her face, kissing her over and over as hot tears pricked her eyelids.

"Goodbye, Emma."

"But stop! Where are you going?" Emma's voice was raised in concern, her lisp pronounced.

"I'm going away. I'll be back soon."

"How soon?"

"Soon."

"All right. Stay safe." Wriggling, Emma wanted down, satisfied that Hester would be back soon.

Hester held her tightly, kissed her one last time, and set her on her feet.

"Bye!" Emma called, running across the yard to the house. Hester stood at the edge of the forest and lifted her right hand, a small smile on her face and tears coursing down her cheeks. It was almost Hester's undoing, this saying goodbye to little Emma.

She knew nothing of the world she was about to encounter. The forest, the surrounding mountains were not alien or terrifying. But she was leaving a world that was safe and cloistered, where ministers led her in the way of righteousness, parents made decisions, and her identity was taking shape. But she had to go. There was no other way. Annie was Hans's lawful wife, his wife in God's eyes.

Still she hesitated, her eyes taking in the stone house, strong and magnificent in the evening light. The green slope fell away to the long stone and log barn, surrounded by split-rail fence, keeping the animals safe from predators.

Long, straight rows of vegetables lay in perfect symmetry with the rows of trees, the springhouse, the new corn crib. Each year, the Hans Zug farm prospered and grew.

She would leave all this and become no one, a runaway, hiding, always moving, for she had no home now.

She stood tall, her green skirts lifting, blowing slightly, her hair barely visible beneath the starched white cap.

Her face shone with an inner light; her eyes contained immeasurable sadness. Her posture was erect, upright. Her heart beat strong in her chest. The blood in her veins sang the song of the Lenape.

She would go now. Etched forever in her heart was the stone farmhouse, the ways of the Amish, the Bible, the work she had learned, the preserving of food, the cleaning and cooking, the way to keep clothes pure with lye soap made of wood ashes.

Down in the shadowy hollows below the barn, a cow bawled for its calf's return. A horse thumped against the wooden gate, causing the hinges to creak. All common noises of the farm, dear, familiar. She would carry them with her in her heart forever.

Turning, she faded into the overhanging branches of a maple tree, into the Pennsylvania forest that would be her home.

The End

GLOSSARY

Ach, du lieva—A Pennsylvania Dutch dialect phrase meaning "Oh, my goodness."

An shay kind—A Pennsylvania Dutch dialect phrase meaning "A nice or beautiful child."

Auferstehung—A Pennsylvania Dutch dialect word meaning "resurrection."

Au-gvocksa—A Pennsylvania Dutch dialect word meaning "tight, sore, aching muscles, which relax when massaged."

Behoft—A Pennsylvania Dutch dialect word meaning "possessed."

Boova Shenkel—A Pennsylvania Dutch dialect phrase meaning "beef- and potato-filled pastries."

Bund der lieva—A Pennsylvania Dutch dialect phrase meaning "bond of love."

Dat—A Pennsylvania Dutch dialect word used to refer to or address one's father.

Dein villa geshay, auf Erden vie im Himmel—A Pennsylvania Dutch dialect phrase meaning, "Your will be done on earth as in heaven."

Denke, Gute Mann—A Pennsylvania Dutch dialect phrase meaning "Thank you, good Lord."

Denke schöen—A Pennsylvania Dutch dialect phrase meaning "Thank you very much."

Der Herr—A Pennsylvania Dutch dialect word meaning "God."

Die gichtra—A Pennsylvania Dutch dialect word meaning "seizures."

Doddy—A Pennsylvania Dutch dialect word meaning "grandfather."

Dum kopf, or *dumbkopf*—A Pennsylvania Dutch dialect word meaning "dumb head."

Dumb heita—A Pennsylvania Dutch dialect word meaning "foolishness."

Englische leit—A Pennsylvania Dutch dialect phrase meaning people who aren't Amish or Native American.

Englische schule—A Pennsylvania Dutch dialect phrase meaning "a school run by people who aren't Amish or Native American."

Fa-sarking—A Pennsylvania Dutch dialect word meaning "caring for."

Faschtendich—A Pennsylvania Dutch dialect word meaning "common sense."

Fa-shput—A Pennsylvania Dutch dialect word meaning "mocked."

Fishly—A Pennsylvania Dutch dialect word meaning "the best cut of deer meat fried in lard."

Fore—A Pennsylvania Dutch dialect word meaning "leading the song in church."

Freundschaft—A Pennsylvania Dutch dialect word meaning "family," usually "extended family."

Gaduld—A Pennsylvania Dutch dialect word meaning "patience."

Gile chplauwa—A Pennsylvania Dutch dialect phrase meaning "blacksmithing."

Glay Indian maedly—A Pennsylvania Dutch dialect phrase meaning "little Indian girl."

Goot—A Pennsylvania Dutch dialect word meaning "good."

Goot opp—A Pennsylvania Dutch dialect phrase meaning "better off."

Gott im Himmel—A Pennsylvania Dutch dialect phrase meaning "God in heaven."

Grishtag Essa—A Pennsylvania Dutch dialect phrase meaning "Christmas dinner."

Grosfeelich—A Pennsylvania Dutch dialect word meaning "proud, cocky."

Guten morgen!–A Pennsylvania Dutch dialect phrase meaning, "Good morning!"

Hans sei Kate—A Pennsylvania Dutch dialect phrase meaning "Hans's wife, Kate."

Harrich mol sell—A Pennsylvania Dutch dialect phrase meaning, "Listen to that."

Häse—A Pennsylvania Dutch dialect word meaning "hot."

Heiland—A Pennsylvania Dutch dialect phrase meaning "Christ" or Savior."

Herr Jesu—A Pennsylvania Dutch dialect phrase meaning "Lord Jesus."

Hexary—A Pennsylvania Dutch dialect word meaning "witchcraft."

Hinkle dunkus—A Pennsylvania Dutch dialect phrase meaning "gravy."

Hinna losseny—A Pennsylvania Dutch dialect phrase meaning "the ones remaining after a death."

Ich vinch da saya—A Pennsylvania Dutch dialect phrase meaning, "I wish a blessing for you."

Kindish—A Pennsylvania Dutch dialect word meaning "childish."

Knabrus—A Pennsylvania Dutch dialect word meaning "buttered cabbage and onions."

Komm—A Pennsylvania Dutch dialect word meaning "come."

Leberklosschen—A Pennsylvania Dutch dialect word meaning "dumplings filled with chopped liver and onions."

Lebkuchen—A Pennsylvania Dutch dialect word meaning "a loaf cake."

Lunga feva—A Pennsylvania Dutch dialect phrase meaning "lung fever."

Mam—A Pennsylvania Dutch dialect word used to address or refer to one's mother.

Maud—A Pennsylvania Dutch dialect word meaning "maid," usually employed by a family after the birth of a new baby.

Mein Gott, ich bitte dich, hilf mir—A Pennsylvania Dutch dialect phrase meaning, "My God, I ask you to please help me."

Mein Gott, vergebe mich meine Sinde—A Pennsylvania Dutch dialect phrase meaning, "My God forgive my sins."

Mol net die Annie—A Pennsylvania Dutch dialect phrase meaning "Certainly not Annie."

My gute frau—A Pennsylvania Dutch dialect phrase meaning "my good wife."

Nay—A Pennsylvania Dutch dialect word meaning "no."

Net heila—A Pennsylvania Dutch dialect phrase meaning, "Don't cry."

Oh, Gott Vater, in Himmelreich, Un deine gute preisen—A phrase from a hymn in the Pennsylvania Dutch dialect meaning, "Oh, God our Father in heaven, we praise your goodness."

Ordnung—The Amish community's agreed-upon rules for living, based on their understanding of the Bible, particularly the New Testament. The *ordnung* varies from community to community, often reflecting leaders' preferences, local customs, and traditional practices.

Paradeis—A Pennsylvania Dutch dialect word meaning "Paradise."

Pon haus—A Pennsylvania Dutch dialect phrase meaning "scrapple," a dish made with ground pork, broth, and cornmeal. After it congeals in a loaf pan, it's sliced and then fried.

Rivels—Small dumplings made of eggs and flour.

Roasht—A Pennsylvania Dutch dialect word referring to the traditional main dish served after an Amish wedding, made of cooked and cubed chicken and stuffing.

Rote birdy—A Pennsylvania Dutch dialect phrase meaning "red bird."

Schnitz und knepp—A Pennsylvania Dutch dialect phrase meaning "ham cooked with dried apples and dumplings."

Schnuck—A Pennsylvania Dutch dialect word meaning "cute."

Schnucka galena—A Pennsylvania Dutch dialect phrase meaning "cute little."

Schpeck und bona—A Pennsylvania Dutch dialect phrase meaning "ham and green beans."

Schpence—A Pennsylvania Dutch dialect word meaning "ghost."

Schput—A Pennsylvania Dutch dialect word meaning "mock."

Schrift—A Pennsylvania Dutch dialect word meaning "Scripture."

See iss an chide kind—A Pennsylvania Dutch dialect phrase meaning, "She's a sensible child."

Seeye, der brautigam kommet; Geht ihm entgegen—The lyrics of a wedding song, in the Pennsylvania Dutch dialect, meaning, "Watch, the bridegroom comes; Go now to meet him."

Smear käse—A Pennsylvania Dutch dialect phrase meaning "spreadable cheese."

Sodda schnuck—A Pennsylvania Dutch dialect phrase meaning "sort of cute."

Souse—Congealed cooked and seasoned meat from pigs' feet and heads.

Unfashtendich—A Pennsylvania Dutch dialect word meaning "unbelievable."

Unglauvich—A Pennsylvania Dutch dialect word meaning "unbelieving."

Unser Jesu—A Pennsylvania Dutch dialect phrase meaning "Our Lord Jesus."

Unser Vater—A Pennsylvania Dutch dialect phrase meaning "Our Father," referring to God.

Voss geht aw?–A Pennsylvania Dutch dialect phrase meaning, "What's going on?"

Voss hat gevva?–A Pennsylvania Dutch dialect phrase meaning, "What gives?"

Voss in die velt?–A Pennsylvania Dutch dialect phrase meaning, "What in the world?"

Vossa—A Pennsylvania Dutch dialect word meaning "water."

Wunderbar goot—A Pennsylvania Dutch dialect phrase meaning "wonderful good."

Ya—A Pennsylvania Dutch dialect word meaning "yes."

Ztvie dracht—A Pennsylvania Dutch dialect phrase meaning "tensions" or "divisions."

Other Books by Linda Byler

Available from your favorite bookstore or online retailer.

"Author Linda Byler is Amish, which sets this book apart both in the rich details of Amish life and in the lack of melodrama over disappointments and tragedies. Byler's writing will leave readers eager for the next book in the series."
–*Publisher's Weekly* review of *Wild Horses*

Lizzie Searches for Love Series

BOOK ONE

BOOK TWO

BOOK THREE

TRILOGY

COOKBOOK

Sadie's Montana Series

BOOK ONE BOOK TWO BOOK THREE TRILOGY

Lancaster Burning Series

BOOK ONE BOOK TWO BOOK THREE

The Little Amish Matchmaker
A Christmas Romance

The Christmas Visitor
An Amish Romance

Mary's Christmas Goodbye
An Amish Romance

About the Author

Linda Byler was raised in an Amish family and is an active member of the Amish church today. Growing up, Linda loved to read and write. In fact, she still does. Linda is well known within the Amish community as a columnist for a weekly Amish newspaper.

Linda is the author of the *Lizzie Searches for Love* series and the *Sadie's Montana* series, as well as the *Lancaster Burning* series. She is also the author of *The Little Amish Matchmaker* and *The Christmas Visitor*, as well as *Lizzie's Amish Cookbook: Favorite recipes from three generations of Amish cooks!*

Hester on the Run is the first book in her series, *Hester's Hunt for Home*, set among the Amish and Native Americans of eastern Pennsylvania in colonial America.